QUEEN
OF THE
AMAZONS

Also by Judith Tarr

QUEEN
OF THE
AMAZONS

Judith Tarr

A Tom Doherty Associates Book

New York

QUEEN OF THE AMAZONS

Book design by Michael Collica

A Tor Book
Published by Tom Doherty Associates, LLC
175 Fifth Avenue
New York, NY 10010

www.tor.com

Tor® is a registered trademark of Tom Doherty
Associates, LLC.

Library of Congress Cataloging-in-Publication Data

Tarr, Judith.
 Queen of the amazons / Judith Tarr.—1st ed.
    p. cm.
 "A Tom Doherty Associates book."
 ISBN 0-765-30395-7 (acid-free)
 1. Hippolyta (Greek mythology)—Fiction. 2. Alexander, the Great, 356-
323 B.C.—Fiction. 3. Iran—History—Macedonian Conquest, 334-325
B.C.—Fiction. 4. Conquerors—Fiction. 5. Amazons—Fiction. 6. Queens—
Fiction. I. Title.

PS3570.A655Q44 2004
813'.54—dc22

                                                        2003061396

First Edition: March 2004

Printed in the United States of America

0 9 8 7 6 5 4 3 2 1

PART ONE

The Child Without a Soul

ONE

The queen's daughter lay in her cradle. Her hands and feet paddled aimlessly as a newborn's will. Her skin was beginning to lose the redness of the very young; one could see that it would be ivory and her hair would be ruddy gold. Her eyes were wide-set and lucent blue, and perfectly blank.

"She has no soul," said the seer.

She had come long days' ride to look on this child and conjure her name, traveling to the westernmost edge of the hunting runs, where Queen Hippolyta had paused to give birth to her daughter. The celebrations were just dying down when she came. The last of the wine was going round, and the birth-festival of a royal heir advanced toward its ninth evening.

Selene happened to be abroad in the camp when the seer was sighted riding up the steep track to the summit of the hill. She had gone altogether blind since last Selene saw her, but she had acquired no servant or acolyte. Her little bay mare was all the eyes she needed for the road. In camp she had the goodwill of the people to guide her.

She hardly needed a guide to bring her to the queen's tent and the child in it. The Goddess led her, bringing light where others could see only dimly if at all. Selene followed in silence, soft-footed as a hunter, but she knew the seer was aware of her.

Hippolyta was not with her daughter. Her attendants had persuaded her to snatch a little sleep while the child slept, and Selene had set guards to keep her there until she was rested. Charis was watching over the child, rocking the cradle with her foot while she suckled her own daughter.

She rose at the seer's coming and offered reverence. The seer passed her as if she had been invisible.

The child was awake, watching the play of light and shadow on the tent wall. She took no notice of the figure that bent over her. The seer's nostrils flared. She straightened abruptly and said the thing that Selene had been thinking—and dreading—since the day the child was born.

"She has no soul."

Selene's throat closed. It was impossible, and yet the seer had seen it at least as clearly as she had. This beautiful child, this first-born of the queen, was as empty of soul and self as an image carved in ivory.

"How can that be?" said Charis. "She lives, breathes. She eats. She clasped my finger just now. Surely she can't be—"

"There is no soul in this body," the seer said. "The breath of life is in it, but no spirit fills it. There is nothing here to name."

"We name animals," Charis said. She was stubborn, and she had formed an attachment to the child.

"This is less than an animal," said the seer. She turned her back on the cradle. The child's eyes never flickered, her face never changed. The seer might not have been there at all, for all that the child knew of her.

The seer found Selene that evening by the cookfires, tending a pot and pondering imponderables. She did that when she needed to think long and hard: found a pot or a spit and a bag of herbs and created something for people to eat.

She looked up from seasoning the pot to find the seer standing over her. She sighed, making no effort to hide it. "Still pursuing me, aunt?"

"Always," her aunt said. She had been Kallinike before she left her name behind to become a voice for fate and the Goddess.

"The answer is still no," Selene said.

"And my response is still that this is not a choice. The gift is given. You must take it."

"I refuse," Selene said. She was calm—a warrior's calm, with powerful resistance beneath. "My gift is to ride and fight and defend my queen. I am not meant for the gift you wish on me."

"Never my wishing," the seer said with great sadness. "Believe that, child. Never mine. The Goddess lays Her hand on whom She wills."

"Not this one," Selene said.

That was an old fight, as old almost as Selene. Time was when the seer had tried to press her. They had both been younger then. Selene had fled to the queen and found asylum there. The seer had accepted that defeat, but it was only a single battle in a long war.

"I am not a seer," Selene said. "I will not accept the visions. I will not be the gods' plaything."

"In the end," her aunt said, "that will not be your decision to make. May the Goddess help you then, for I may not be alive to do it."

Selene turned her back on her, just as the seer had done to the queen's daughter. It was a monstrous rudeness.

The seer did not lash her with anger. The air was full of regret and long-suffering patience.

Selene shut her mind to it. When at length she looked over her shoulder, her aunt was gone. Selene prayed it would be a long while before they spoke to each other again.

"Kill it," Phaedra said.

She had called the clan-council, then once it had met, she had done most of the talking. No one seemed to mind that a mere commander of ten was ordering them all about. She was the queen's sister-daughter; until Hippolyta's daughter was born, she had had fair claim to the rank of royal successor.

Hippolyta was still asleep. They were hoping to resolve the matter before she woke, and have it settled and put firmly out of mind.

Not one of the elders and clan-leaders, not even the warleader of the tribe, ventured to protest Phaedra's blunt words. Selene was there on sufferance, mute and supposedly meek in the warleader's shadow. Ione was silent, listening, betraying nothing in her expression. Selene wanted to shake her, to shout at her to say something, do something, wield the power of her rank to strike Phaedra down.

"Yes, kill it," Phaedra said. "Kill it before our lady wakes. We should have disposed of it when it was born, when we saw the emptiness in its eyes."

They growled like men, struck with a sudden hunger for blood. Phaedra smiled.

Selene could not bear that smile, its smugness and its deep self-satisfaction. "You never saw anything!" she burst out. "None of you did. You never knew—"

"Child," said Phaedra with an air of patient kindness, "you're forgiven. We all know how you love our lady. But this thing she gave birth to is flawed beyond recall. Best be rid of it. Once she recovers from the birth, she'll go to the men again and make another."

They seemed to be wise words. They sounded sensible. Yet they set Selene's teeth on edge. Phaedra was not thinking of the queen, and she certainly was not wishing her well.

Phaedra nurtured a deep sense of injustice: her mother had been queen, but when she died suddenly, the late queen's sister had been chosen to rule after her. Phaedra had been a child, not yet come to women's courses. She had been aggrieved then, and the grievance had only grown as she grew older.

Few ever seemed to see the heart in her, only the smile and the soft words. In this council, where everyone was so much of the same mind, she said exactly what they all wished to hear.

"There are wolves in the wood beyond the river," said the chief of the priestesses who were in the camp. She did not say it gladly, but neither did she flinch from it.

Phaedra shook her head. "Wolves aren't certain enough. Let us offer the thing to the Lady of the Wolves, as a sacrifice for the good of the people."

Again it was reasonable; it was right, surely, after the seer had refused to give the child a name. The child was not a human thing; it was a shell, a husk of flesh around a core of nothingness. And yet Selene's heart would not let her bow to Phaedra's will, however skillfully she had imposed it on the queen's council. Even Ione had given way to it.

Selene has been resisting the Goddess all her life. A single mortal woman was nothing beside that. "The queen—" she began.

She had expected to be shouted down. She had not expected absolute silence.

Once the seer had told the council what she had seen, she had retreated to a corner and, it seemed, fallen asleep. Now it was clear that she had been wide awake. She did not move or speak, but the words died in Selene's throat.

The seer seemed to do nothing, simply sat in her bit of light and shadow: a bone-thin woman, not young, with a lined plain face and the milky eyes of the blind. And yet she held in her the beauty and majesty of the Goddess through Whose eyes she saw.

She drew the silence to herself. When all of it was centered on her, she spoke. Her voice was soft; they strained to hear. "There will be no wolves and no sacrifice. This child will live."

"Live!" cried Phaedra, forgetting herself for once. "But you said it has no—"

"That is the will of the Goddess," the seer said.

"How can the Goddess will *this*? What is She thinking? Did She simply forget to provide a soul for it? Will She force us to leave it open to any demon or dark spirit that may happen by?"

"She is protected," said the seer, as soft and serene as ever. "The wolves will not take her, nor will any power for ill."

"Why?" Ione demanded, speaking at last and to the point. "Tell us, lady. What do you see?"

The seer stood erect. Her clouded eyes were fixed far beyond the circle of women, over the long roll of the steppe and the vault of the sky. "The child will live," she said.

"Then you must name it," said Phaedra. "If it is to live, it must be named."

"A name will come to her," the seer said. "Wait and be patient. You will see."

She walked away from them then. She did not walk quickly, nor did she ask for guidance. Any one of them could have caught and held her, but even Phaedra lacked the power to move.

The seer had left them with far more questions than she had

answered. The priestesses knew no more than any. The Goddess did not choose to enlighten them.

Selene left the circle as it erupted in confusion. They would shout at one another until the sun went down, and some would shout the moon across the sky, but it would all come to nothing. They were railing at the wind.

The shouting had died down by morning. As the first rays of the sun touched the hilltop on which the royal clan had camped, a new and quieter commotion brought out everyone who was not already up and about.

Selene had snatched a few hours' sleep among the horselines. She had not wanted the seer to find her, and it seemed she had succeeded. What she could not escape were the dreams.

They came to her out of the dark, each one whole and complete: visions of places she had never been and people she had never known. She saw a woman who she knew was the queen's daughter, a woman very like the queen, tall and strong, with hair the color of ruddy gold, and eyes as blue as flax flowers. There was life and self in those eyes, an intelligence so keen and a spirit so strong that in her dream she caught her breath.

The vision neither faded nor vanished, but the woman was gone. Selene saw a man on a black horse. His hair was as bright as gold and his eyes were as blue as flax flowers. The spirit in him was like a living fire. He rode across a dim and half-seen country, and an army of men followed him.

The eyes of her vision rose up from the earth until she hovered like a bird in the sky. All the world spread out below her, with all its tribes and nations, its kingdoms and empires. The man of her vision swept across them like a storm over the plains.

He came from the setting sun. The lands he swept across would matter, she knew in the way of dreams, without reason or logic. She would remember them, just as she would remember this dream, because she had dreamed true.

She was almost at ease, almost ready to accept what had been given her. But the spirit inside her, whether it was the giver of the gift or some adversary, twisted the dream and tore its fabric. She struggled to escape, but she was powerless as always. She had to stand transfixed, and see what she had seen in the first dream that she remembered.

She was very young. She could ride—every sister of the people could from the time she was old enough to sit upright on a horse's back—but she had not yet learned to shoot a bow. Her mother would teach her in a year or two.

Her mother was chief priestess of the royal clan. Even so young, Selene expected to receive the same calling and the same office when she was old enough. She was gifted, everyone said, and wise beyond her years. There could be no doubt that the Goddess loved her.

When people spoke of the Goddess, she saw her mother: tall, strong, beautiful. That was the face she saw when she prayed, and the voice she heard when the priestesses told her the Goddess spoke through the things of earth: the whisper of wind, the fall of water, the shifting of stone. Her mother was everything that was wonderful. When people said that Selene would grow up to be the same, she was ineffably proud.

Today she was weeping with anger. Her mother had gone away without her—the first time that Selene could remember, and if she had anything to do with it, it would be the last. She did not know or care where Dione had gone, only that she was elsewhere and Selene was here, in the camp of the clan. The queen's sister of the image, binding her to the Goddess and the people, Phaedra sprang between. Her eyes were blazing; her hands were clawed. "You cannot do this. This is not a human thing. It is an abomination—a horror; a visitation of the Goddess' wrath upon the people."

Hippolyta looked her in the face. She could hardly avoid it; Phaedra was all but pressed against her. "Cousin," she said mildly, "you are interrupting the rite."

"There can be no rite! There is nothing to offer but an empty husk."

"I offer Her what She has made," Hippolyta said.

"You will not," said Phaedra.

Hippolyta's eyes narrowed slightly. She was still far more self-possessed than the one who faced her. "Are you telling me what I may and may not offer to the Goddess Who made me?"

"This is an insult to Her," Phaedra said.

"How can She be insulted by Her own creation?"

"It is monstrous," said Phaedra.

"It is my daughter," said the queen. "My heir, the firstborn of my body."

"This cannot be your heir."

Then at last Hippolyta's composure broke. Her face went stiff. She thrust Phaedra aside as if she had been made of bundled grass, and laid her daughter in the Goddess' lap. "By heaven above and earth below," she said in a voice that throbbed in the watchers' bones, "by all the Powers that dwell beneath the moon, I swear: This is my daughter and my heir. This and no other shall be queen of the people. This alone shall rule when I am dead. If this oath be broken, may the earth gape and swallow me; may the sky fall and crush me; may my soul die forever to the memory of the light."

To a woman they shuddered; some of them gasped and made futile gestures against the terror of that oath. There was none

Hippolyta was looking after her, and Selene adored Hippolyta. But she was not Selene's mother.

Daughters of the people learned to weep in silence, but Selene made sure everyone knew how angry she was. Her head ached and her throat was locked shut.

Hippolyta fed her a cup of warm milk laced with honey and wine. It had gone down before she understood that it would make her dizzy and then make her fall asleep.

In sleep she saw her mother. Dione was inside of walls. Selene recognized the temple of the Goddess to which she had gone with Dione the summer before. It was not a tent such as the clans lived in, but a house of wood from trees that grew all around the Goddess' hill.

Lamps flickered in it. The image of the Goddess loomed in the dimness. She had a fire in Her belly. Selene was not afraid of Her, though She had no face, only the huge breasts and burgeoning womb. She was the Goddess, Mother and beloved.

Selene's mother prayed with other priestesses. It was a great rite, very holy, very secret. Selene knew that the way one did in dreams, without doubt and without question.

It was a peaceful dream, full of the Goddess' warmth and Her blessing. Selene let it lull her. It took away the worst of her anger at being left behind.

That first time, Selene did not see exactly how it began. Later, when the dream came back again and again, she saw the gust of wind that shot like an arrow through the hole in the roof and scooped the fire out of the Goddess' womb. Sparks flew.

The wood of the temple was very old and very dry, and had been covered over with the black water that bubbled out of the ground not far away. It was thick and oily, that water, with a strong smell, but it kept wood alive long after it should have rotted.

The temple went up like a torch. The priestesses in their rite were caught without hope of escape. The one door, the walls, the roof were sheets of flame.

Selene watched them burn. In her dream she could not close her eyes or turn away. She saw the flesh melt from her mother's bones, and yet she still lived. She was alive long after her body was a charred ruin. When at last the fire consumed her, it had gone beyond mercy, even beyond cruelty.

Selene woke screaming. She screamed until her voice was gone. Nothing that anyone could do would comfort her. And the worst of it—truly the worst—was that when she dreamed that horror, it had not happened yet. She could not speak of it, or warn anyone.

Three days later it happened, and it was her fault. If she had not been so far gone in horror, if she had told anyone what she saw, her mother might still be alive. The priestesses might not have died. She would not have to live that nightmare over and over, night after night, until she dreaded sleep and shrank from dreams. Nor would she ever, though the Goddess Herself commanded it, accept that she was born to be a seer.

On this morning, the ninth day of the soulless child's life, Selene left the dream of fire behind and crawled wearily out of her blankets. The murmur of voices roused her to something like consciousness. She sat up, blinking in the pale early sunlight.

People were up and moving, gathering toward the sunrise side of the camp. The queen's tent was there, and the shrine of the Goddess that went with her wherever she traveled.

A cairn of stones had stood in that place since the people first came to the sea of grass. The shrine was set within its circle, laid

on a broad flat stone: a canopy made of spears, with a roof that was a war-cloak, and beneath it the image of the Goddess that was older than the oldest memory of the people.

It was a black stone that was said to have fallen from the moon, too heavy for a single woman to lift. In its rough shape one could discern the outline of a head and shoulders and the curve of a swollen and fecund belly. It had no face, no eyes or mouth, and no feet or hands. The more skittish of the priestesses could hardly bear to touch it; it was too strong, too heavy with age and power.

Hippolyta was standing in front of it. Her hair was free, flowing down her back. She had put on the garment that from the beginning had marked the Penthesilea, the ruler of the people: a girdle of knotted cords, red as blood. No other garment was ever worn with it, nor was it made for modesty. In it a woman was utterly a woman, and all the more so this one, with her belly still slack from the weight of the child, and her breasts heavy with milk.

She held her daughter in her hands, lifting her up before the Goddess. The child was still, but she breathed: Selene saw the lift of her breast.

Selene was not the last to come there. The elders were behind her, and the priestesses bleared with sleep, and Ione the warleader with an air of one who had been expecting this—the only one of them all who had.

Phaedra came late and last, looking as if she had drowned her sorrows in a vat of wine. Her voice rose like a hawk's cry above the murmur of shock and astonishment. "You cannot do this! It has no name. The seer—"

The queen took no notice of her. She offered her child to the sun and the sky, to the four quarters of the earth, and last of all to the Goddess. Just as she would have laid the small body in the lap

greater or more binding. She had condemned her soul for the sake of a creature who had none.

She had condemned the rest of her people, too, as some declared, loud and long—and Phaedra louder and longer than any. None of them pointed out that if Phaedra had held her tongue, she might not have driven the queen to this. She had spoken when she should have kept silent. The queen had named her heir—and that heir had neither will nor living spirit.

It was done. It could not be undone, however vehement the protests. Hippolyta lifted her daughter from the lap of the Goddess and cradled her to her breast, where with blind persistence the child sought the nipple and began to suck.

Selene had been as shocked as the rest, though maybe her anger was less. That gesture, as simple and natural as any in the world, for some unfathomable reason melted her heart. She could still see the emptiness within that body, but she saw too that it was her queen's child whom she had carried beneath her heart, whom she loved with a mother's intensity.

Selene had miscarried her first child in the winter. The child would have been a son—a lesser tragedy, she was told, than if it had been a daughter. Her womb did not know that. It was empty and her arms bereft. Her breasts still ached, although the milk had long since dried.

Maybe the Goddess guided her. Maybe it was her own foolish will. She looked at this child and loved her, though the child would never return that love, or any other human emotion. She belonged to Selene's queen; she would be Selene's queen—and how the Goddess would bring that about, only She knew.

Selene approached Hippolyta. She laid her right hand on the queen's breast over the beating heart and her left hand on the child's soft head. Steadily she spoke the words that bound her to the queen who was and the queen who would be.

She thought she would be alone, but after a stretching pause, Ione followed her. Others were at her back: warriors, hunters, but no priestesses. Not one, of the dozen in the camp who were consecrated to the Goddess.

When the last of them had come and gone, Selene reckoned the tally of those who had taken the oath. It was a little more than half of the grown women of the clan—but it was enough for the moment. They were stronger than those who held back; they had more skill in weapons. If it came to a fight, they would win.

"You are mad," Phaedra said. "You'll destroy the people, all of you—you and this monster that you serve."

Maybe so, Selene thought. Maybe not. That was in the Goddess' hands.

TWO

Not even the queen would name a child whom the seer had refused to name—even though she was the queen's heir. But the children were not bound by strictures of magic and custom. They called her Etta, which was the sound a child makes in pointing to a thing that it wants but has no other word for. *Etta*—"that thing." Even Phaedra had to admit that it was fitting.

Phaedra had retreated into an uncharacteristic silence. In the autumn of Etta's first year, she led her friends and kin on a hunt that proved to be years long. They had not removed themselves by rite or ritual from the rest of the royal clan, but they were gone; they did not come back. In the gathering of the clans the next spring, rumor had it that Phaedra's allies had left the people's lands and made a tribe of their own, somewhere beyond the world's edge.

Hippolyta took no public notice of their absence. She returned with her heir and the remainder of her clan to the heartlands of the people. There she began the great circle, the pilgrimage to the nine shrines of the Goddess, to present her daughter at each and take the blessings that the Goddess had to give.

However unwilling her own priestesses had been to accept her oath, the priestesses of the temples made no effort to turn her away. What was done was done. They would proceed according to the Goddess' will.

It was all as it should be for a queen who had proclaimed an heir. The oath was sworn and irrevocable. The rest had to unfold in orderly fashion.

Sometimes in the dark before dawn, or on the long marches across the sea of grass, Selene wondered what madness had possessed them all—what insanity had led them to bind themselves to an empty shell. No soul came to fill it, wandering in months and then years after its time, to take up residence like a traveler who had got lost on the road. The body lived, grew, thrived; it ate and slept and seemed to dream. But nothing lived inside it. It was perfectly empty.

After a while waiting became habit. It was no longer patience; it simply was.

The seer had left the royal camp before the queen named her heir. She did not come back to the clan the next year, or in any of the years after that. Rumor began to spread that she had died; that somewhere on her solitary journeys, wandering blind and aged through the world, she had taken leave of her body.

Selene did not believe it. There were other seers among the clans, but only one whose name had been taken away, who was simply *Seer*. She would not let go of this world until she had found a successor.

It was too much to hope that she had given up her campaign to force Selene to bow to the Goddess' will, but she had withdrawn a considerable distance. If the Goddess was kind—if She was capable of kindness—the seer would die before she troubled Selene's peace again. For it was most certain that whoever succeeded the seer, it would not be Selene.

In the seer's absence, Selene had discovered a strange, a wonderful thing. It came to her slowly, but little by little it dawned on her that when she was set on guard over Etta, she did not remember her dreams. Only when she was away from the child on the queen's business or on the hunt did she descend into nightmare.

At first she did not believe it. It was a deception, or simply an odd coincidence. Then she tested it.

For a whole month she set herself to guard the queen's heir by day and night. In all that time, her sleep was deep and peaceful. Come the new moon, she took a horse and her bow and sought the solitude of the plains.

The first night away from the camp, she dreamed, but remembered only dim fragments. The second night, the visions came flooding, so swift and so strong and so numerous that she felt like a dam breaking. They ended as always in the horror of fire. She woke screaming, as she had not done since she was a child.

If she had truly been strong, she would have essayed a third night. But she was weak. She mounted her horse and turned back toward the camp of the clan.

Even before she came to it, she felt the shield that was Etta, the emptiness that in its way was power. In that void the visions were lost, scattered. She was safe.

She had had time to think, through the month of peace and the bare three days of visions. She went in search of the queen.

Hippolyta was sitting in the weavers' circle, spinning thread for the looms. She smiled at Selene's coming. Selene checked her stride as always, caught by that golden beauty and amazed that it should warm so for her. She was only one of many guards about the queen, but she imagined sometimes that Hippolyta looked on her with a fraction more affection than she showed to the others.

That was foolishness, of course. Hippolyta did not choose favorites. She was evenhanded always. That was her gift, and it was one strong reason why the last queen had chosen her over her own daughter. Phaedra could not be evenhanded. She was incurably partisan.

Nonetheless, the warmth of that smile was like a fire in winter. Selene caught herself smiling in return. She sat beside Hippolyta and lifted a spindle from a basket of carded wool, and took up the rhythm of spinning. Some of the weavers were singing a sweet twining song with words so old that no one remembered what they meant.

With that song for descant, Selene said, "Lady, I have a favor to ask."

Hippolyta bent her head. She was always gracious, which was another of her gifts.

Selene let it out all at once, before her resolve failed her. "Give me to your daughter."

That raised the queen's brows. "Why should I do that?"

It was a reasonable question. Selene had prepared an answer. "She has no self, but she has will enough. She goes where she pleases, and no one seems able to stop her. A little while ago, I saw her nearly walk through a campfire. Someone was there to turn her aside. Someone usually is. But if that should fail, what then? She grows older and stronger and, in her way, more willful. Will she live to a woman's years?"

"Do you believe that you can make it so?" asked Hippolyta.

Selene lowered her eyes. Her cheeks were warm. "Maybe I get above myself. Maybe I can do something. If I were hers completely, with others to allow me time for sleep and rest, maybe she would be well enough protected."

"A company of guards," Hippolyta mused as she spun the cream-pale wool. "That's not an ill thought. With you as its commander—"

"I wouldn't ask for that," Selene said a little hastily. "Just to be a part of it."

"Why?"

Selene bit her lip. No one but the seer knew what she was. She had never told anyone, not even Hippolyta, of the dream that had tormented her since she was small.

If she spoke now, Hippolyta would have to force her to accept the burden. It was the queen's duty. She upheld the will of the Goddess, and through it ruled the people.

Selene answered with a truth, if not the truth. "I feel a calling. This is my place."

Hippolyta pondered that. Selene held her breath. For her sanity's sake, she needed this. But she could not say that. She had to wait upon the royal will.

At last Hippolyta said, "I think you are already given to her. Choose six more to stand guard with you—young warriors, fast and strong and infallibly watchful. You may train them as you will."

Selene bowed to the ground. It was not a thing one did among the people, except to the Goddess, but her gratitude was too deep for constraint.

She leaped up. The weavers and spinners glanced at her, some with curiosity, some not. Her grin was hectic. She had found a way—by the Goddess, she had found an escape from the thing that would drive her mad.

———

In the spring after her daughter was born, the queen had gone to the men in the town near the sunset temple and chosen one who was strong and beautiful and had sired many daughters. Nothing came of it—not that year, not the year after, nor the year after that. And Etta grew, and the older she was, the more beautiful she became. It was painful to see, that beauty, because it had no soul.

She was willful as Selene had expected, but her seven guards followed her wherever she went. They kept her safe, and protected her from herself. That did not grow easier with time, as unlike an ordinary child she did not learn. She did as her body pleased, with no regard for sense or safety.

Early in the sixth spring of Etta's life, after a winter that had been more bitter than most, the royal clan still had not left the hot springs that were their winter camp. It was green in the hollows even when the snow was deepest on the hilltops, and the heat of the waters kept the camp warm in the worst of the cold.

The people were slow that year, thick with cold and winter lassitude. But the turning of the stars told them that spring had come, and that the men would be waiting in the villages to the south. The rest of the clans would already be moving, riding toward the gathering and the long festival. They would come and go through all of the spring and summer, and some even into the autumn, as the hunt and the clan-leaders' whim took them. There had been no wars to distract them since before Etta was born.

The omens had been as sluggish as the people, but there was no one who was willing to read them. When Phaedra left, the royal clan had lost all of its priestesses. Thereafter, none had come to take their place.

Hippolyta had not seen fit to ask the temples for others to replace those lost, nor had the temples offered. It was their way of recording their disapproval of her choice of heir, and her way of informing them that she would not be swayed by it.

This bleak spring was like a spell or a dreamcasting, as if the camp had been caught outside of the world. Only Etta seemed real. She had been walking since the end of her first year, tumbling about like a healthy young animal, so headlong and heedless that Selene had fashioned a harness for her to keep her somewhat within bounds. Her guards were sometimes hard put to keep pace with her—her Immortals, they called themselves with the irony of the young, after the picked troops of the Great King of the Persians, far away over the mountains.

The day the seer came, Selene slept uneasily and woke late and slow. She was too sluggish to understand the import of that shiver under the skin, or to be disturbed that it had come even in Etta's presence. The sky when she came out of her tent was the color of ash on snow, the air neither warm nor cold, and the wind was absolutely still. The stink of sulfur from the springs was strong, with no breeze to blow it away.

There were a few women up and about. The gaggles of children lacked their usual enthusiasm; the few that she saw were huddled in circles, whispering or playing some secret game.

The shiver crawled to Selene's spine and prickled there. This was an enchantment, insidious and slow. She had to force her feet to walk along the well-worn path to the queen's tent.

Etta was outside it, running circles at the end of her tether, while that hour's guardian stood like a post in the middle. However blank the child's eyes and however empty her spirit, she was a strong young thing, agile as an Indian monkey. Selene had discovered not long ago that she could catch a ball if anyone tossed it toward her, though she was as likely to stand staring at it as to throw it back.

She was thoroughly occupied this morning, running round and round, sunwise as Selene happened to notice, with her hot-gold hair flying. Her watcher had the same half-drugged expression Selene had seen in everyone else. Etta never spoke or acknowledged a human presence. The girl Nikia blinked sleepily as Selene passed, but did not return her greeting.

The air in the tent was heavy and still. Selene could barely move against the weight of it. Hippolyta was standing as motionless as Nikia, but her eyes were brightly and fiercely alive.

The seer was sitting in the chair that had followed the queen of the people from camp to camp for time out of mind. It was made of wood and covered with sheets of gold. The back of it was carved with a gryphon in flight; the arms were shaped like an eagle's talons and the legs were the legs of a lion. It was an odd and extravagant thing, sometimes difficult to transport, but insofar as the queen of the people had a throne, it served that purpose.

It was not quite startling for the seer to be sitting in it. She was beyond presumption. Her blind eyes turned toward Selene; she smiled.

Selene tensed to turn on her heel and stalk away, but that milky stare held her rooted. "Child," the seer said. "You come in good time. Have you been dreaming dreams?"

"Dim dreams," Selene answered before she thought. It was all part of the spell on this place and this season.

"Tell us," the seer said.

"It's yours," Selene said. "Isn't it? This is your enchantment."

"I make no spells," the seer said. "I am only a voice. Speak."

"I don't remember my dreams," Selene said sullenly.

"Pretend that you do," the seer said.

Hippolyta was watching them, saying nothing. Selene could not meet her eyes.

"Dimness," Selene said to the air beside the queen's face. "Shadows and heavy cloud. A temple on a hilltop, a village below. Phaedra with a knife in her hand, and your blood on it: the only bright thing in all that dream."

"Phaedra is gone," Hippolyta said.

"Phaedra has come back." Selene looked up into that sky-blue stare. "A messenger rides to the camp even now. She carries a lie."

Hippolyta showed no sign of surprise. Selene wished she could have said the same for herself. She had not known what she knew until she said it.

The seer was not smiling, not quite, but some tension had gone out of her. As if, Selene thought, she had heard what she had long hoped to hear. She had hunted her quarry with endless patience. At last she had brought it to bay.

There had been no dream of fire. The greyness, or Etta's presence, or maybe both, had swallowed it.

Sound crept through the silence: a murmur of voices, and beneath it the thudding of swift hooves. The chill in Selene's spine settled deep and determined to stay.

She did not want this. She did not want to know how it would begin, how the game would play out, or how it would end. She wanted simple mortal ignorance and the life of a warrior of the people, the queen's own, the heir's guardian.

The Goddess will not be denied. That was the seer's voice, but she had not spoken aloud. Before Selene could think of a response, the commotion had come as far as the queen's tent.

A woman thrust through the flap. She wore the circular cloak of a messenger of the Goddess, and the boots laced high; she cradled her rod of office in her arm.

The messenger was Selene's age perhaps, or a little younger; she had the narrow oval face and slanting eyes of the eastern clans. Those eyes slid toward the seer. They were wary; they were not wise enough to be afraid. Somehow, although there was no physical resemblance, she reminded Selene of Phaedra. It was her expression: sweet but sly, with an undercurrent of long-standing grievance.

She turned her shoulder to the seer. Selene she did not deign to notice at all. She bent her head to the queen in what might have been taken for respect, and said, "Lady. I come from Eos temple with the approval of the high priestess there, but my message comes from another."

She paused. The queen made no attempt to fill the silence. Selene's hackles had risen. She could feel the world shifting, her winter lassitude fading.

After some little while the messenger grew weary of waiting for the queen to prompt her and said, "Your kinswoman, royal lady, has taken refuge among us. Her heart is changed: she has made peace with herself and with the world as it is. She begs leave to settle your differences and, she hopes, restore her place among the people."

Hippolyta's expression changed not at all. If she was taken aback, she hid it well. "My sister-daughter knows that she may return to us whenever she wishes. She was never exiled by any of us, whatever she may have done to herself."

The messenger bowed. Selene's eyes sharpened. Here, she thought. Here it was. "Lady, it's been so long, and she left under such a cloud, that she begs your indulgence. Will you come to her in Eos? She understands that what she asks is presumptuous; the supplicant should come to the queen. But Eos is a sacred place, blessed of the Goddess. She wishes your reconciliation to be witnessed and consecrated for all the people to know. Will you grant her this request?"

"I shall consider it," Hippolyta said. "Go now. Rest; eat. Share whatever my people have to offer. When my decision is made, I'll summon you."

A messenger, even one as arrogant as this, could not contest a royal dismissal. Selene moved to withdraw as well, but Hippolyta said, "Stay."

Selene bent her head in obedience. As the messenger's presence withdrew through the camp, Hippolyta sank down to the heap of furs and rugs and cushions that was her bed, and sighed enormously. "Tell me what you think," she said.

She was not speaking to the seer. "Does it matter what I think?" Selene asked. "Surely you should—" She gestured toward the seer, who seemed asleep, hunched in the golden chair.

The queen's eyes were piercingly blue. They drew out the words, just as they had drawn the dream.

"I think this is a trap," Selene said.

"Tell me what you see," said the queen.

So this was what it was to be a voice, Selene thought. She thought she should be angry. She could only speak; she had no other choice. "I see Phaedra's face," she said, "reflected in her messenger. It's not reconciliation she wants. She wants you— your name, your life. All that you are."

"She's always wanted that," said Hippolyta.

"You're not afraid?"

"I'd be a fool if I weren't," Hippolyta said with a faint snap of impatience. "Six years. Why now? Has she raised an army?"

"That I can't see," said Selene.

"Of course not," Hippolyta said. She sat up abruptly. "We leave in the morning. Fetch Ione—tell her. She'll choose twenty warriors. Ten will ride with me. Ten will ride ahead and determine if they can what trap my sister's daughter has laid."

"You're not going," Selene said. "Send Ione, yes, but as a messenger—to bring Phaedra here, free and willing, or bound as a renegade."

"That would be wise and sensible," said Hippolyta, "but I'm going to Eos."

"Why?"

"You know the answer to that," said Hippolyta. "Fetch Ione. It's past noon already; we've much to do before we ride."

"But if you leave, and Phaedra expects that; if she has an army, if it's waiting, if it falls on the camp in your absence—"

"So many ifs," said Hippolyta. "Ione. Go."

Selene was babbling, and Hippolyta was losing patience. The seer might be able to talk sense into her. Most certainly Selene could not.

"Interesting occupations are earned," Ione said. She pulled the girl to her feet. "Report to the cooks. If drilling with weapons is too dull for you, maybe tending cookfires will prove more stimulating."

Callista was in no grateful mood. With luck and the Goddess' help, she would have time to think, maybe even to learn. But she could only see that her existence had gone from bad to worse.

Ione dismissed the rest of them just as the captain of the heir's guard appeared with Hippolyta's message. Ione had had a thought of an hour's rest in a quiet tent, then perhaps she would take Callista's suggestion. The game that had grown thin and scarce over the winter was coming back slowly now: geese flying north, small creatures emerging from their dens. Fresh meat would be welcome.

But the queen's summons was not to be refused. Selene was somber, almost grim. That it had something to do with the Goddess' messenger who had come in not long before, Ione was certain. War? She rebuked herself for hoping so. At heart she was no more or less silly than the girls she trained in weaponry.

As Ione and Selene approached the queen's tent, they found the heir's Immortals in a circle outside it. Etta was in the midst of them. She had got hold of a short hunting spear, gripping it in her small hands. She was ducking, darting, turning.

It was the drill to which Callista had objected so loudly, perfect in every particular. The child must have been watching, although Ione had not seen her. The blank face, the empty mind, had somehow absorbed and remembered.

The child's guards were grinning as they watched, as if they had found themselves a performing ape. Selene picked up the

THREE

Ione the warleader was drilling the young women with spears. They were as draggingly reluctant as they had been all winter, scowling and snarling and fighting every step, but she would not let them slacken.

"There hasn't been a war in years!" Callista burst out. She had been rumbling to a boil since the clan first came to winter camp. Ione had pressed her hard today, choosing her as an example for the rest. She snapped as Ione had expected, and said aloud what they had all been muttering to one another.

The girl had flung down her spear in her fit of temper. Ione swept it up, whipped it about, and caught her behind the knees. She fell sprawling. "It's not only war you have to think of," Ione said. "When your life needs defending, what will you do? Shriek and hide behind a man as women do in the rest of the world?"

Callista was little cowed and in no way silenced. She scrambled up on her elbows. "I can fight. But where's the use in drilling ourselves into a stupor, day after day, when we can be doing something interesting, like hunting for the pot?"

two closest by the scruff of the neck and shook them until their teeth rattled, then set them down without gentleness. The rest were gaping, a circle of wide eyes and open mouths.

Ione stepped through the gap that Selene had made in the circle. The child, having completed the spear-drill, had grounded the butt and stood still. Ione set a finger under her chin and tilted it up. Her eyes were as flat as blue stones, reflecting the emptiness of the sky.

Ione gripped the spearhaft. She barely saw the child move, or the sudden shift of the spear, but the light pressure of the point against her throat was unmistakable.

She would not allow her breathing to stop, but it slowed appreciably. She was vividly aware of the world about her: the guards staring, the camp bustling, a thin wind blowing. There was no soul to appeal to, no power of reason to call upon.

A wild beast has in it some living awareness. In this human-seeming form she saw none. Her first thought, that the child had been put up to it by Ione's disgruntled pupils, slipped away and vanished. There was nothing here but blind instinct.

Ione's fingers were still closed about the shaft of the spear. Very, very carefully she straightened her arm.

The spear shifted. The child never blinked. A figure, striding swiftly through the motionless and gaping guards, snatched up the small body just as Ione thrust the weapon away.

Etta lay limp in Selene's arms. The captain of the guard had done what none of her subordinates had had the wits to do. She cradled the child with no sign of fear or loathing.

"That is a warrior," Ione said of the child with unabashed admiration. Her glare raked the guards. "Unlike the rest of you."

"That is a wild animal," one of them dared to say—it seemed to be a day for young women speaking out of turn. "She almost killed you."

"And whose fault was that?" Selene demanded. "You are dismissed. The queen will judge you when she sees fit. Until then, you are relieved of your duties."

These children were not as defiant as Callista had been. Their duty was less interesting but more momentous, and they knew it. They left in a pack, shoulders slumped and steps dragging.

Selene set the child on her feet but kept a grip on her hand. "I cry your pardon," she said.

"No need," said Ione. "I was the fool, to do what I did. Goddess knows what possessed me."

"If the queen's enemies hear of this," Selene said, "it's not you they'll reckon possessed."

"There is no ill spirit in this child," said Ione. "Do you remember what I taught you long ago? The body knows."

"And the mind too often confuses," Selene said with the flicker of a smile. "I do remember. You have hope for her."

Ione looked down at the child who had almost pierced her throat with a spearpoint. Etta was watching the play of light and shadow as sun chased cloud across the clearing sky.

"She sees nothing that breathes," Selene said. "Only the Goddess' pure creation. No animal, no walking or flying or crawling thing—but grass, clouds, moon or sun, those she somehow perceives."

"She can fight," Ione said. "She'll be dangerous as she grows older, unless she has teaching."

"How do you teach a mindless pupil?"

"Goddess knows," Ione said.

"You were in the council," Selene said, "the day she was born. You would have killed her then. Will you kill her now?"

Ione looked into Selene's eyes. They were grey, like rain, and they were as full of life and soul and self as the child's were empty.

"She was nothing then—a ruined creation. Now she is the queen's heir."

"She is still a ruined creation," Selene said.

"Or one that is still to be made," said Ione. "I'm not a seer, but I'm not blind, either. In time I learn to see."

Selene flushed faintly. "I didn't mean—"

"Of course you didn't," said Ione.

There was a silence, brief and awkward. Selene tugged the child closer to her, like a shield of sorts. "I have a company of guards to inspect," she said, "and discipline to administer. Go if you will— the queen is waiting. I'll see that the heir is taken care of."

It was true: Ione had a summons to answer, and this diversion had taken her too long away from it. She inclined her head in respect. Selene's flush deepened, but she kept her head up.

Ione concealed her smile until she had turned away. All the young women were terribly shy in front of the warleader—even this captain of guards, who was young for her position, but still she should know better.

She would do well enough with that deadly child. Ione would help as she could. She would teach herself to teach a pupil who had no soul. And if that meant she spent time in the company of the captain—well then. Duty and pleasure need not always be kept apart.

FOUR

It was a month's ride from the winter camp to Eos temple, from south and somewhat west to the eastern edge of the people's lands. Hippolyta did not ride hastily; she paused more than once to receive guests and embassies and to hold audience. She was making Phaedra wait.

In that time the weather broke. Winter passed into summer with hardly a day between: from icy chill and spits of snow to heavy, sodden heat. Swarms of stinging flies pursued them. They gained no advantage by riding at night: the heat was much the same, and the flies if anything were worse.

Ione had sent ten riders ahead as Hippolyta commanded, but the escort that rode with her was thirty strong. Ione had insisted on it. With baggage, remounts, and packhorses, they were a small army.

Etta rode among them. Hippolyta would not leave her with the rest of the clan—not so much for mistrust as for unwillingness to let her daughter out of her sight.

Selene was the child's keeper. She had pondered the incident in front of the queen's tent, considered the offenders, and dismissed them all. She would have to find others, and soon. But for the moment, no one else could be spared. No one in this riding was either willing or able to keep watch over such a notoriously unpredictable creature.

Selene found her predictable enough in her way, as the wind could be, or the passage of a storm across the steppe. Certain things drew her: food, water, a weapon left lying about. A horse, too, as Selene discovered early in her sole guardianship, when she woke from too sound a sleep to find her charge gone. The horse-lines had snared her. She was perched on the back of the most perilous of the mares: The queen mare, moon-white, who was never ridden except by the queen.

Etta rode as she fought, with the surety of instinct. A number of idiots were attempting to undo the sacrilege—for it was that; even a queen's heir should not ride the queen mare. The mare, who had been grazing peacefully until she became the center of a mob, had turned on them with the ferocity of a mother whose child is threatened. Etta kept her seat perfectly easily even when her mount whipped about and charged a fool who had come too close.

Selene dispersed the crowd with a few well-chosen words and the judicious application of her fist. Those who did not yield to such blandishments she lifted bodily and pitched out of the way. Then the mare was quiet, although her ears were still flat and her rear hoof was noticeably restless.

Selene moved in carefully, wary of the mare's teeth and heels. She made her body quiet, a vision of harmlessness, soft and calm. The mare rolled an eye at her but held still. Selene caught the child and drew her unresisting into her arms, then backed away.

Etta showed no sign of distress. She was limp in Selene's embrace, as she always was. Yet as Selene carried her away, her eyes remained on the mare for as long as the horses were in sight. It was the first moving, breathing thing she had ever focused on.

Hope was as foolish as any expectation of an omen: that the queen's heir had gone direct to the queen mare, and not only mounted her but been permitted to ride. There was nothing behind those eyes, no more than there had ever been. Etta had seen a living cloud, that was all, an alluring white shape on which she had been moved to climb. There was no more to it than that.

The seer rode into their camp on the day of the new moon. She had not ridden from the winter camp with them, and should have been far behind at the speed so old a woman, mounted on a lone and aging mare, could manage. And yet she was here, looking as if she had sprung up out of the grass.

She was no more or less frail than she had ever been, but something in her had changed. To Selene's eyes it seemed as if she stood still and the world retreated from her. She was letting it go.

It was nothing to do with Selene, even when her eyes, blind to all else, turned and fixed, and her hand stretched. Selene did not want to take it, but her arm had a will of its own. The seer's hand was as fragile as a bundle of twigs. "It is time," she said.

Selene tried to pull away, but those eyes and that hand held her fast.

"Take me to the high place," said the seer.

The queen's guards had drawn back. Hippolyta stood beyond them, watching, perfectly still.

The seer turned and waited. Without a word Selene lifted her onto the bay mare's back. She had no weight to her at all.

One of the queen's guards was standing just beyond them, holding the bridle of Selene's own mare. Selene could have refused, could have ordered the mare returned to the horselines. She took the rein instead and swung astride.

She did not think as she did this. She was out of the world, as she had been in the winter camp. But this was not dull or remote. It was intensely real—too real for the world, as the seer herself was.

Deep within Selene, resistance set hard. She went where she was led, did as she was bidden. It was a courtesy to her kinswoman. She had not given in to the Goddess, nor did she intend to. When this was done, she would come back to Etta, who silenced her dreams. Etta was her protection. That had not changed because the seer had decided that it was time to die.

There was only one high place near the camp, a hill that rose abruptly to the westward; they had ridden around it to make camp where a spring bubbled out of the ground. The hill was gaunt and bare, windswept, with the power in it that such places took to themselves through their nearness to heaven.

The seer had let go while they rode. When they came to the foot of the hill, she was lying limp over the bay mare's neck. She was alive, but only barely. Selene lifted her down with care and cradled her.

The seer's smile was a faint glimmer in starlight. She thought that she had won. Selene did not choose to disabuse her of the notion.

It was a hard climb, carrying a limp body in her arms, but it was necessary—a sacrifice, as befit a warrior. The burning in her lungs, the ache in her legs and arms, were proof that she was alive; that she was strong.

The sun set while she climbed, and the vault of stars opened above her. She made her way by instinct rather than by earthly sight. The seer barely breathed, but there was still life in her. She fed on starlight: a thin sustenance, but it held her to the earth for a few heartbeats longer.

The summit was rough and stony but level enough. In its center was a ring of stones. Power gathered itself there, shimmering with starlight. It sang softly as Selene approached, and settled to a low melodic hum when she stepped into the circle. Gently she laid the seer in its center.

The seer groped for her hands as she had in the camp. Selene cradled them carefully, but they caught hers in a grip that was startlingly strong. "You will see for the people," the seer said, "but your sight will wander far. It will lose itself, then find greater strength than I ever knew."

No, Selene thought. She felt odd, remote. This must be the world of the sight, where time was strange, and past and present and future were all one. "I am not—I will not be—"

"No one ever asks for this," the seer said. "Often those who want it least are most blessed with the gift—or curse, if you would call it so. I, too. I was young once; I had a name that no one now remembers. I had a clan, friends, a sister whom I loved. Then the sight took me away. It will take you, but by ways and to places that you may never expect. Expect the unexpected, child. Even with the sight, some paths are dark, and others lead to false turnings. Nothing in this world is certain; and the sight will often confuse more than it will make clear."

"So you taught me," Selene said. "You thought I wasn't listening. I remember every word."

"You remember," said the seer. "Now believe."

"I will not," Selene said. Her voice shook. "I refuse."

"There is no refusing this." The seer's grip tightened to the threshold of pain. "No one runs from this, however hard she may try. Accept it, child. Bow to it. It's a great gift."

Selene's heart was beating hard. She was dizzy, sick with anger and resistance that, she feared, was altogether useless.

The wind had begun to blow, a soft shrilling above the hum of the stones. The stars turned in their slow dance. In their patterns, all against her will, she saw multitudes. Tribes and nations. Armies marching. A great wave of conquest that swept from the sunset to the sunrise. She saw lovers in one another's arms, and enemies locked in the embrace of death. She saw Phaedra's face, and Hippolyta's, and Ione's. She saw Etta, but the child was turned away from her, showing the curve of a shoulder and a plait of red-gold hair.

If she must see, she should see more—should see what was directly before her, what waited in Eos temple. But the sight was not a tame beast. It was in the mood to offer grand scope and the sweep of ages. She could not force it to focus more closely.

Maybe she did not want to. While it showed her wars and armies, it did not torment her with visions of fire.

"In time," said the seer, hardly more than a whisper now, "you will master it. Be patient; let it grow in you. It will bear fruit."

"What if I turn my back on it?" Selene demanded.

"It will pursue you. Be sure of that. Have a care, child, that when at last you turn to face it, you have the strength to be its master. I failed in that. I lost my name, my place, my clan and tribe and nation. I became its slave, blown by every wind and driven to go wherever it led."

"You? You failed? You were the greatest seer in the memory of the people."

"Memory is short," the seer said. "I was weak enough to lose my self. Maybe you will not be. Maybe all your resistance will serve you in the end—or it will destroy you. That choice is yours."

"What if I choose neither?"

"You will choose," said the seer. "Now open the passage. Set me free."

"I don't know how."

"Look within. Listen to your heart."

Selene bit her tongue. The iron-sweet taste of blood brought her somewhat to her senses. The seer asked that she act as a priestess; that she perform the office of the dying. She was not a priestess and never a seer. She was a hunter, a fighter, a protector and a guard.

And yet she knew the rite, clear and immediate at the sound of the seer's words.

"Words are a guide," the seer said, hardly more than a whisper. "Let the spirit move through them."

The spirit was in her. She had not felt it come in. Maybe the seer spoke the truth; maybe it had always been there.

She began the chant on a clear high note that, sustained, bred the next and the next. The seer sighed under her hands. Her joy was vivid, singing in Selene's heart. She could not help herself; she had to share in it. It was overwhelming. It drowned her.

As the seer passed, she shed old age like a skin and emerged all new. Just before the light took her, she turned. Her smile dazzled Selene, blinding her to the light.

When Selene opened her eyes again, the light that met them was earthly sunrise, and the wind that scoured the hilltop was clean and cold. The seer's body lay in the circle, arms folded on its breast. The life was gone from it.

Selene could not find it in her to grieve—and not only because she had hated this woman for so long. In the end there was no hate and only dim resentment. There was no sorrow in this death, no pain. All that was drowned in joy.

Selene met the queen's riding half a day out from the camp in which the seer had found them. They had not been keeping too strong a pace: Selene's mare was breathing lightly, still fresh from a night's rest and grazing on the hilltop.

Mare and rider came alone. The seer's mare had been gone when Selene looked for her, vanished into the sunlit air.

No one spoke to Selene of what she had done in the night. It was like a gift of the Goddess, a veil of forgetting.

Maybe that was Etta's gift. Selene took charge of her, to the visible relief of the royal guards who had been watching over her. In her presence, as always before, the press of the world eased. The sight receded. Selene was a simple woman of the people again, without power or great destiny.

It should have felt wonderful. It felt oddly cramped: as if she had been standing on a high peak but had descended from it into a dark and stifling space, as narrow as a grave.

She set her teeth. This she had chosen. This she would keep. Not for her the dizzy heights, or the horrors that slept beneath them.

FIVE

Eos temple was a half-ruined tower on a high hill, with a village
of round stone houses below. It was the oldest of the temples of
the people, the first that they had raised in the Goddess' honor, so
long ago that the count of years was forgotten.

The Goddess had dwelt on the height before the people came.
Others had worshipped her before, and gathered the stones that
in time had been raised into the tower. The sense of age, of holi-
ness sunk in the earth, grew stronger the closer Selene came,
pressing like a hand against her face and body.

Of treachery she felt nothing. No foresight came to her, no
rush of vision. She was as simply and mortally blind as she could
have wished to be. The words she had spoken in the winter camp
had been empty wind. There was nothing here that should not
have been here.

Hippolyta's scouts reported no armies gathering, no threat
impending. Phaedra was lodged in the circle of stone houses far-
thest from the hill, with most of the clan-sisters who had gone
away with her, and a handful of others: women of eastern clans

who had elected to ride with her. They were hiding nothing that anyone could find. The priestesses had them under guard, unobtrusive but unmistakably present.

Hippolyta professed herself content. She paused in sight of the temple and prepared herself to be seen in public: she put off her riding clothes, shook her hair out of its plaits, and put on the scarlet girdle of her office. Ione brought the queen mare for her to mount.

The mare was unwontedly irritable. She snapped at Ione; she half-reared and spun as Hippolyta approached. For the queen she would stand, but once Hippolyta was on her back, she whirled and bolted westward—away from the temple, back the way they had come.

Hippolyta mastered her. She did not yield easily, but she was obedient to the stronger will. She turned back toward the temple and suffered herself to be ridden through the gate. It was dangerous for anyone to ride too close; her heels were restless, her tail switching with temper. She snapped at one of the priestesses who had flocked to the gate, so sudden that the woman barely escaped.

Selene rode behind Hippolyta with Etta perched on her mare's shoulders, resting quietly in the circle of her arms. Without warning the child turned boneless and slipped free and darted toward the queen mare. She was up in front of her mother before anyone could move.

The queen mare shook from nose to tail and heaved an enormous, groaning sigh. Her ears lifted; her eye lost its wild glare. She plodded peacefully forward as if her eruption of temper had never been.

Selene saw the flick of fingers here and there among the gathering of priestesses, gestures of warding against the untoward. Their faces were wary; some were afraid. Those, Selene thought, had been listening to Phaedra.

Of Phaedra's followers she saw nothing. A priestess was waiting for them in front of the innermost house, which was larger
than the rest, with a carved lintel and a wooden door. She stood
by respectfully as Hippolyta and her escort dismounted, then
bent her head as a servant of the Goddess should before the ruler
of the people. "Be welcome in Eos temple," she said in the sweet
trained voice of a sacred singer. "Your presence honors us."

"I give honor to the temple," said Hippolyta, "and thanks to
you who welcome me to it."

The priestess inclined her head again and beckoned. "If you
will, lady?"

Most of the escort remained outside with the horses and the
baggage. Ione followed Hippolyta with a pair of strong women,
and Selene somewhat behind. Etta was in Hippolyta's arms, and
Selene was Etta's guardian. Where the child went, she was obliged
to go.

The high priestess' house was wide and almost airy within.
Light streamed through the center of the roof, illumining a circle
of rooms and alcoves round the broad circle of the hearth. The
fire was banked on this warm, close day; a young priestess dozed
by it, snapping awake as they all entered. There was no one else in
the hall.

She helped their guide to offer hospitality: water for washing,
bread and cheese and clear water to quench hunger and thirst,
and tanned hides on which to sit or rest. It was no more or less
than the courtesy of the people, and yet Selene itched in her skin.
Just as she gathered herself to rise and hunt down Phaedra, voices
sounded without.

Half a dozen women entered, but Selene's eye fixed on the one
who led them. She was not the ancient who had been priestess
here when Etta was presented to the Goddess; she was much
younger. Yet she wore the golden fillet and the long tunic of white

leather, open at the sides, and the heavy collar of gold and amber that Selene remembered. She had a queenly air about her, a sense that she knew her own importance and was most careful of it. Had she not kept the Penthesilea herself waiting upon her convenience?

There was a strange sourness in Selene's thoughts. She had been in this temple before and found it both restful and holy, but now it made her twitch. Maybe it was Phaedra's presence, however unseen; maybe it was the queen mare's uncertain mood. Maybe it was the sight that hovered just out of reach, tormenting her with uncertainty. Whatever it was, she could not settle.

The new high priestess was exquisitely courteous, her words and her gestures of respect perfectly calculated. There was nothing to object to, nothing to justify the deepening sense of wrongness that had Selene leaping nearly out of her skin.

None of the others appeared to sense it. Ione was alert as always, but her stance was easy, her hands at her sides, some small distance from her weapons.

Selene drew back toward the wall. The curtains were down in the alcoves. She thought she heard movement within: a rustle, a whisper. Her hackles rose.

The queen and the priestess were still speaking together, a murmur of voices, distant and inconsequential. Selene hunted the thing that sent a prickle down her spine.

She slipped from shadow to shadow. The first alcove was empty. In the second, a priestess nursed a pair of infants, one at either ample breast. The third was empty again. They were all empty except for the one. Selene's ears must have deceived her.

She returned to Hippolyta's shadow, which was the most familiar of them all. She loosened her long knife in its sheath; she let herself fall into the guard's stance, light, watchful, ready to leap at the first sign of trouble.

No one spoke of Phaedra, not even the mention of her name. It was as if she did not exist. There were matters enough to consider, affairs of the clans and the people, rites and courtesies—a long waste of time in Selene's estimation. Her nerves jangled more, the longer it went on.

They went from greeting to lodging in alcoves of the great house, and from there to a feast of welcome. For that they left their weapons behind according to custom. Selene's uneasiness grew as she took in the empty scabbards and the missing bows and spears.

The priestesses had slaughtered an ox and roasted it whole. There was warm bread and strong cheese, honey in the comb, and new greens of spring, fresh and clean to the taste. It was a wonderful, a perfect feast, and Selene barely tasted it.

The wine was a delicacy, a rarity in this land of barley beer and spring water. It had come from the lands to the south and west; it was strong and only lightly watered. Hippolyta and her people were careful of it, but even a little of that vintage was enough to make a woman's head spin. Selene stopped well short of a cup and took shelter behind Etta, who could feed herself well enough, but not particularly tidily. Feeding her bits of roast ox and leaves of green stuff made Selene invisible. She was a servant, a menial, and therefore beneath notice.

One by one, for all their efforts, Hippolyta's escort succumbed to the wine and the feast. The warmth of the hall, the heavy scents of wine and roast meat and crowded humanity, weighted Selene's eyelids. She fought to stay awake.

Etta was restless in her lap, wriggling as she did when she had to relieve herself. Selene heaved them both up and stumbled toward the door.

No one seemed to notice that she was escaping. Her heart contracted at the thought of leaving Hippolyta in that place, but the child's struggles had become insistent. Selene stretched her stride.

The night air was surprisingly cool. It revived her. She got Etta to the privies in time; when the child was done, Selene found herself reluctant to return to the hall.

Driven by an impulse she did not question, she sought the field where the horses were. The queen mare stood glimmering in starlight, grazing quietly, but with an air of watchfulness that Selene could well understand. Selene set Etta on her back. The mare snorted softly and shook her ears, but offered no other commentary.

The child was safe. Selene straightened as if relieved of a burden. Her weapons were in the high priestess' house, left in her lodgings according to the courtesy of banquets. She would have to do what she could without them.

She went softly, with a hunter's stealth. Maybe it was foolish, but it did no harm. If the Goddess was kind, Selene would come again to her queen's side and find all as it should be.

As she approached the high priestess' house, she heard voices. Shadows moved in the gloom: figures advancing toward the glimmer of light from the door. They could have had honest business there; this was a temple, and it was nearly time for the midnight ritual. But the prickle in Selene's spine said otherwise.

She counted a score of them, and more too deep in the dark to see. Selene slipped in through them, moving as softly as they. The voices were farther ahead. One she could have sworn she recognized, but maybe she was hearing what she wished—or dreaded—to hear.

After the dim starlight, the light of lamps in the high priestess' house was painfully bright. Selene kept to the darkness but peered within. Figures slipped past her. There were others inside, and two were speaking. One was the high priestess. The other, as she had expected, was Phaedra.

She had aged, Selene saw as her eyes grew accustomed to the light. Years and bitterness had eaten away at her beauty. She was thinned to the bone, and her hair was shot with grey. But her voice was the same: its false sweetness; its gift of persuading the weak and the gullible.

It seemed the high priestess was either or both. She leaned toward Phaedra with the air of a woman besotted.

Phaedra's women had scattered through the hall. They were armed with knives. All of Hippolyta's people were down, some snoring, some sprawled in deep and silent sleep. Hippolyta was sitting upright with Ione beside her, but her eyes were shut and her body slack.

Selene strained to hear the words that Phaedra spoke. She caught only snatches. *Death . . . regret . . . Hippolyta.*

All of the women with knives had gone into the hall. Only Selene was left outside, hidden in shadow. She measured the distance from the door to Phaedra, and from there to Hippolyta. Phaedra's followers closed in on the sleepers.

Selene felt the rush of air, a buffet like a sudden gust of wind. It flung her into the hall. But no one had eyes for her. The storm that burst through the door had the shape of a moon-white mare, and on her back a child with empty eyes.

The queen mare hurtled through Phaedra's followers, flinging them down and trampling them, until she stood over the sleeping queen. There she took her stand, ears back, neck arched like a striking snake's.

She had scattered the would-be murderers, but Selene's eyes were on Phaedra. Hippolyta's rival wore an expression of absolute frustration. She had waited too long and plotted too deeply to be deterred by any omen, even one as powerful as this.

Selene moved even before Phaedra began, with no thought in her, only speed. She paused once, a swift stoop and sweep, coming erect with a dagger in her hand. The woman who had held it would not get up again: the mare's hoof had crushed her skull.

The blade fit sweetly across Phaedra's throat, the point resting light and easy just where the great vein pulsed beneath the skin. She stood frozen in Selene's grip, breathing shallowly.

"Wake the queen," Selene said to the high priestess, who stood staring, her face the color of curdled milk.

The priestess' eyes rolled like a startled foal's. Selene let the dagger's point bite just enough to bring forth a drop of blood. The priestess flung herself to her knees, crawling toward the mare and the queen. "Lady," she said, hardly more than a gasp, but her voice found itself quickly enough. "Lady, wake!"

The mare stamped. Her hoof rang on the packed earth of the floor. Hippolyta stirred, murmuring, frowning as she swam up out of sleep.

Phaedra's body tensed infinitesimally. Selene gripped her about the neck and flung her down, knee pressed to her throat, knife shifted to her cheekbone just below one wide and hating eye.

Hippolyta rose unsteadily, still fogged with sleep, but coming swiftly to consciousness. Her glance took in the hall, the fallen women, the knives scattered across the floor, and the queen mare now standing behind her with Etta still clinging to her back. It settled briefly on the high priestess, then came to rest on Phaedra. Selene watched her wake to understanding.

"Let her up," Hippolyta said.

Selene widened her eyes. Hippolyta frowned slightly. Reluctantly Selene drew back from her captive.

Phaedra lay for a long moment as Selene had left her. Selene barred the way to the door. Others of Hippolyta's women had roused and drawn in in a circle, with Ione foremost, simmering with anger at her own weakness.

At length Phaedra drew herself to her feet. She bowed with rather less irony than Selene might have expected. "Lady," she said. "You have strong defenders."

Hippolyta gave her no title of either respect or kinship. "I had thought better of you," she said.

"It was a clever plot," said Phaedra. "It would have succeeded, but for . . ." Her eyes slid toward the white mare.

"But for the Goddess' help," Hippolyta said. "I was a fool; I thought to face a threat in daylight. This night of knives shames the blood we share."

"It would have made me queen," Phaedra said.

"Never," said Hippolyta. "Not in this world."

"Nothing is certain while we live," said Phaedra. She lifted her chin. "Will you kill me? Are you brave enough for that?"

"Neither brave enough nor wise enough," Hippolyta said. "I cannot be a kinslayer, even to save myself."

"You *are* a fool," said Phaedra.

"Certainly," Hippolyta said, "but I am the Goddess' own, whatever level of idiot I may be."

Hippolyta pronounced sentence under the open sky, in the clear light of morning. Phaedra stood naked, her wrists bound, her hair cropped short. The morning was warm, but she shivered convulsively.

"You are no longer of us," Hippolyta said in the hearing of her escort and of the priestesses of Eos temple. "You are forgotten. Your kinship is broken. Your name is taken away. Nameless, kinless, clanless, I cast you out. I condemn you. I doom and damn you to wander forever beyond the ends of the world. At your death none shall mourn you. No kind spirit shall inter your bones. Your soul shall be scattered to the winds of heaven. Never again shall you be reborn. Your life is as nothing; your death shall be absolute."

She stooped and took up a fistful of dust and cast it on Phaedra's head. "You are dead to us. You are gone to us. You are forgotten."

Phaedra sank down. The knobbed curve of her spine, the pebbled white skin, struck Selene with pity that she had no desire to feel. She struggled to harden her heart.

The queen mare knew no such weakness. She had endured the humans' ritual with tail-switching impatience. Now she had had enough. She charged upon the exile, gripped her arm with long yellow teeth, and dragged her to her feet, then hounded her as if she had been an outcast of the herd: nipping, harrying, driving her away.

Long after the mare and the exile had vanished over the long hill to the east, they all stood silent. Whether it was grief or awe mattered little. It was never a joyful thing to cast a sister from the people.

None of Phaedra's followers had chosen to share her sentence. They would take whatever punishment the queen decreed, rather than endure involuntary exile. And that was the saddest thing of all, even sadder than Phaedra's casting out from the clan.

There was still the matter of the high priestess. The queen pardoned the lesser priestesses—to their heartfelt and babbling relief—but she could not close her eyes to the treason of one so highly placed. The woman was stripped of her rank and her office, set among the lowest of the servants, and condemned to menial labor until she either died or proved herself repentant.

Her guards were Phaedra's followers. If one of them turned traitor again, they all died, every one. If their charge escaped or corrupted anyone but herself, they would die. Their sentence was death—in their natural span if they served the queen well; summarily if they did not.

Hippolyta rode away from Eos three days after she had come to it, mounted on the white mare who had preserved her life, with her daughter riding before her. There was no more word of sacrilege, and no audible murmur against the abomination. The Goddess' hand had shown itself in the child. She was sacred now, a living image of the One who had created her.

Selene rode behind them in silence. The people would accept the queen's heir—perforce, but they could not deny the Goddess' will.

She should have been happy. She was relieved, yes, but there was an odd sadness in her. She did not grieve for Phaedra—never—but Hippolyta did. However little love there had ever been between them, they were close kin. That bond of blood could not so easily be forgotten, even after the rite of banishment.

Hippolyta's choice, like Selene's, had no reason or logic in it. She had done what she must. She had chosen the child of her body, however deeply flawed, over her sister's daughter. She could pray, and must with every day's rising, that she had chosen rightly.

Selene's own prayers were frequent and heartfelt. She could not shake the ongoing sense of foreboding, and the awareness that this was not over. But Hippolyta was safe for a while. That much her bones knew. That while would stretch for as long as Hippolyta's loyal women could manage. Years. Decades, maybe. Then there would be a price to pay. But, Goddess willing, they would all be prepared to pay it.

SIX

The moon was full: a soft spring moon, blurred with haze and scented with flowers. Selene stepped through the door of the potter's house into a wash of blue-white light.

She drew a long breath. Her duty to the clan was done. She had lived out her month with a man of suitable breeding and intelligence, who was also a considerate lover and an amusing companion. It had been a pleasant time, but as she stood in the moonlight, she knew that nothing had come of it. She had been barren since she lost her son, the winter before Etta was born—how long ago?

A dozen years. Six years since Phaedra was stripped of her name and cast out from the people—and since the seer had passed her gift and curse to Selene. Selene had said nothing of it even to Hippolyta. It was asleep in her, waiting for the moment when it would wake and possess her and single her out from the people.

That moment was not yet. If Selene was strong enough, it would be never.

She ran her hands down her body. The years had been kind to her. Her skin was smooth, her face unlined, her hair untouched with grey. But then, she thought, she was bred for that. Her mother had been beautiful when the fire took her, when she was well past her fortieth year; and Selene had been a late child, born when Dione was past thirty.

Selene was just shy of thirty. There was still time to bear a daughter for the people. Maybe when her guardianship of Etta was done, the Goddess would free her to raise a child of her own.

Etta had been under others' care for this month. She had been well: Selene had seen her when she came in the day before, riding with hunters who had brought back a boar from a covert north of the men's village. Hunters often took Etta with them as a talisman, because she had an infallible instinct for tracking and killing game. She was better than a pack of hounds, they said— though not, if they could help it, where Selene or Hippolyta could hear.

Selene glanced back. The interior of the house was aflicker with lamplight. Dion the potter lay in the rumpled bed: a bare brown shoulder, a tangle of fair curls. She smiled at the memory of his hands on her skin, but she turned away with remarkably little regret. *Men are for breeding,* her mother had taught her. *Women are for love.*

The people were dancing under the moon, away below the village, in the green bowl that had been both shrine and dancing ground for as long as anyone could remember. The drums were beating; the pipes were wailing. Voices were singing the old songs, the chants of moonlight and darkness: sweet voices of women and now and then the deeper voice of a man, striking notes that one seldom heard in the camps of the people.

Hippolyta was not there tonight, but Etta was. She was naked as many of them were, slender as a young tree, swaying in a wind that no one felt but she.

Selene stopped short. The moon softened some shapes, but others it caught as brightly as if in daylight. Etta's skin, golden in the sun, was silver-white under the moon. The limbs were a child's still, thin and angular, but no eye could mistake the budding of breasts.

Warmth moved beside Selene. She started slightly and looked into Ione's face.

The warleader had seen what she had; Ione's brows were raised, her expression quizzical. "It did have to happen," she observed. "The body is as healthy as any other young animal's."

"One never expects it," Selene said, "in any of one's children. With souls or without."

Ione's lips twitched. Her arm settled about Selene's shoulders. The moon was bright, the music was wild, the queen's heir was dancing like a wind over the grass. Figures swirled together and dropped away in pairs all across the field, or came back arm in arm, smiling a warm and secret smile.

Selene had been in awe of this woman since she was a child. She had never dared approach her with anything but the utmost respect. But respect was not in Ione's mind tonight. In a very little while, it vanished from Selene's as well.

Hippolyta was no blinder than either Selene or Ione. She saw what had become increasingly obvious: that her daughter was no longer a child.

As the spring gathering wound to its end in the solstice feast and the great rite of the Goddess, she sat in the circle of elders beneath the tree that was the heart of the men's village and said, "My heir will be a woman this season."

The elders glanced at one another. "It is evident," said Dorcas of the Dun Mare clan. "Has she begun her courses?"

"In the moon's dark," said Selene.

Once more the glances went round. Someone murmured the phrase that was proper: "She has the Goddess' blessing."

"Indeed she does," said Hippolyta, "and in a blessed time. We'll celebrate her feast before the clans disperse to the summer pastures."

That met with perfect silence. Even Ione could think of nothing to say. Very briefly she caught herself missing the one who had been cast out. That one had always said the things that no one else would say; as Hippolyta's sister-daughter she had had a certain immunity, and rank enough to escape the royal wrath.

No one was going to speak. Maybe it was best, but Ione's heart would not let her be. The words came of their own accord. "Lady," she said, "she has no name, no self. She can speak no words, share in no rite. How can she be accepted into the tribe?"

"A woman is a woman," said Hippolyta, "whether she can speak or no."

"A woman has a name," Dorcas said, now that Ione had opened the door, "and even if she be mute or deaf, she still has a soul."

"There is nothing in the traditions that says such a thing," Hippolyta said. "Only that when a daughter of the people comes to the age of her courses, she be reckoned a woman. My daughter is a warrior, a hunter. The Goddess has blessed her. She brings no shame to the people."

"She has no soul," said one of the priestesses.

Hippolyta rose, with Selene a shadow behind her. "We will feast before the clans disperse."

For some time after she was gone, the elders sat without speaking. None seemed angry. At length Dorcas said with a heavy sigh, "We should have expected this."

"Is there any harm in it?" asked her clan-sister Melanthe. "It changes nothing, commits us to nothing. It's not as if she's to be initiated into one of the temples."

"Will you wager on that being next?" said the priestess who had spoken before. "She's forced that thing on us from the moment it was born. She won't stop until it has every rank and privilege of a live and breathing sister, as if it were capable even of knowing that such a thing could be."

Ione bit her tongue. She had not been fool enough to think that Phaedra's exile had cast out such thoughts from the people, but she had hoped not to hear them spoken so plainly. Etta's existence festered beneath the surface always.

Maybe it was best to lance the wound. She did not say what she would have said, either the rebuke or the defense of her queen. She let them speak, pouring out years of resentment, fear, incomprehension. Even the priestesses—especially the priestesses—had forgotten or chosen to ignore the Goddess' omens.

When she judged that it had gone on long enough, she said, "So. You would foment another rebellion. A war. An uprising against the queen."

Their shock seemed honest, as did the horror on the faces of those who had spoken the loudest against the heir. Dorcas spat at the roots of the tree and made a warding gesture, sharp and angry. "Goddess, no! What makes you think that? We're loyal to Hippolyta. But isn't it our duty to question her decisions, if those decisions are ill-judged?"

"Is the Goddess guilty of bad judgment?"

"The Goddess is incalculable," said the priestess.

"How convenient," said Ione. "You object to the queen's decision. Well and good—I'll tell her. But you're fools if you think she'll give way for that."

"We are not fools," Dorcas said. Her voice was cold.

"I would hope not," Ione said.

The day before the queen's feast, the clans began to move from the gathering place. They packed up their tents and loaded their wagons and rode away.

It was a slap in Hippolyta's face. Selene would not have faulted her if she had gone to war over it, but she simply said, "One day they'll bow at her feet—and no one will force them."

Selene kept her thoughts to herself. She had enough to do to keep Etta clean, fed, and intermittently clothed; tomorrow the child would sit at the feast, however few the revelers and however forced the merriment.

"It's better this way," Hippolyta said, reading her as easily as always. "I know who is loyal—and I know who was too honest to lie about her misgivings."

Etta sat like an ivory image in the firelight, crowned with flowers and dressed in the girdle of white doeskin that marked a new-made woman. The rite that consecrated her had been simple.

Because no priestess had come, the queen had celebrated it. Etta had had no words to speak; she stood where she was made to stand, rapt in contemplation of a fiery sunset, while the hymn was sung and the sacrifice made and the Goddess invoked.

The likeness between mother and daughter was striking: the same red-golden beauty, the same clean-carved cast of feature. But there was no light or life in the child's face.

That had long since ceased to grieve Selene, but tonight it ached like an old wound. This was a young girl's gladdest night, when she left her childhood behind and became a woman, a full sister of the people. But Etta could know nothing, no joy, no sorrow, only the intermittent fascination of the firelight, and the stars overhead, and the taste of roast meat on her tongue. She had no preference for anything that was fed her; she ate it all impartially.

Selene savored it because Etta could not: tasting each bite, relishing the richness of fat, the crack of bones and the sweetness of the marrow. She was aware of Etta beside her and Hippolyta beyond, and Ione some little distance along the circle—with a brief and surprising pang of jealousy at that: was she sharing a cup with one of the women from the warband?

Etta stirred. Selene's hackles rose. There was no reason for it; the child had only straightened somewhat and shifted, turning slightly. Maybe her body was uncomfortable. Maybe she liked the warmth of the fire better from that angle, or found the moon's light more pleasant on her face. And yet Selene had reacted with a hunter's instinct, that could distinguish between the wind in the grass and the passing of the quarry through it.

Etta stilled again. Gradually Selene's tension eased, but she remained alert, watchful. She ate and drank more sparingly. She even forgot to watch Ione, but that resolved itself: the warleader came in time to sit beside her, not touching, simply being there.

Selene meant to tell her that something was amiss with Etta, but somehow the words never came. Ione said nothing. After a while she stretched out beside Selene, head in her lap, and went peacefully to sleep.

Selene stroked the long dark-gold hair, but kept her eyes on Etta. The child did not move. She was focused on something, if such a thing could be, but it was not anything in the circle of the clan. It was something beyond—far beyond, maybe, to the south and west. Selene stretched her own sight as best she could, but saw only darkness and the cold gleam of starlight.

A man's voice startled her into a different kind of alertness. He was speaking from nearer the fire, where some of the men from the village were passing round a jar of their rich brown ale. "Yes," he said: a deep voice and resonant, pitched by nature to carry. "I heard it from the traders who came in just after the full moon. The world is changing, away to the westward. New kings, new empires—worlds being conquered."

"Worlds are always being conquered," said another of the men: a lighter voice, and familiar; Dion the potter had come out for Etta's feast. Selene was touched, a little.

"Not like this, from what I heard," the first man said. "Kings come and go, rise up and kill one another and then someone kills them, but there's a new king who means to rule the world."

"Don't they all?"

Laughter ran round the circle. "Men out there," said someone new, "they're not like us. They're savages."

Did he sound a little wistful?

"Savages armed with bronze," said the first man, "and marching in thousands. The Great King of Persia is sorely beset, they say. He's been invaded from the west, and the invader is a god, or the son of one—no one's exactly clear on the point, except that there's divinity in it somewhere."

"His queen must be very strong," said a younger voice, slurred with wine.

"His mother is a priestess," said Dion, "and a queen." They all stared. He spread his hands. "I didn't say I believed it! I heard it, that was all. It's a good story. How she lay with a god and conceived a son—not a daughter, which tells you how preposterous it is. How the son grew up to be a king. And how his heart will never rest until he rules the world."

"Preposterous," they all murmured, except the first man.

"Goddess knows," the first man said, "men in the west are strange—even if some of them are our kin from long ago."

"They went away in fear of the Goddess," Dion said. "They defied Her and She cursed them. They were cast out."

"Now they're coming back," said the first man, "with armies."

"They won't come here," said Dion. "We're protected as we've always been. No one invades us. The Goddess stops them."

"Pray the Goddess that be so," his friend said.

The conversation wandered away after that. Selene wondered at herself for listening as long as she had. The affairs of men in the western countries had nothing to do with her. War could break out here; invasions did not. The land was warded and the people protected, as the man had said.

SEVEN

Selene woke with a start. She had not meant to doze off; she had been half awake, half in a strange wandering dream.

The sky was lightening with dawn. The fire had died. Bodies were scattered across the field, some snoring, most deeply and soundlessly asleep.

Etta was on her feet, stalking softly as she did when she hunted, picking her way through the sleepers. Selene staggered up and followed her.

Etta moved with purpose, if such a thing could be said of her. Her track was as direct as the ground and the various obstacles would allow: west and somewhat south, in the direction she had been facing since the night before.

For this Selene had been waiting, hardly even aware that she had been doing it. It was time; and Etta was the sign and the omen.

Selene barely paused to gather what she reckoned to need: a bag of bread and cheese and dried meat, a skin of water, a horse. Etta paused for nothing but the horse. Somewhat to Selene's surprise, she did not choose the queen mare, but clambered onto the back of one of her daughters, a young mare, heavily dappled, who had just been broken to a rider in the spring. She was notoriously difficult, but for Etta she was as calm as her mother. The mares knew what she was, however blind their human servants might be.

Selene made no effort to hide herself. Etta was oblivious; the mare clearly did not care, except to warn Selene's mare to keep a respectful distance.

None of the people followed. They were all sleeping off the night's revelry. She rode through the remnants of the greater camp: black scars of quenched fires, trampled grass that marked paths and the positions of tents, and the turned earth where the privies had been.

Etta ignored it all. Her eyes were fixed on the horizon. Although the sun was behind her, her face was full of its light. For a moment as Selene stared after her, Etta was wrapped in light, sending off rays of blinding splendor. She had become the sun, and the sun had filled her, delighting in her emptiness.

Ione's sleep that night had been heavy, as if drugged. She had drunk deeply enough, but her head for the men's strong ale was legendary; it should not have felled her as hard as it had.

Her dreams in that leaden sleep were strange, not quite nightmares, but not pleasant, either. In them she wandered a dim country with companions whom she could not quite see, who spoke words she could not quite hear. She took into waking a memory of strangeness and an odd sensation in her middle, as if she had been fighting a hard and fruitless battle all through the night.

The sun woke her, shining in her eyes. Others were groaning, stirring, rising. She did not know what made her look for Etta first, before even Hippolyta.

The child was gone. Not a child now, no—last night's feast had made her a woman. But to Ione she was still a small feral creature with empty eyes, who fought as she breathed, with utter and instinctive ease.

Not only Etta was missing. Selene was nowhere to be found. That need mean nothing; they could have gone to the privies, or ridden out in the bright morning. But the taste of Ione's dream was still on her tongue. She roused Hippolyta with a word.

Hippolyta had the same half-stunned, half-bemused expression Ione had felt on her own face at waking. The fog of dreams was on her, too.

The queen gathered a hunting party, a dozen strong riders, raiders and trackers, who could fight well if they must, and ride fast and far. It should have seemed absurd or overwrought, but Ione felt the same breathless urgency.

They picked up the trail at once. Neither Etta nor Selene had tried to conceal their tracks. They had taken good horses; Ione would have been astonished if they had not. Their path led west and somewhat south—toward Persia in the end, though they would cross a good part of the people's lands and pass through a fair number of tribes on the way there.

For a few wild moments Ione knew that Selene had abducted the heir and was taking her away to sell to one of the tribes beyond the borders, to be a plaything for a bearded chieftain or a victim for his wives. But that was preposterous. Most likely they had only gone hunting. There were herds of deer and gazelle where they had gone, and wildfowl in abundance, and fish in the rivers. Etta was a tireless hunter. She would find good quarry, capture or kill it, and bring it back to feed the clan.

That might be so, but Hippolyta continued to follow Etta, and

Ione followed Hippolyta. The ones they pursued, lighter and superbly mounted, with several hours' start, drew ahead as the day wore on, but never so far that Ione began to fret.

The quarry were not hunting. They were riding by as straight a way as they might, as if they had a destination in mind. They paused only as often as they must, to water the horses and give them time to graze a little. They must intend to stop for the night; they had no remounts, and must spare the horses as much as they could if they meant to travel far.

Had Ione's madness been sanity after all? Had Selene lost her mind and taken the heir away?

She was not leading; the smaller, lighter rider rode ahead. Etta was the guide. The Goddess must be in her, must be drawing her onward.

So did She lead Hippolyta, who had not spoken a word since she began that ride. They were all being led on this odd hunt.

It was easier, once Ione understood that, to ride and be silent— to be a hunter purely, and follow the quarry wherever it led.

Selene was aware that they were followed. She had expected it. Hippolyta would wake and find her daughter gone, and know that it was no ordinary hunt that had taken her. Selene would have paused to wait for her, but Etta would pause for nothing but the horses' welfare—and that, her mount decided for her.

It was nine days before Hippolyta's party, better provisioned and provided with remounts, with less need to hunt or forage, came within sight. They were nearly to the western edge of the people's lands, where the mountains of Anshan began to rise along the horizon. The hunting was easier, the game more

Judith Tarr

numerous, but the land was more difficult; it rose abruptly or fell
into sudden ravines, preparing itself for the mountains ahead.

Just past such a headlong descent, as the sun sank behind the
wall of mountains, Selene made camp in the shelter of the hillside. It had rained earlier; she was still damp. She gathered bits of
turf for a small fire, feeding it with cakes of dried dung.

Etta was sitting on the western side of the circle, face fixed as
always toward the sunset. The young mare grazed beyond her.

Suddenly the mare lifted her head. Her nostrils fluttered in a
whicker.

They came softly through the dusk, a dozen women of the
clan, with Ione and Hippolyta last of all. Selene's heart leaped at
the sight of them. She rose in respect for Hippolyta, and managed, just, not to fling herself into Ione's arms.

Hippolyta took in the camp with a glance and nodded to herself. "I did well to trust you," she said.

That was all she said, but it warmed Selene considerably. Still,
the real warmth, the warmth of the heart, came later, when Ione
brought her blanket and folded it on top of Selene's and slipped
beneath. Then Selene could rest, secure in those strong arms.

They rode on together, following Etta. Selene had gone beyond
the people's lands before, but never in such a way, with no knowledge of where she went or why, or how long she would be gone.
Nor had she ever ridden so far into a world that knew little or
nothing of the Goddess.

The bandits fell on them as they ascended into a country of
deep forests and stony mountainsides. There were forts on some
of those peaks, occupied by veiled and suspicious people who,
said Tanis who had traveled to this country when she was

younger, kept their women in cages and let their dogs and their tough little mountain ponies run free.

Hippolyta's riders had made no effort to prove the veracity of her story. The land fed them well enough; they were not of a mind to visit the houses of strangers. In any event, Etta's track led away from the hill forts and through the mountains.

This time when Selene's back felt eyes on it, there was little expectation that those who followed would be friendly. She glanced at Ione. The warleader had fallen back on the steep track as if to rest her horse, but her expression was wary. She had uncovered and strung her bow.

Selene judged it wise to follow her lead. Others were doing it, too, one by one down the line. They were armed and ready when the walls of the mountains closed in and the robed and shrilling attackers dropped from the heights.

Selene put an arrow through the eye of a bandit who fell almost on top of her, gagging at the unwashed reek of him— there could be no doubt that he was a man; no woman stank so powerfully. The next was too close to shoot. He grappled with her, struggling to pull her off her horse. Her mare snapped at his throat. He recoiled. Selene slashed her knife across his veiled face. He shrieked and fell away.

They were all men, and all smaller than she: wiry little creatures, armed with a startling array of weapons which they must have stolen from travelers and traders. They swarmed over the riders, relentless as locusts.

Selene could not press forward toward Etta or Hippolyta. The way was too narrow, too rocky and steep. At least, she thought in a dim corner of her mind, they were in a ravine and not on a ridge. The attackers could not fling them off the mountain.

Her hands were bloody to the wrists. There was no elegance in the way she fought. She hacked blindly at bodies that came and came. Her lungs burned. Her arms ached. She had wounds, she supposed. She could not feel them.

Charis was down. Tanis stood over her. Selene heaved up a wailing bandit and flung him headlong into the pack of his fellows.

Maybe that ended the battle. Maybe the battle had been ending before that. The ravine was strewn with bodies, some moving or screaming, some crumpled and still. Only one was of the people. All the rest were bandits. Their living fellows had fled, clambering back the way they had come.

Hippolyta and her riders brought Charis up to the open mountainside, out of the confinement of those stony walls. There was no time for a proper rite—Etta was straining away from the sister who held her. The queen entrusted Charis' soul to the Goddess and her body to the winds of heaven. They set her upright against a stone with her face toward the sunrise, and bound her so that she could not topple, and laid her bow and sword in her hands and her round shield at her feet. Then they cast earth upon her head, each of them, with a murmured word, so that her soul could be free.

Etta broke loose even as the last of them gathered up her fistful of stony dust. She was on her mare's back and riding relentlessly, with the blood of the slain still upon her hands and splashed on her legs and feet. The rest were given a choice: follow or be abandoned.

Selene followed, with Hippolyta close behind her. Ione sent half of the warriors after them. The others she kept with her, to pursue the bandits and assure that they would not lay another ambush.

"I'll catch you when I can," Ione called out to Hippolyta. "Don't wait for me."

"Guard yourself," Hippolyta called back. "Come back to me alive."

"On my honor," said Ione.

She said nothing to Selene. Selene expected nothing, but her heart knew the pain of yet another parting.

Almost she turned and galloped back. Hippolyta would not stop or fault her for it. But she was bound as tightly as Ione by bonds of honor and of duty. She rode with Etta. She always rode with Etta; that was her fate, as clear to her as the most vivid of visions.

EIGHT

They came down from the mountains of Anshan to the shores of the sea: a broad expanse of blue water stretching to the horizon. This was a different world, a world all of strangers, few of whom spoke any language that Etta's escort could understand.

Ione had caught them before they left the mountains, leading a caravan of mules and donkeys. Her coming was doubly and trebly welcome, and more useful than Selene might have expected. Ione knew a smattering of Persian, learned from a man who had occupied her bed for a while long ago; it was enough to win them passage and buy them food and teach them how to ride through this barbarous country. The caravan that Ione had won from the bandits gave them the wherewithal to buy what they needed, and clothed and armed them as well. They rode in Persian dress, which was enough like their own that they were at ease in it.

Ione's command of the language, such as it was, served another purpose. They had the news that ran through the villages even swifter than the couriers of the king. The Great King was dead, murdered by his own satraps. The new Great King was the vaunting boy, the invader from the west, whose name no one here could properly say. They called him Sikandar, but the riders heard his true name spoken once or twice: Alexander.

He was in Zadrakarta, in the city by the sea. War was raging across this country, which was called Hyrcania; but he had paused to celebrate a victory before he went on to win even more of them.

Etta was riding direct to the city, caring nothing for any obstacle that might present itself. Sometimes that obstacle was a company of men—raiding parties from Persia or Macedonia—and as often as not, that company saw a caravan apparently guarded by eunuchs and perceived it as fair prey. Hippolyta's women added to their store of weapons and trophies, and left behind a swath of dead or badly cowed men.

Sometimes the obstacle was other than human. On a windswept day just outside of Zadrakarta, a wild boar slashed Sardis' leg to the bone and killed one of the horses. While they tended the wounded and butchered the boar, a tiger took exception to their claiming of the prey. As if somehow it knew what she was, it leaped straight for Etta.

Ione shot at it, but the arrow clipped its ear and flew onward. Selene went after it with a boar-spear.

Just before the spear struck, it whipped about. She met its wild green glare. This was the face of death: fiercely striped, snarling, with blood matted in its fur.

Etta swooped down on its back, knife in hand. Before it could become fully aware of her presence, she had twisted up its jaw and cut its throat. It was a powerful stroke, slashing through the thick fur, straight to the great vein. The hot blood sprang. The tiger convulsed. Etta dropped, scrambling away from its death-throes. One of its wildly flailing paws caught the hem of her coat and shredded it.

Selene snatched her to safety. The tiger stiffened suddenly and coughed, and then was still.

They dined well that night on the flesh of the boar. Etta had the tiger's skin for a carpet, flickering like flame and darkness in the light of the campfire. She was quiescent as always after sundown, but her face would not turn away from the no longer distant city.

The younger women were spinning grand tales of the battles they had fought, all the way back beyond the mountains. Sardis, whose voice was sweet, had made a song of their exploits. Tanis had a flute; Phoebe fashioned a drum from a cookpot.

Selene rose softly and retrieved her bow and spear and sword, and went to sit out by the horses. The music and the singing were clear to hear from that distance, but she could, if she focused, hear the sounds of the night.

It was warm here in this season. The wind had died with the sun's setting; the air felt thick and damp after the cold clarity of the mountains. People crowded in here: the camp was almost within sight of a village, and from the hilltop beyond, had it been daylight, she could have seen the walls of the city.

She acknowledged Ione's coming with a slight shift of the body toward her, but no relaxation of vigilance. The warleader settled beside her, creaking somewhat, with a gust of wry laughter at the betrayals of age. "They're lively tonight," she said of the women by the fire.

"All this way," Selene said, "and they've never learned caution. They killed a tiger—what can men do to them, after all?"

"They didn't kill the tiger," said Ione. "Etta did. We're safe enough, I think. The king yonder, this Alexander—he's tamed the people hereabouts, by every account. Unless his own patrols fall on us, we'll not suffer an ambush within reach of Zadrakarta."

"No doubt," said Selene, but she did not put her weapons away.

Ione sat quietly beside her. The music had paused. The night was full of rustlings and chitterings. Far off, something grunted. Boar, maybe, or bear, if there were any in this country. Selene did not think it was another tiger.

Wild beasts did not frighten her. Men . . . she did not trust them. At all.

There were men nearby, camped closer to the village. They were much quieter than Hippolyta's women. She had had to listen hard to be sure, but there was no mistaking the sounds of a troop of horses, or the snores of the men who had been riding them in the women's wake. Following? She was not sure. In this country it was always wise to be suspicious.

She levered herself up with her spear. "Will you keep watch here?" she asked Ione.

She could just see the warleader's face in the starlight, how her brow lifted. "Are you wise to go alone?"

"Not wise," said Selene, "but safe enough. Be sure the child doesn't move before morning."

"I'll watch," Ione said.

Selene brushed her lips with a kiss and slipped off into the night.

The men were camped beyond a copse of trees. Selene had seen such camps at a distance as she approached Zadrakarta: strictly ordered, occupied by men who looked and spoke altogether differently than anyone she had seen before. Their language had an odd likeness to her own; she could, if she strained, begin to understand what they said to one another. They came from a country called Macedon, away in the west; they were of the same kin as the young king, the conqueror Alexander.

This was a hunting party from the look of its weapons and the line of perches for falcons, and the dogs tethered near the horses. Most of the men were Macedonians, but there were a handful of tents off to the side in which slept a small company of Persians.

In their coats and trousers and their long curled beards they were quite unlike the close-cropped, short-bearded or clean-shaven, bare-legged Macedonians. The two nations were not particularly amicable, although they hunted together. The Persians kept scrupulously separate; those Macedonians who were still awake did not offer to share wine or company with them.

Or so Selene thought as she lay concealed in the copse, until a stir within the largest of the Persian tents ended with the lifting of the flap and a sudden dazzle of light.

It was only the light of a single lamp, but it was blindingly bright in the darkness. The man who held it was Persian, very tall as some of them were, and richly dressed. Silk gleamed in the lamplight; he wore jewels set in gold. The man whom he ushered out into the night was Macedonian, less tall but still of substantial height; the light limned a face of rather remarkable beauty, clean-carved, with skin like darkened ivory. He wore no ornaments and only a simple linen tunic, but he carried himself like a prince.

He was laughing as he came out. The Persian said something in a language they both understood, and the Macedonian clapped him on the shoulder, easy and companionable. They embraced as friends would, in a warm haze of wine. Then they parted, the Macedonian staggering slightly but moving with grace nonetheless, seeking one of the tents in the greater camp.

The Persian stood looking after him, still smiling, but a kind of sadness had come over his face. Selene was rather surprised that she could see it; she was not accustomed to fathoming a person's expression through a thicket of beard. But this man seemed less opaque than most of his countrymen.

He turned, light and perfectly steady on his feet, and vanished into his tent. So: there was guile in him after all. If he had drunk as much as he pretended, she would have been surprised.

She withdrew softly into the underbrush. These men were not hunting the caravan, or patrolling the country, either. They had their own prey and their own purposes. It was happenstance that they had come across Hippolyta's track.

Even so, she watched them until the dark before dawn. She trusted nothing and no one here. The Goddess might be leading Her children, but She expected them to look after themselves.

The men beyond the copse were still asleep when Etta rose to ride. Selene had returned a little while before. Her eyes were gritty and her belly tight with lack of sleep, but her mind was clear enough.

Hippolyta called them all together just before they mounted. "Today we ride to Zadrakarta," she said. "You know that; you know who leads us. But I've been led as well. I've dreamed. The fate of our people is in that city. Our destiny is there."

No one spoke. Selene heard someone swallow a yawn. They had celebrated late, and drunk a great deal.

"Ione," said Hippolyta. "Selene. You ride with me. The rest of you, take the caravan and lead it away from the city, up into the hills. Make a war-camp there and wait. We'll get word to you when we've done as we must."

That roused them. They burst out in protest. Sardis' voice was loudest: "You can't go alone! They'll eat you alive."

Ione snorted. "Those aren't tigers yonder, they're men. When has any of us ever been afraid of a man?"

"Never," Sardis shot back, "but we've never faced a whole city full of them, either. They're worse than tigers. They hunt in swarms and they live for treachery. They're only ever safe when we raise them the way we raise our horses: constrained from birth to the discipline of the whip and the headstall."

"And if they're too obstreperous—horse or man—we geld them," Ione said. "I'm still not afraid of these men, or of their king, either."

"Time's passing," Hippolyta said. She was already mounted, blocking the path of Etta's mare. Etta looked ready to leap off and run afoot toward whatever it was that had called her so far.

Ione nodded sharply. "You have your orders, sisters. Take the caravan and go."

They were not happy, but orders were orders. Even the most rebellious of them would submit to the discipline of the clan. Selene resisted the urge to look back over her shoulder as she rode away. Everyone she loved was here, riding beside her—but it was a great temptation to wish she were riding away from this blind destiny and not toward it.

NINE

Zadrakarta was full of Macedonians: big, rough-spoken men who filled the taverns and roistered in the streets. Word in the villages had been that their king kept decent discipline in war, but in the flush of victory it seemed his army could do as it pleased. There were games in the Greek style, to which women were not admitted, and which the townsfolk found frankly embarrassing: all the men in them were naked.

Ione found them lodgings in an inn that was neither too rough nor too ostentatious. Travelers of middling rank and decent manners frequented it; soldiers passed it by, finding its beer watery and its wine worse. But its cook knew how to roast a fowl, and he had a fine hand with a sweet cake. Better yet, it had a room for the four eunuchs as they were taken to be, with a door that could be bolted, and clean beds; and its stableman both recognized the quality of their horses and proved able to look after them. It was a pleasant enough place, and quiet, which had much to be said for it.

As soon as they passed the gates of the city, Etta had gone quiescent. She followed where the others led; the intensity that had animated her was gone. The Goddess had let her go.

Hippolyta on the other hand was almost feverish with excitement. She was like a child, insisting on seeing everything, dragging them from one sight to the next, reveling in the richness and variety of a market swelled by the loot of an army.

Selene had decided some while since to learn a few words of whatever language would be most useful in this country—Persian, certainly, and Greek. Greek was easier in its odd likeness to the language of the people. Persian twisted her tongue in knots, but she relished the challenge.

Ione had taught her as much as she knew, enough that Selene could haggle in the market or order dinner in a tavern. She learned more from listening, from following Hippolyta and keeping track of Etta and eavesdropping on conversations whenever they paused for long enough to glean more than a few words.

Hippolyta spoke Greek. She was rather fluent, in fact. "My father," she said when Selene asked, back in the inn in the evening, over good wine from the market and one of the cook's succulent roast fowl. "He came from Argos. Mother kept him long enough to teach me his language, then she let him go. He was pining for his own country."

"She kept him? In the clan?" Selene had heard the rumor from the time before she was born, but she had never believed it; it was an old story, much embellished, or so she had thought.

"She kept him in her very tent," said Hippolyta. "It was a scandal at the time—even I was aware of it, though I was too young to understand what was so outrageous. A man in Artemisia's tent, traveling where she traveled, riding when she rode. He was a great hunter; they had contests, which he sometimes won, to see who could bring home the most or the largest or the most dangerous prey."

"Greeks are obsessed with contests," Ione said. "They'll fight over anything, and lay wagers on who will win or lose. Every one of them has to be the best, or he can't bear to live."

"There can only be one who is best," Selene said. "What do the rest of them do?"

"Resolve to win the next contest," said Hippolyta. She fed bits of meat wrapped in bread to her daughter. "Tomorrow we shall see what these Greek games are like."

Selene's brows rose. "Will they let us in?"

"Why not?" said Hippolyta.

Why not indeed, Selene thought. One thing she had learned in the world in which men called themselves master: they never expected to see a woman where women were forbidden.

"They say the king will be at the games tomorrow," Hippolyta said. "I should like to see him."

"And let him see you?" asked Ione.

Hippolyta shrugged. "That will be as it will be."

In Persian dress, with scarves over their faces, Hippolyta and her companions ventured the games. They were not stopped at the gate. There were other apparent Persians in attendance, though most of the crowd were Macedonians; they were stared at but not interfered with. Macedonians took their games seriously, and were not to be distracted from them, even by the sight of trousered barbarians.

The games were not unlike those of spring and autumn among the tribes, when the young warriors tested their skill, and the men came to be judged for their fitness to be the fathers of daughters. Selene saw a few on the field whom she might have been glad to take to her bed, but they were not her main preoccupation, or Hippolyta's, either. They looked for the one who ruled these men, the king who was still, by all accounts, little more than a boy.

He was not sitting in the high seat above the field, though that was surrounded by men decked out in gold enough to ransom half of Persia. Selene had been listening in the streets and the taverns; she looked for a sturdy man, not tall, with hair the color of new gold.

Soon enough she found him. He was down on the field, running with men who as often as not were larger than he.

He did not always or even often win. The victors were not afraid of him, either, nor did they yield the prize to him. The one who tried had to see it given to the man who had come in last, with a stern warning not to do such a thing again. Alexander wanted his victories whole, well and honestly won.

This was not the usual run of men—or kings, either, from anything Selene had heard. Past that first unknowing glance, when she saw him as ordinary eyes could see, she was blinded, dazzled, confounded. He was like a rioting fire.

Such a soul came direct from the spheres of heaven. It was too strong for living flesh to bear.

This one would never live to grow old. The fire of the spirit would turn his body to ash long before age took him. But ah, Goddess, what a light he would shed before he consumed himself!

Not since that night on the hilltop when the seer died, when she had opened her eyes upon the light of the Goddess unveiled, had Selene seen so clearly or with such breathtaking intensity.

She had been living in a dream, wrapped in a shroud of shadows. Suddenly she was swept out into the light.

It was astonishing; breathtaking; maddening. It had taken her completely by surprise. Even Etta's presence was not enough to thrust it aside.

She dragged herself back by main force to the duller but far more welcome world. Hippolyta was watching Alexander, but not as one who is rapt in awe. She was studying him, narrow-eyed, judging as a queen must judge.

Etta had been sitting between them, as blank as ever. She startled them both by leaning forward over the tier of benches. Selene gripped her tightly before she tumbled down. Etta took no more notice of her guardian than she ever did. Her eyes, for the first time that Selene could remember, had something like an expression. They were fixed on Alexander.

She who saw nothing human or animal save only the queen mare, saw this child of light. She tugged at Selene's hand, struggling to break free. Selene set her teeth and held on tighter. Ione, beyond her, lent a hand. Etta began to fight in earnest.

Just before she escaped from them both, Selene realized that Hippolyta was no longer beside them. She had risen and begun a leaping descent through the tiers of the amphitheater.

On the field below, the races had ended. Men were challenging one another, offering tests of combat.

No one challenged Alexander, although he had not left the field—until a clear and all too familiar voice rang out over the clamor of the crowd. "Alexander! Alexander of Macedon!"

He whipped about. He was fast, and light on his feet, even after a long day of games. He looked up to where Hippolyta was standing in her Persian guise. His eyes were blue—Selene could see them clearly as she came down beside Hippolyta.

Ione was still above, slowed by age and scars, but making what speed she could. Etta crouched at their feet, clear blue eyes fixed on Alexander. This was what she had come for; this had brought her over the mountains of Anshan. She had come for this light, this power; her emptiness called to it, as if in its nearness she could be filled.

"Alexander," said Hippolyta in her rough but serviceable Greek, "I wager that you cannot best me in combat."

"Indeed?" Alexander said. His head tilted. "What will you wager?"

"This," she said, laying her hand on her daughter's head.

Selene's breath caught. Alexander's brows were up. "A boy? He's pretty; I've seldom seen a prettier. But I'm no Persian king. I've no need of boys to ornament my palace."

"This is my own child," Hippolyta said, "my blood and bone. What will you wager, king of Macedon? What will I take with me when I win?"

Alexander grinned at her. "You have gall, I grant you that. I'll give you . . ." He paused. His brows knit. Suddenly he laughed, light and free, as one who wagers everything on certain victory. "I'll give you whatever you ask that is in my power to give. Only ask it, and it is yours."

She bowed to him. Selene could not see her expression beneath the scarf, but her eyes were clear and steady. "That is a good wager," she said. "Shall we fight?"

They fought with swords, sharp blades unblunted. Alexander's guards and servants were appalled, but his men cheered him on. They loved his crazy courage, to fight naked against an unknown, shrouded, and most likely armored enemy. They could not know what Goddess was in him, driving him, giving him strength—but never as much as She gave Her daughter, Her beloved, the queen of Her own people.

He was lethally fast and brilliant in battle, but Hippolyta was the Penthesilea, the daughter of war. She danced a sword-dance about the heavier, slower, more quickly tiring man, with grace that caught at Selene's heart.

In the midst of the dance, as he rallied and pressed hard against her, the bindings of her headdress parted, then fell away. Her hair, bright copper-gold, made the watchers cry out softly. Alexander, who could see her face, checked for the space of a breath, astonished: like all Greeks and their kin, he never expected to see a woman on the field of battle.

Hippolyta had been winning before then, in Selene's estimation, but once he saw what she was, there was no battle left. She beat him back with ringing blows, forcing him to defend himself, but he was crippled, defeated; he could not strike, only parry. She drove him to his knees and thrust her sword in the sand between them, and said coolly, "I had thought better of you."

He was a high-colored man, ruddy even at rest, but as he knelt at her feet, he went crimson. He surged up in pure blind rage.

Her arm caught him and thrust him down again. But he was beyond reason. The third time he fell, her blade came softly to rest across his throat. A gasp echoed in the amphitheater; guards lurched forward with swords drawn or spears in hand, but there was nothing any of them could do. If she was minded to kill Alexander, she would do it. She would die as soon as it was done, but that would not save their king.

His eyes cleared. As suddenly as it had risen, his fury died.

Hippolyta lowered her sword. The tension in the theater eased a fraction. Alexander stood slowly, stiffly, bleeding from a score of small wounds. He was exactly as tall as she.

Her eyes ran over him in sincere appreciation. "If I needed a child," she said, "I would ask you to give me one."

"If you asked," he said as civilly as a man could who had just been soundly and publicly defeated in combat by a woman, "I would respectfully decline the honor."

"Would you?"

"Some things cannot be forced."

"Yes," said Hippolyta.

He looked hard at her. Selene thought he might say something cutting, but when he spoke, it was only to say, "Come to dinner with me."

That was a command, and she was a queen. But she chose to suffer it. She followed Alexander out of the crowds and the sun, past men who stared and murmured, in a flurry of rumor and speculation. It had not been clear to any but Alexander what had come out of the crowd to fight him. They still were thinking that Hippolyta was a Persian, a fighting eunuch, intent on avenging the conquest of his country.

TEN

Alexander fed his odd guests royally, but not in the crowds and confusion of a royal feast. There were a few friends and companions, somewhat wide-eyed when they saw Hippolyta and her escort bathed and unveiled. Alexander with the courtesy for which he was famous had sent servants to offer them a selection of garments, both women's dress and men's. They had chosen the silken coats and loose trousers of Persian nobility, richer versions of the clothes they had worn to the games.

They ate in a smaller dining hall of the palace, within sound and scent of the sea. Selene barely noticed what she ate. She was intent on the faces of those lords and generals, warriors to a man, as they understood at last what her people were. Alexander laughed like a boy. "Legends! Old tales riding down from the mountains. You are—you really are—Penthesilea?"

"I am the Penthesilea," Hippolyta said. "My ancestors have borne that title for years out of count."

"And you came to see me." He tilted his head in the way he had. "To teach me a lesson?"

"To see what you were." She smiled at him. "And to teach you a lesson."

"Did I learn it? Or am I still being taught?"

"That will be clear in time," she said.

"So," said Alexander. "You won a gift from me. What can I give you out of all that I have?"

"It's not yet yours to give," she said, "but when it is, I will ask for it."

"What, the other half of Persia?" That was one of his generals, a big man, black-bearded, with an air about him of one who needed a good thrashing with the flat of a blade.

Selene would have been happy to oblige, but this was not her country. She could only watch him along with the rest, and tend Etta, who would not eat for her unceasing fascination with Alexander. Selene persuaded her at length to take a bit of bread dipped in honey, which she ate neatly; she had grown into a clean creature, whatever she lacked in wits or will.

The black-bearded man was watching them. He was looking for weaknesses, Selene thought, and more than pleased to find one. "Well, Alexander," he said, "whatever you have to pay for losing the fight, at least you won't be nursemaid to an idiot."

Selene tensed to rise, to teach him the lesson he so badly needed, but Hippolyta caught her hand. "Selene," she said: only the name, but it bound her. Hippolyta regarded the Macedonian with the hint of a smile. "One may be forgiven a lack of understanding," she said. "This is my daughter, my heir. She is blessed of the Goddess. If your king had won her, he would have won a queen of the Amazons."

The Macedonian's lip curled, but Alexander spoke before he could insult them further. "A great prize," he said, "and a great gift." He looked into Etta's face and smiled. And she, who had never shown a human expression, mirrored that smile exactly.

"She's very beautiful," he said. He did not add, even with his eyes, that it was a pity she had no heart or spirit to give that beauty substance. He stretched out his hand. She reached in turn to clasp it. "Good day to you," he said with courtesy that could not be learned; it was born in a rare few, almost none of whom were kings.

Of course Etta did not answer, but her eyes never left his face. She was basking in the light of him, as if he had been the sun.

He bade a servant bring a chair to set beside his own, and drew her to it. Through the rest of that banquet, he ate with one hand, because she would not let go the other.

He pressed his guests for tales; he was insatiably curious, eager to learn all that he could. He had heard every myth and legend of the people he called the Amazons, from the most preposterous to the merely foolish. It was a pleasure to enlighten him; he had a child's willingness to learn, and it troubled him not at all to be corrected.

"You really are all women?" he asked. "No men at all?"

"Men in villages," Hippolyta said: "potters and weavers and farmers. We hunt; we wage war when it comes to us. We speak before the Goddess. In the spring we go to the men, and we make children."

"And the menchildren? What becomes of them?"

"The fathers keep them," said Hippolyta. "The daughters go to their mothers. What, did you think we killed our sons?"

He shrugged uncomfortably. "The story is that you leave them out for the wolves. Or," he admitted, "you send them to their fathers."

"Half of what you heard is true." She sat back, turning the

golden cup in her hands. It was shaped like a stag's head; it had come, Alexander said, from the royal hoard of Persia.

Selene watched them both, and Etta between them. There was a startling likeness there, a cast of feature, and in the king and Hippolyta, a habit of movement and expression. Their coloring was very similar: the fair skin that went red in sunlight, the brightness of the hair. They could have been close kin.

"How do the men feel?" Alexander asked after a pause. "What do they think? Is it hard for them?"

Hippolyta's brows rose. "You think it must be hard? How so? They live well. Those who grow restless are free to wander, but most of them come back."

"But in the rest of the world," he said, "they're lords and masters. Whereas in your country . . ."

"In my country," she said sweetly, "they know their place."

Alexander burst out laughing. His companions were taken aback, but Hippolyta smiled. "Lady," he said, "I think your world would defeat me."

"Ah!" cried one of the Greeks, an attenuated personage with a rim of elaborate curls around his bald skull. "Nothing can conquer Alexander—and certainly not a nation of women. With all due respect, great lady," he said, bowing toward Hippolyta.

She kept her smile, though it must have cost her no little effort. Alexander did not trouble with such tact. "Don't be a fool, Callisthenes," he said. "You yourself have said no man can conquer Alexander. You never said anything about women."

Callisthenes gaped like a fish. The rest of the king's companions laughed, some loudly. It appeared Callisthenes was not the most highly respected man in this court.

He sputtered and gurgled, but he had no words to say. The conversation turned away elsewhere.

They sat together until well after sunset, but although there was wine in plenty, it was well watered. They did not suffer the infamous excesses of a Macedonian banquet.

Some of the king's companions, Callisthenes and the black-bearded man among them, excused themselves—to escape, Selene supposed, to a more comfortable gathering. The rest lingered. They had some share of Alexander's thirst for knowledge, and some of his quick intelligence. She caught herself warming to them, helped perhaps by the wine, although she had drunk little of that.

Soon after the sun went down, when the sky was still full of light, a newcomer joined the gathering. Selene started a little at the sight of him. She had seen him in light rather like this, on the other side of a copse outside of Zadrakarta. He had come out of a Persian tent in the same way that he came into the hall, passing a handful of men who were departing, laughing at some sally that she did not catch.

Alexander did not leap up or wax effusive, but she saw how he warmed from the inside out. "Hephaistion," he said. "Come here, sit with us. Do you know who is here?"

"I heard," Hephaistion said, bowing gracefully to Hippolyta. "Lady, you honor us."

Hippolyta inclined her head. Hephaistion sat on the other side of the king, easily, as a friend or a close kinsman.

Selene found him even more beautiful in full lamplight and close by, but it was Alexander who drew her eye. Although he was good enough to look at, he lacked the carved perfection of that profile or the clear ivory of the skin. And yet the soul in him, the fire of his spirit, overwhelmed everything near it.

Etta was altogether besotted. When at last it was time to go, she would not leave the king.

Selene had expected that. She was ready for the silent battle, braced to heave the child over her shoulder and carry her out if need be. But Alexander said, "Beautiful one, you should sleep. In the morning you may come to me; we'll visit the horses together."

Etta could not have understood him; words to her held less meaning than the cries of birds. Yet she let go his hand. She turned her eyes from him at last, bent them down, and permitted Selene to lead her away.

ELEVEN

As long as Alexander was in Zadrakarta, Hippolyta and her companions stayed as his guests. They were housed in the palace and given a servant, and a groom for the horses.

Ione was gone. Hippolyta had sent her away the day after they dined with the king, bidding her find the caravan and send it back to the people. Ione did not go willingly. Not at all. "I will come back," she said, "when my message is delivered. You will not be all but alone in a world of strangers."

To Selene, the night before she left, Ione said little more. It was a long night, but not particularly passionate. Passion was for the easy times. This had to last. "I will come back," she said as she had to Hippolyta, but this was solemn and a vow, sworn on the joining of their bodies.

Hippolyta was Alexander's guest, treated with honor and even awe as word spread of what and who she was. The king's chamberlains and the servants of this palace had been in a quandary at first as to how to regard their strange charges, but they quickly decided that these were royal guests of indeterminate gender. That comforted them remarkably. Courtiers had a great need to put everything in its proper place.

Etta had abandoned her mother. As much as she could, she attached herself to Alexander, following him about side by side with the great hulk of a dog that he called Peritas, crouching at his feet when he sat to eat or hold audience. Alexander was remarkably gentle with her, and strikingly tolerant; he was fierce in protecting her against both mockery and disapproval.

Selene learned one of the whys of that a handful of days after the king's banquet. She was still Etta's guardian regardless of where Etta happened to be. She followed Etta as Etta followed the king—a procession of shadows, as one wag observed in her hearing.

On that particular day, Alexander had caroused until dawn with his Companions, slept an hour, then risen refreshed to deal with a day's worth of royal duties. Hippolyta had gone hunting with Hephaistion and some of the Companions. Selene would have been glad of a wild ride under the sun, but duty bound her to Etta, and Etta was bound to Alexander.

Often as Selene watched them together, she remembered the elders' fears long ago, that the child without a soul would become a vessel for some power of ill. Instead she had been called to light and fire.

Toward noon the press of petitioners eased somewhat. Alexander withdrew for rest and food and a visit to the garderobe. Peritas, who had been sleeping in the little room behind the hall of audience, roused and lumbered over to lay his heavy head on Alexander's foot. Etta curled beside him in comfort.

When Alexander had eaten and drunk, he yawned and stretched until his bones creaked, then said, "Here, beautiful one. My wits are scrambled and my eyes are crossing. Let's run away for a little longer."

Etta did not know or care what the words meant, only that he held out his hand for her to take. He smiled at her, and won as always that luminous reflection. Selene rose softly from the corner in which she had been waiting.

Thus far Alexander had let Selene have her invisibility, but today his eye fell on her and lingered. "You could go," he said. "You're not bound here."

"I am," she said, "lord king."

He looked a little surprised. "So. You speak Greek."

"A little," she said. "I cannot go. I belong with her."

"You don't trust me?"

That was beside the point. She shook her head. "I am bound."

"By oath? Love? Criminal sentence?"

Her lips twitched at that. "Duty," she said, "and oath. I belong to the queen, and to this her child."

"Ah," he said. "A captain of guards. I understand. But if you'll trust me, and if you like, you really can go. I promise by my mother's Goddess that I'll protect your charge with my life."

Selene was sorely tempted. But she said, "I ask your pardon, lord king—but no."

He opened his mouth as if to say more, but clearly reconsidered. "Well then," he said. "Come with us."

He had the gift of grace: once he had acknowledged the position she chose, he let her settle back into it. He allowed her to be a shadow. Silent in his wake, bound to her queen's heir, she followed him through some of the less frequented ways of the palace.

Selene had done a little exploring when Etta was asleep or in Hippolyta's care. She knew that these passages led to the royal quarters, a suite of rooms that looked out over the sea. She heard its murmur and sigh even before she came to the room he had been aiming for.

It was pleasant, not large as this palace was old and somewhat cramped, but airy and light, with its shutters open and the salt air blowing through. There were a few good furnishings, most pushed back against the wall to allow space for an extraordinary thing: a city in miniature, full of people and animals going about their various business. Outside the walls were two armies facing one another. One wore trousers as the Persians did; the other marched in ranks bristling with long spears, and a man in golden armor led them, mounted on a black horse.

It was beautifully made, each piece carved with care and skill. A man was kneeling by it, peering down at the battlefield. As they paused, Peritas pushed past them, great tail waving, to thrust his wet nose in the man's neck.

The man gasped and laughed and turned. He was a strong man, broad in the shoulders, with a pelt of black hair and a heavy beard. He looked as if he should have been a soldier, a fighting man of Macedon. But there was something unformed about him: a softness, a blurring about the edges. His mind and soul were a child's, nor would he ever grow to manhood.

"Alexander!" he said in open delight. "Look! I have a new army. See, Petros made them for me. There's you and there's the other king and—"

"Arrhidaios," said Alexander. His voice was gentle, with no edges to cut, but it stopped the spate of words. "Brother, look. I brought friends to meet you."

Arrhidaios' grin faded. He scowled at Etta and Selene, but particularly at Etta. His finger stabbed toward her. "She is empty. She has nothing in her at all. Except," he added after a pause, "except . . . you. She's full of you."

"She has no soul," Selene said. It was not her place, but the spirit moved her.

"No soul," said Arrhidaios. "No person. Just a body."

"Just a body," Selene agreed. "And your brother. Your brother is like the sun to her."

"He is the sun," said Arrhidaios. "He shines in the dark. Why does she have no soul? Did you take it away from her?"

"She was born that way," Selene said.

He pushed himself to his feet, clumsy-graceful, and stretched out a hand toward Etta. Selene restrained the purely instinctive urge to strike him away. She remained on guard as much for his sake as for Etta's—the child could be lethally fast—but he brushed his fingers over Etta's face and shoulder without harm to either of them.

"Empty," he said. "Pretty. She's so pretty. When she gets her soul, she'll be beautiful."

"You think she will?" Selene asked—for who knew, he might have an answer.

He did not seem to hear her. He tugged at Etta until she folded on the floor beside him, and set the carved king in her hand. Her fingers closed reflexively about the thing, but her expression never changed. It only did that for Alexander.

Arrhidaios patted her as if she had been a dog. "Good," he said. "I'll play. You watch."

Selene would not have called it watching, but it seemed to have drawn Etta's attention from Alexander. As Arrhidaios drew back, Etta remained where she was, eyes fixed somewhere between the miniature city and the endless reaches of her own emptiness.

"I hope you don't mind," Alexander said to Selene. "My brother is a gentle soul. He won't harm her."

"The dog likes him," Selene said. Peritas was sprawled beside the king's brother, as content as if the man had been Alexander.

"Animals understand him," said Alexander. "He understands them. Not that your princess is any such thing. But—"

"My charge is less than an animal," Selene said. "You don't need to be polite. We know what she is—just as we hope that someday she'll be more."

"The gods can work miracles when it suits them," Alexander said. Then after a brief pause: "If you like, she can come here every day and play for a while. My brother's guardians are trained to look after those who are lacking in wits. You'd have an hour or two to yourself then."

Selene opened her mouth to say that she needed no such thing, but the words did not come. She was tempted, and sorely—to see more of this city; to walk free under the sky; to ride by the sea.

Alexander snapped his fingers. Three men emerged from an inner room. Two were guards in armor. The third was a milder man, dressed like one of the Greek philosophers who trailed after Alexander, but he lacked their bluster. His eyes were kind.

"This is Petros," Arrhidaios said to Etta. "Petros made my city."

"It's a splendid city," Alexander said. "Someday Petros will have to build one for me in real brick and stone, with real people in it."

Arrhidaios clapped his hands. "Yes! Like the one in Egypt? Only better?"

"Certainly better," Alexander said. He turned to Selene. "Are you reassured now?"

"Very much so," she conceded.

"Then go," he said. "Come back when you like. Petros will see to it that your princess is safe."

Petros smiled and nodded. "It's a great honor," he said, "to attend the princess of the Amazons."

Selene had left Etta in the care of her own people often enough; it was not as if she had been bound to the child for every moment of every day. But these were not her people.

Her heart told her to trust them. It offered no intimation of danger. Etta was safe, as Alexander had promised.

Selene left while she could—before her misgivings overcame her. Etta did not care what she did or where she went. Arrhidaios was busy with his city, arraying the armies in a new order. This time the trousered, veiled commander rode side by side with the king in the golden armor.

Selene felt like a child who had run away from her tutors: a confusion of guilt and excitement. Where she would go, what she would do, she did not even know. She could not follow Hippolyta; Hippolyta was Goddess knew where. She was free to do as she pleased.

She wandered for a while around the palace. She knew some of the people she passed, by now; some stared, some greeted her courteously. None gave her reason to pause.

She had every intention of going out into the city, and maybe even riding outside it, but she found herself atop one of the towers, looking out across the sea. The wind was brisk; it buffeted her with gusts. She laughed in the teeth of it.

There was someone else on the tower. He had been sitting so still, so much a part of the stones of the parapet, that she had not seen him until he stirred.

It was one of the Persians who were housed in the palace: prisoners, some of them, but others had allied themselves with Alexander against the rebels who had murdered the Great King. This one had a certain look about him that Selene had learned to associate with the royal house: very tall, very straight, with a profile from one of the many carvings and paintings that cluttered the palace.

She had seen so many like him that it was a moment before she remembered where she had seen him before. This was the Persian who had been hunting with Hephaistion before she came to Zadrakarta.

He rose. She was tall here; people said she was as tall as a man. He towered over her. She was not accustomed to that. It made her bristle a little, then laugh at herself.

He bowed to her with the grace of his people, with more courtesy and less discomfort than she had seen in most of them. They disapproved of women who rode and fought like men, who wore scars with evident pride, and never veiled their faces. But this one did not avert his eyes, and he regarded her with candid interest. "Lady," he said in Greek considerably better than hers.

"My name is Selene," she said. "And yours?"

By Persian standards that was so abrupt as to be rude. He did not seem to take offense, although he blinked a little. "My name is Nabu-rimanni," he said, "lady. But mostly here, they call me Naburianos."

"Nabu-rimanni," she said.

He smiled. "You remind me of my mother," he said.

She let her eyes ask the question.

"The queen," he said. "Sisygambis. Someday you should meet her."

"I have heard of her," Selene said. "Alexander is in awe of her."

"And so he should be," he said. "We say she should have been born a man. No doubt you would say that she should have been born an Amazon."

"We would say that she was born where the Goddess wished her to be born."

"Your people are wise," he said.

"Does that surprise you?"

"Queen Sisygambis is my mother," he said. "Do you think I could be surprised at a woman's wisdom?"

"I know little of men," she said, "and less of Persians. I don't know what would surprise you—even with such a mother as yours."

"I'm the odd one," he said: "the idler, the scholar. I don't like to fight, though I will if I must. They say I should have been born a woman."

"Among us, that would be the highest compliment."

She had startled laughter out of him. "Then I shall take it as such."

She leaned on the parapet. She never tired of watching the sea: the endless blue; the heave and toss of the waves. "Where I come from," she mused, "the sea is grass. This is more turbulent. Wilder."

"I'm a son of mountains," he said, "but I've sailed in ships."

"I've been in a boat on a river," she said. "I was horribly sick. I need the earth underfoot or a horse under me."

"I prefer a horse to a boat myself," he said, "but ships can carry us where no horse can. The islands of Greece are all mountains and sea."

"They have horses in Greece," she said.

"None like yours," he said. "Even our Nisaians can't compare."

"Our horses are the Goddess' own," she said. "She made them; sometimes She takes flesh through them and lives among us. It's a great blessing when She does such a thing."

"I should like to learn of your Goddess," he said, "if it's permitted."

She glanced over her shoulder. He had an expression she knew rather well: a thirst to know, to understand. She had not seen it in a man before, except in Alexander. Mostly men in this world did not care to understand, only to rule and to possess.

She was remarkably comfortable in his presence. Talking to him was like talking to a woman.

Truly he should have been one. He would have made a fine sister of the people.

That was not a thing she could tell him, even as pleasing as she found his company. He was a man after all, and a Persian—royal Persian at that. Some things even he might not regard as a compliment.

TWELVE

The year drew on toward winter, but Hippolyta showed no sign of leaving Zadrakarta. Ione had come back in late summer, all whipcord and leather, with the news that the caravan had gone back over the mountains.

Selene was deeply glad to see her. She was weary of this city; she yearned to go home. But Hippolyta would not go. "I dreamed," she said, "and that dream must play itself out." But she would not say what the dream had been.

Selene was not about to argue with it. She had no dream of her own, and for that she was glad. The sight that had threatened to overwhelm her in Alexander's presence had receded again. She was as safe as she had ever been, with Etta for her shield and protection.

The queen came in one dark and early evening, windblown and damp and spattered with mud, for it had been raining that day, a cold raw rain. She had gone hunting nonetheless; blood spattered her coat, and she carried the hide of a stag. Its meat would be in the kitchens, roasting for their dinner.

Alexander was out fighting. There was a great deal of Persia still to subdue, and he was much preoccupied with it.

To everyone's amazement, Etta had not tried to follow him to his war. As if some communication had passed between them, a promise that he would return, she settled to days in Arrhidaios' company and nights with her own people—always with the same blank calm.

She was sitting by the fire in the room that Alexander had given her, staring blindly at the flames, when her mother passed the door. Hippolyta came in shivering; Ione went swiftly to fetch dry clothes for her. Selene warmed the cold hands in her own and led her to the fire, sitting the queen down beside her daughter. Etta was rapt in contemplation of the fire.

Hippolyta ran a hand lightly over the red-gold curls. "It's time," she said. "Winter comes; the people need us. It's time to go home."

Selene's heart leaped. But she could not stop herself from saying, "This one may beg to differ."

"She may," said Hippolyta. She was warming slowly; the chattering of her teeth had eased. She took the cup that Ione brought, with a smile of thanks, and sipped the wine heated with spices. Between sips she said, "If my daughter chooses to stay, and if the king will agree to it, she may."

Selene was silent. She tried to be expressionless, but she was not Etta. Her eyes never failed to give her away.

Hippolyta's own eyes were kind. "I release you from your charge," she said. "You've kept it admirably for years longer than you must ever have expected. Now you may lay it down. She herself has chosen her keeper. You are free."

"No," Selene said from somewhere inside herself. "I can't be free. Not while her soul is bound apart from her body."

"Not even to go back to the people? Not even to be what you were born to be—warrior and captain, protector of the tribe?"

Selene's heart was torn in two. Everything in her yearned to give way, to accept the gift, to go back to the world in which she had been born. And yet there was the truth, the thing she had been evading for half as long as Etta had been alive. If she went back without Etta, the sight would be waiting. The dreams would fall upon her. She would drown in a madness of fire.

That was cowardice. So be it. It was also destiny, after its fashion. It led her to say, "I protect my queen's heir."

Hippolyta looked long into her face. Selene kept it as still as she could. At last the queen lowered her eyes and bent her head. "As you will," she said.

Selene hated her then. It was not fair or right, but she could not help herself—even knowing that in truth it was herself whom she hated: her own fear, her own cowardice; her long defiance of the Goddess' will.

The choice was made. It was done. There was no undoing it.

Only then, and far too late, did she remember Ione's presence. She looked into that beloved face, and saw both the understanding and the deep hurt. Her own heart was like to break, but she could not unsay the words.

That night the sight took its revenge. Selene had no warning. One moment she was half-asleep in a bed to which Ione had not come—nor had Selene expected her. The next she was buffeted by such a storm of visions that she spun like a feather in a whirlwind. She could not grasp them; they were too many. They overwhelmed her, drowned her.

"Child," said Ione's rough-sweet voice. "Child, come back to us."

Selene clung to that presence, to the sound of that voice, following the thread of it through the tumult. Snatches of memory, past or to come, brushed past, too quick to follow. She glimpsed faces—Hippolyta, Etta, Alexander, Phaedra. She saw flickers of movement: the flash of light on a sword-blade, the lift of wind-blown mane on a horse's neck. She saw Etta, clear-eyed, half-smiling—aware. Etta blessed with the gift of a soul.

She opened her eyes on Ione's face. There was real fear in it, transmuting into the sharpness of temper as Selene came to herself. "Selene!" she snapped. "Come out of it, damn you!"

"I am out," Selene said thickly, throwing up a heavy hand to fend off Ione's slap. "I was—I dreamed—"

"You were damned near lost to the world," Ione said, her voice still edged with anger.

That anger stung, but it brought Selene back to herself. The torrent of dreams was fading. Only the last of them was clear: Etta's eyes, alight with life. There was no nightmare of burning. No flame-charred horror. The only fire was that of Alexander's spirit.

"That's it," she said suddenly. "That's Hippolyta's dream. That's what she sees. But I shouldn't be seeing—I don't know why—"

"Sleep on it," Ione said. Her fit of temper had passed; she cradled Selene in her arms and rocked her, crooning to her. "Rest; let the dreams find their own way."

"Once I might have known how to do that," Selene said. "Now, after what I've done or not done . . . I don't know what I'm capable of doing."

"It's all the same," Ione said. "The people may be different. The sky may not be as wide. But it's still the Goddess."

"This is not my country," Selene said. "It never will be. I belong among the people. And yet I also—I must—I swore an oath. I can't break it."

"Honor is a damnable nuisance," said Ione.

"It's not honor," Selene said. "It most certainly is not that."

There was no way Ione could have understood. And yet somehow, in some way that went beyond the simplicity of truth or deception, Selene felt that she did. The hurt was no less, nor the grief of inevitable parting, but there was some small comfort in the warmth of that regard.

"Of all the times and places for the Goddess to give me a clear and unmistakable omen," Selene said, "this may just be the worst. I don't want to be told what I know already. I don't want to stay in this country."

"But you have to," Ione said.

"I don't have a choice."

"I wish you did."

That was as blunt an admission as Ione would ever make. Selene pulled away, though not in rejection; she needed to see Ione's face. Because, she could not help but think, she might never see it again.

Ione's eyes were steady. She never wept; it was not her way. But her simple words had made Selene's heart constrict. Ione knew the truth of things. That was why Selene loved her. Even when the truth was hard; even when it hurt.

Hippolyta left in the morning, quietly, with only Ione for escort. Etta was with Arrhidaios; farewells meant as little to her as any other human rite. Selene went with the queen and the warleader to the gate.

She would have been glad if the rain had continued, and glad-

der if it had turned to ice. But the storm had blown away in the
night. The air was warm and washed clean. It was a beautiful day
to ride. The horses were fresh; they pawed and stamped, impa-
tient to be gone.

There were four of them. Selene had decided, though it
wrenched at her heart, to send her mare back to her own world
and her own kind. The young queen mare, who had brought Etta
here, chose to follow her herdmates. It was not an abandonment
but a promise: that their riders, however long the parting, would
meet again. That the wanderers would come home.

Selene could have ridden with them a little way if she had chosen, but she had never been one to prolong the agony. Ione
embraced her so tightly her ribs creaked, but said nothing. Hippolyta's embrace was hardly less strong. "You'll see me again," she
said. "That I promise you."

Selene bent her head. She was cold inside. This choice, this
madness—she could revoke it. She could run after them, vault
onto her mare's back, ride away.

She stayed where she was and watched the two slim upright
figures ride through the gate and out into the city. Long before
they actually left Zadrakarta, they had gone out of sight.

She turned her back on the gate. The palace that had become
so familiar was all strange. She walked in a fog. Without Ione and
Hippolyta to anchor her, she had nowhere to look, nothing to
focus on, to hold her to the world.

She stumbled through a doorway into a place of light. It was a
garden such as the Persians made more perfectly than any nation
in this world. Roses were blooming in sheltered corners. Most of
the trees had dropped their leaves, but their bare branches had a
beauty of their own, drawn fine against the stones of the wall.

There was a pool with fish that had not yet been brought in
from winter's cold. They gleamed like gold and silver, crowding

toward her, leaping over one another in their eagerness for whatever largesse she might have brought.

She had a bit of bread in her coat, which she had saved as a farewell offering for her mare and then forgotten. The fish were glad of it. She sat on the rim of the pool and scattered crumbs across the water.

Close by her, something breathed. She stilled, listening.

It was human. It had come in behind her and paused, perhaps in surprise to find her there. She turned without haste.

She had seen him at a distance now and then, moving in the king's orbit, or in company with the Persian nobles who had attached themselves to Alexander's court. He and his brother the prince Oxyathres were often invited to dine with Alexander when he was in the city.

In spite of her almost-promise to teach Nabu-rimanni the ways of her people, she had not spoken to him since their meeting on top of the tower, months ago now. Sometimes he had tried to catch her eye and smile, but nothing had come of it. He had been too much a part of this country for her comfort, just then.

It was difficult to ignore him here, with him looming over her, watching her with an expression that she was not sure she wanted to read. If he had been a man of the people, she would have called it presumptuous. In this place it was merely determined. "Lady," he said, "you look as if you want to weep."

She should have set her lips together and left him standing there. But her heart was raw. "I do want to weep," she said. "My queen is gone away."

He did not pretend to misunderstand. "Did her people call her back?"

"Her duty did." Selene glowered at him. "What are you doing here? Aren't you supposed to be out waging war with Alexander?"

"I was," he said. "I came back with relief for the garrison. He'll follow in a little while." He paused. "She wouldn't go. Would she?"

"She has no will," Selene said. "She's like a flower, and he's the sun."

"And you are the gardener who tends the flower."

Her lip curled. "Nothing so poetic," she said. "I'll get over the tears soon enough. This is a grand adventure, after all; a story to tell my granddaughters, long after I've gone back to my people."

"It is that," he said, "and of course it suits you to be brave. But if you ever need to cry or shout or hit someone, do keep me in mind. Even a warrior of the Amazons needs a friend, surely."

He was more than presumptuous. He was outrageous. And yet she caught herself succumbing to his smile. "Don't tell me you learned *those* manners in the court at Persepolis."

"Certain persons will tell you I grew up in a barn," he said, "and others, that I was buried in a book when my brothers were being instructed in proper manners and deportment. I'm quite an appalling creature, all things considered."

"You are that," she said, but the damnable smile would not go away. "Very well then. Since you insist, I'll take your friendship. Who knows? I might need it."

"You might, at that," he said gravely, but his eyes were glinting.

A friend, she thought. A man—but one could hardly have everything. She would take him and be glad of it. Friends were not common anywhere, least of all here, where women lived in a hidden world, and men knew nothing of them.

PART TWO

King of All Asia

THIRTEEN

Selene was beyond hunger. She was almost beyond thirst.

She had lost count of the days since Alexander had begun the crossing of Gedrosia. That it was a desert, he had known before he began, but for once he had listened to bad advice. He had thought that he could travel easily enough from well to well, and rest in oases that, as he had discovered, did not exist.

Gedrosia was a horror of heat, thirst, and endless marches without hope of water or forage. The sea mocked them with its immensity; so much water, and every drop of it bitter with salt. Those of the army who went mad and drank it went even madder then, and died of thirst.

They marched by night, which was almost as cold as the days were hot. During the reign of the sun, they took what shelter they could. Most had left their tents behind long ago, with all the rest of their baggage, and the loot of years of conquest: all the way to India, until they had come within days, it was said, of the stream of Ocean; and now they were going home. Their bodies were burden enough to carry here, without food, without water, without relief from relentless heat and bone-numbing cold.

All too many had given up. The path of the march was lined with their graves, a long trail of mounds in the sand. Selene had no doubt that carrion creatures would dig them up as soon as the army was out of sight, and feast on meat that was abundant and nearly fresh. But she never said anything of that to the men with whom she traveled. It would only appall them.

They were used to her now, to be sure. Five years in Alexander's army, walking and riding in Etta's shadow, had made her a veteran. She was familiar and even, somewhat to her surprise, not too greatly disliked: the king's Amazon, the odd rangy woman who strode about like a man and, more to the point among these men of war, fought like one.

On a day out of count, under the hammer of the sun, Selene lay strengthless in the shade of a dune. The sea surged and sighed on the other side of it. Etta was asleep, drawn into a knot. She was as whipcord-thin and sun-baked as the rest of them; her hair was bleached nearly white. Asleep, with those empty eyes closed, she was heartbreaking in her beauty.

There were dark shapes scattered all down the strand: men as exhausted as Selene, and horses with staring coats and prominent ribs, standing with heads low, too weak even to switch tails at the flies. Their own mares were stronger than some, but even they had begun to struggle.

Selene's eyes were aching and burning. She closed them and sighed. There was a tiny bit of water left in her waterskin, but she was saving that for Etta, for when the sun set and they dragged themselves up again for another night's grueling march. Somewhere, someday they would find green again, and water that was not burning with salt.

She lay in her private darkness. Her soul tugged at its bonds. She had not been letting it wander—if she did, she would lose it. The sight that had not seen fit to warn her of this horror was quiescent except for a vision, or perhaps only a yearning: a cascade of water through lush greenery, so vivid that she could feel the coolness of spray on her face, and smell the wet earth, and taste the sharp cleanliness of grass and balsam.

She rested in the vision, taking sustenance from it. After a while, in the dream, she rose. Her strength was renewed, her body supple again, kneeling easily by the pool that spread across the green bowl. The grass was soft under her knees, a softness she had forgotten in the harsh sand and sharp stones of Gedrosia.

She bent over the pool. It was motionless here in spite of the turbulence above, reflecting the soft blue of the sky.

Slowly an image took shape, a vision within a vision. She looked down on a camp of her people, circle within circle of tents, the herds of horses and the herds of goats and sheep and cattle. She recognized the place: the autumn camp of the royal clan, raised up on a hill beside a river that ran deep even in that season. Her heart ached to see it, to be there, to walk those paths again; to hear her own language spoken in the voices of her own people.

She circled like a hawk in the blue air. People moved below in the ordered dance of a living camp. Some had gone to the horses and readied them to ride, armed with the weapons of the hunt. The queen was among them, and Ione a little thinner and little greyer and a little lamer on the bad leg, but still her beloved and familiar self. Selene recognized each of the others: her sisters, her kin.

It was a grand hunt. Selene followed it on her swift and unseen wings. They started a stag in the thickets along the river, and chased him into the tall grass. He leaped and darted, until a sudden doubling flung him full upon the queen's arrow. It flew straight and true, and lodged deep in his heart. He was dead before he struck the ground.

They dressed and gutted the stag and loaded it on one of the packhorses, leaving some of the younger women to guard it as they followed more slowly. The rest set off in pursuit of wild boar: the most dangerous and most succulent of prey.

As the hunt went on, the clarity of the sky darkened. Clouds heaped on one another. Far away, thunder rumbled.

The air grew heavy and strangely still. The hunters could not fail to be aware of the storm that was coming, but they had found a scent, and the hounds were baying. They were the Goddess' children. They laughed at lightning.

Selene hung above them, empty of thought and feeling. She was pure vision.

They brought the boar to ground in a shallow cave. The hounds closed in, bellowing and snarling. The hunters followed with boar-spears at the ready. The boar crouched at bay. Foam flew from its tusks. Its eyes were blood-red.

The queen laughed as she always did in battle, tossing her hair that was still as bright as a new coin. She sprang down from her white mare's back and balanced the heavy spear in her hand, stalking slowly, delicately, like the lioness she was.

One of the hounds screamed. The boar had gutted it in a blindingly swift slash. And yet it was still fighting, still leaping in toward the quarry, tripping and tangling in its own entrails.

The boar charged straight at the queen. She grounded the spear, driving it as deep in the tumbled earth as she could, and braced, and waited.

It was a voluntary sacrifice. The boar drove itself on the point of the spear, its little hooves scrabbling, its great body heaving, until it snapped its bloodied tusks in the queen's face. There it gasped and died.

She rose a little shakily. The others had begun the death-chant, the warbling hymn of triumph and praise. She set her foot on the inert body and wrenched the spear free, and lifted it high.

The Goddess took her just then, in supernal mercy, with great blessing. Selene saw the bolt come down, the fire from heaven. It pierced her from crown to sole. It seared her body to ash. Her soul spun free, brighter than the lightning, singing like a lark as it soared up to heaven.

Selene fell headlong into her body—into the heat, the thirst, the pain of a mad march. Her heart was still and cold. She was in shock. The blood had stopped running in her limbs; her mind was numb.

It had been no dream, what she saw, and no vision of things that had yet to be, that might still be prevented. This had happened. This was done. She had seen the truth. Her queen was dead.

She scrambled up wildly and all but flung herself toward Etta. Etta who was now her queen. Etta who lay sound asleep.

No soul came to rest in that body. No living spirit filled her emptiness with splendor. The queen was gone. Etta was as blank, as vacant as ever.

Selene had no tears, but still she wept. She sprang to her feet, staggering with effort. But once she was erect, however unsteadily, she could not move. Where would she go? What path would she take, that she had not set foot upon already? Her horse was nearly dead. Her body clung to life by sheer will. She could go no faster, drive herself no harder.

There was nothing she could do but sink down in her burrow of sand and give herself up to mourning for her kinswoman, her beloved, her queen.

Gentle hands lifted her, turning her onto her back. She was distantly aware of them, and somewhat less distantly she felt the trickle of warm wetness into her mouth. It was water, tasting strongly of leather and earth, but delicious in the face of her thirst.

She opened her eyes. The light was fading; the sun had set. The sky was crystalline. She saw it, and the first glimmer of starlight, beyond a face she knew quite well.

Nabu-rimanni was gaunt and his beard was grey with dust, but he had kept his elegance even in this place. He wrung a second napkin of water onto her tongue. She thrust away a third.

"Don't," he said in a rasp of a voice, such as they all had of late. "There's plenty. Hephaistion found one of the oases—thank the Good God, almost where the guides said it was. He sent back enough water for everyone, and we'll be at the oasis before dawn."

Selene did not want to hear good news. She wanted to hear grief, sorrow, anguish. But her body needed the water.

She struggled to sit up. He set a cup in her hands. Etta had another, drinking from it blindly as she always did. There was still no soul in her.

Selene had been a fool to think that when the queen died, her soul would enter into the queen's daughter. It had never even been a coherent thought, only a remote and wordless hope.

The queen was gone—truly gone, taken away in the Goddess' arms. When she came back, if she came back, it would be in another body, the body of an infant. That was the right way, the way the Goddess had always willed it, except for Etta.

Nabu-rimanni saw more clearly than he had a right to. He knelt beside her, taking the cup from her slack fingers, and said, "Tell me what it is."

Selene should have refused to answer, or else laid the blame on Gedrosia, but his quiet presence, his undemanding silence, drew the words out of her. "My queen is dead," she said.

He sat on his heels. "Today?"

She nodded. He did not question the truth of what she was saying; he simply accepted it. That acceptance made her go on, though her throat was nearly shut. "She's gone. My heart is empty. It's years since I saw her, months since I had word from her, but as long as she was in the world, it didn't matter. Now . . . I wasn't there. I couldn't be there. I can't go back. I can't conjure wings. I can't—"

He drew her into his arms. She still had no tears, but the dry sobs racked her, tearing at her throat. She clutched his coat, twisting it in her fingers, shaking him in the storm of her grief.

He held steady, saying nothing, simply holding her. He had never done such a thing before—never touched her at all, that she could remember. His warmth was welcome in the chill of dusk, his solidity a blessing.

He did not make her grief less, but he gave her the strength to carry on. After a while the storm passed. It left her with a dull ache in her center, an emptiness that would not go away. But she could rise, compose herself, tend Etta; then when the night's march began, she was ready.

Her heart yearned to run, but her body was doing well to walk, setting one foot in front of the other, step after step, across the waste of Gedrosia toward the west and home.

FOURTEEN

Persepolis was a monument to memory. The bones of its palace rose out of the ruins of Alexander's fire, soot-blackened columns holding up the sky. Processions of stone-carved princes marched in the sun, although they had been carved for the dimmer light of halls and passages. Wind and rain and the scouring fire had worn away the paint from the cool pallor of the stone.

"We offered it up as a sacrifice," Alexander said. He stood before a gate that rose intact, open on emptiness. "Fire is holy, the Persians say. We sanctified this place once we'd taken it, and gave it to the gods."

"We were royally drunk," said his friend Ptolemy, who some said was his brother. Ptolemy was the first to declare that he was a practical man; he had no poetry in him. "There were torches, and Thais had a score to settle with the Persians. It seemed perfectly logical at the time."

"It was more than logical," said Alexander. "It was inspired. The gods were in us, and they were in a mood for a holocaust."

"Zeus knows they got one," Ptolemy said. He rubbed his long jaw and frowned. "Are you really going to let him do it?"

The memory of exaltation drained from Alexander's face. "I can't stop him."

"Well, you should," said Ptolemy. "He's old, but he's sound enough. It will be months, maybe years before his body gives out on him. It's murder to burn him alive."

"Not in his country," Alexander said. "He wants the blessing of fire. How can I refuse to give it to him?"

"Easily," snapped Ptolemy. "You're the king. Tell him you refuse him his request."

"I can't," said Alexander. He was snappish, too, and he would not budge. His mind was made up.

The object of their argument sat on the stump of a column. It was winter, and although the sun was bright but hardly warm, he was naked: a bone-thin, leathery, brown and wrinkled creature with a remarkable quantity of matted greying hair, and a beard that flowed to his navel. He was not shivering; he never showed any sign of feeling either cold or heat. He smiled with extraordinary sweetness, raised a skeletal hand, and crooked a finger.

They broke off their bickering, and with expressions remarkably like those of schoolboys caught in a fight, approached the old man. "Kalanos," Alexander said. "What—"

The old man set his finger to his lips. He pointed to the gate and to the sunlit court beyond it.

"There?" said Alexander. "You want your pyre there?"

The old man nodded. Ptolemy glared. Kalanos reached out with more strength than anyone might have given him credit for, and caught Ptolemy's hand. He drew it to his heart and met the angry eyes, and inclined his head a fraction.

Ptolemy snorted. "You're a stubborn old bastard," he said.

Kalanos laughed soundlessly and patted Ptolemy's cheek. That leathery soldier blushed like a girl.

The king and his friend went to see to the building of the pyre. Selene, who had been passing through when she heard their voices, felt the warmth of Kalanos' regard.

He had been a great sage in India, something between a priest and a philosopher. It was said that he had perfected himself by stripping away all but the barest essentials of the flesh: his body, such little sustenance as would keep it alive, and just enough earth for his two feet to stand on. But one steaming hot day he had fallen from wisdom, when a certain young barbarian king had come to look on the naked philosophers. He had met Alexander's eyes and risen, taken up his staff, and followed him to the ends of the earth.

Just so had Etta done. Soulless or so rich in the gifts of the soul that the body was almost superfluous, it did not matter. They both were bound to Alexander.

But now, half a world away from India, Kalanos had decided that it was time to let go the body. He was not mute, although he seldom spoke; he had never learned a language Alexander knew. Selene had acquired a few words of his language. She could understand more than she spoke, which at the moment was fortunate.

"You do know," he said. "The world binds you tightly, and your soul is far from perfected—by your own will; you live for love and duty. But you know why I do this. You can see."

She shook her head. Words came with difficulty to her now, as they had in the months since Gedrosia. Sometimes she thought she must be dead herself, as her queen was; only she did not know it, but kept wandering among the living, pretending to be one of them. She had no power to feel, to act, or even to think. She was empty, and her heart was hollow.

Or so she had been until Kalanos announced that he was giving himself to the fire. That woke her with a raw and brutal shock.

He understood Greek, she knew; she spoke to him in that language. Her voice was rough with disuse. "I see that fire is the worst death imaginable. The pain is beyond belief. It's horrible; unspeakable. Why do you insist on it?"

"Pain is illusion," he said. "Fear is illusion. Life itself is illusion. Fire is real. It cleanses; it makes all new."

"Fire makes horror. It melts flesh and chars bone. It sears the lungs until they shrivel and collapse. It—"

His fingers brushed her lips, stilling them. "Child," he said in the gentlest voice in the world, "this is not fire that destroys without reason or mercy. This is sacred fire. It will heal you."

"Fire heals nothing."

He shook his head slightly and smiled his sweet smile. "Listen," he said. "Remember. It is time. I am called back to the cycle of death and rebirth."

"Why?" she demanded. "You could have left the Wheel and forsaken this world altogether. Why do you choose to return to it?"

He shrugged. "It is my fate—my karma, as we say. Now it is my duty and my karma to set aside this body."

"By fire," she said with a deep shudder.

"Yes," he said. "You do understand, although you refuse that understanding. So do you refuse the sight that is your gift—all for fear of fire. And yet there is nothing in it to be afraid of. Death is but a change of shape. Fire makes all clean, and eases the passage."

"Nothing?" Her throat was nearly locked shut. "Nothing to fear? You know what I know, and still you can say that?"

"I know what you think you know." He fixed her with eyes as bright and empty of either fear or misgiving as a bird's. "Will you come? Will you say goodbye to me? It's not enlightened of me, of course. I shouldn't care what or whom I leave behind. But that's my flaw. It keeps me on the Wheel."

Selene could not find the words to say. There were too many, and they were all tumbled together, roiling inside her.

His gaze held her rooted. A bird's, was it? A hawk's, then, fixed on its prey. "I will look for you," he said, "when I go to the fire."

Kalanos laid himself on his pyre under the blue winter sky. A great crowd of people had come to say farewell, with as much pomp and ceremonial as Alexander could persuade the old man to accept. Any of them would have helped him to climb up that mountain of timber and pitch, but he waved them all away. He clambered up as nimbly as a young man, stood upright on the summit, then lay down in a graceful movement. His expression was calm. He knew where he was going and why. He was not afraid of the pain that would send him to it.

Alexander lit the first torch. His face was as exalted as Kalanos'. He bowed before the pyre, swept the torch around in a stream of smoke and flame, and thrust it deep into the packed tinder.

Fire was a god, the Persians said. Truly this was a divine fire, a torrent of flame that rose to engulf the wizened figure on the pyre. He lay unmoving; he made no sound. The fire embraced him like the lovers he had long ago forsaken.

Selene had come as he had known she would. Everything in her yearned to run far away, but when she had tried to do that, her feet had carried her here. Her stomach was an aching knot. Her throat had not unlocked since he spoke to her the day before. She had not eaten or drunk. Sleep was the enemy. There was fire in it, and death without beauty or dignity.

She watched him burn with eyes that would not look away. She braced for horror; she steeled herself against the heart's pain.

And yet, as she watched, she realized that there was none. The fire was not a blind and soulless force but a living thing. The spirit enfolded in it was pure, unsullied by pain or fear. It melted into the fire, until it was a flame itself, dissolving into light.

In that light was a torrent of visions. They caught her unawares and overwhelmed her.

The heart of them was as clear as if she had come there in the flesh. She stood once more in the camp of the people, in the circle within circle of tents, surrounded by the herds of horses and the herds of goats and sheep and cattle.

It did no good to resist. She would see it again as she had seen it in the desert, but now as memory rather than vision. She would see her queen, the hunt, the boar, the fire from heaven.

The armor of numbness that had protected her was gone. The pain was as raw as it had been on that burning day in the desert. She had turned her back on it, first in the simple ordeal of survival, then because it was too strong and she too weak. She could not face it.

Now she had to. She could not turn away.

This was Kalanos' last gift to her. He would not care if she wanted it, or if she thanked him for it. He was already gone, riding the Wheel out of this body and into the next. She could almost see where he went, almost know what no mortal was meant to know.

Selene opened her eyes. The light was fading; the sun had set. The pyre had sunk to embers.

Nabu-rimanni was kneeling beside her, a vision of silken elegance as always. His eyes, as always, were kind.

Somehow she had expected to see him there. He always seemed to know when she needed a quiet presence. And that was his gift, as rare in its way as Kalanos'.

She struggled to sit up. He supported her with his arm, saying nothing. There was no need for words.

Hippolyta was still dead. Selene's heart still mourned for her. But Kalanos' passing had caused something within her to shift. She had been like the dead herself. Now, incontestably, she was alive.

She laid her hand over Nabu-rimanni's heart. Its beat was steady and strong. That was life. So was the warmth of the body that contained it.

Her own heartbeat had quickened. Her fingers tensed. Nabu-rimanni was perfectly still.

She drew back carefully. He made no move to stop her. With a sense half of relief and half of regret, she left that place of both death and rebirth.

FIFTEEN

The night after Kalanos' soul returned to the Wheel, Selene lay awake while Etta slept on the other side of the room. The king's palace in Persepolis was as quiet as it ever was. The wind of the world was still, and the sounds of the night had gone silent. Only Etta seemed alive, and that life was without soul or sense.

Hippolyta came in the dark before dawn, just as Selene had known her in life, wearing the scarlet girdle of the queen, with her bow in her hand and a crescent moon on her brow. She smiled at Selene as she had so often. "Beloved," she said in an accent Selene had half forgotten, the accent of their people. "Dear cousin. Are you happy?"

That was a strange question for the dead to ask. Selene answered honestly. "How can I be happy? I live in exile, and you are dead."

Hippolyta laughed, as if Selene's grief could be a matter for jest. "Oh, yes!" she said. "I am dead. Is that why you creep about in such gloom? I'm with the Goddess now in the land of everlasting."

"You should be here," Selene said in unslaked bitterness, "in this body that waits for you."

Hippolyta frowned slightly, although her lips still smiled. "Body? Waiting? It's not my time to be reborn."

Selene had known that; she could hardly escape it. Still she said, "You said—your oath—"

"I swore that she would be queen after me," Hippolyta said. "And so she will. That is as true a vision as it ever was."

"I never had that vision," Selene said.

"The Goddess has not willed that you should have it," Hippolyta said.

Selene shook her head stubbornly. "How can she be queen? The Goddess made her but never finished her. She was never given a soul."

"One waits," said Hippolyta. "Wait and see. It's not long now. The time is coming."

"I am coming," said Selene, "to the plains where I was born. I'm tired of this duty. I'm afraid for the people. They have no queen. Ione can hold them together—but for how long? They need someone to rule them."

"Wait," said Hippolyta. "Be patient. Protect my heir. She's safer by far here than she would have been among the people. They will go to war, cousin; my loyal friends, my warriors, my kin, will fight against those who would proclaim a queen. If you bring her there as she is now, she'll die—and you with her. She will never be reborn. Only souls can take flesh again, and she, as yet, has none."

Selene heard her in a kind of despair. The urgency in her to be gone, to be home, whatever it cost her, flared to ash. If it came back, it would come back transformed.

Hippolyta laid her hand on Selene's head, both blessing and

solace. "Soon," she said. "The time will come; you will know. Wait and see."

Selene set herself to wait. Her heart should have been as still as before, her grief as absolute, but Hippolyta would have rebuked her for the indulgence. Selene made herself rise and tend Etta as she had so many mornings before, then bring her to Arrhidaios, who was still her playmate although he was a greying man and she a blooming young woman.

Over the years Selene had come to an agreement with Arrhidaios' keeper. They looked after their charges by turns. This morning was Petros' watch; Selene was free to do as she would. She was more than half minded to give him his freedom and take guard-duty herself, but in the end she exchanged a few words, forgotten as soon as she had spoken them, then went away as if she had a place to go.

Kalanos' pyre was still smoldering. A few people were hanging about, idle or curious, but there was little to see but embers and ash. Most of the king's followers were gone in wine—celebrating Kalanos' passing, they said.

It was a convenient excuse, Selene thought. They had been celebrating since they came out of Gedrosia, feasting and carousing to make up for the starvation and thirst of the desert. There seemed to be no end to it, and no will to end it. They were caught up in a sort of madness.

Selene stood by the remnants of the pyre. The memory of pain that had tormented her for so long at the sight of flames or their aftermath was gone.

That shocked her somewhat. As she stood there with the wind

tugging at her hair and filling her nostrils with the reek of burning, she felt as empty, as clean and unsullied, as the soul that had
dissolved in the fire.

Kalanos had known. She would not call it healing, no. But
something in her was no longer festering. It had begun, however
reluctantly, to mend.

She bowed to the pyre as to the Goddess Herself. Kalanos
would have refused any such honor, but that would be Selene's
gift to him, well deserved and no doubt unwelcome, but somehow necessary.

She straightened and turned away. The day was no brighter
than it had been before, but the sky seemed cleaner. Her heart
was, if not light, then less heavy than it had been before.

Usually at this time of day Nabu-rimanni was out riding or hunting. He did not carouse as Macedonians did; he had a rather
remarkable sense of measure and restraint, which confined such
excesses as he had to the evenings. Selene would have welcomed
his presence, but the room he favored suited her mood better just
then.

He had retrieved as much of the library of the palace as had
survived Alexander's fire, and added to it treasures of his own.
They were all here, and in among them were other, familiar
things: bits of harness, saddlecloths, a coat of armor and a rack of
spears. In the corner by the window was a cage, the door of which
was always open. An owl came and went at will, flitting on soft
wings.

The owl was asleep at this hour, hunched on its perch. It did
not stir at her coming. She was familiar, and it was deep in sleep.

She was not in the mood to struggle with the Persian she had been learning laboriously to read, and even Greek for the moment was beyond her. She made a nest of saddle-fleeces and settled in it, wrapped in quiet.

She gave herself up to memory; then from memory came sight, filling her irresistibly. She saw Etta again with the light of a soul in her eyes, standing on a hilltop above a windy grassland. A battle raged below. Arrows flew. One escaped the pack and winged toward Selene, direct to her heart.

Sight melted into dream. Alexander was there. He caught the arrow and laughed. "Selene," he said in a voice a good octave deeper than his own. "Selene. You had better not be dead."

She peered through veils of past and future to Nabu-rimanni's face. For a confused instant she thought she saw the arrow in his hand, but he was holding a cup, pressing it to her lips, making her drink until she choked.

The cup was full of wine, heated and rich with spices. The fumes of it were enough to make her dizzy.

It brought her back to herself. She gagged and struggled. Nabu-rimanni set the cup aside.

They were on the floor, and she was in his lap like a child. She staggered up and away from him.

He made no move to stop her. His expression was supernaturally calm.

"I'm going mad," she said. Her voice was almost as calm as his face.

"Are you sure you're not going sane?"

She could have struck him: he would not have resisted. She seized him and pulled him to his feet. "This is something," she said, "that I have never told anyone. If you speak of it anywhere but here, I will hack you in pieces. I am—I was supposed to be— the great lonely spirit and divine exile of the people. I was to be the seer, the voice of the Goddess among the tribes. She chose me. She bred me, raised me for it.

"But I would not. My first vision was a thing of such horror and such overwhelming grief that I cut myself off from it. I refused it. I denied the Goddess Herself.

"I thought I had found the perfect refuge. In my queen's daughter, in her heir who has no soul, I found emptiness of my own. The sight let me be, unless the force of it was so strong that it could pierce even the walls of her oblivion.

"I was a fool. Kalanos knew: he made me face the fire that I had hated and feared for so long. He opened the door to the visions.

"Now I can't close it. All my resistance, all my refusals, are of no help to me at all. Everywhere I look, the world shifts and changes. The veils of time are torn away. I see what was and what is and what will come. I can't stop it. I can't control it. I can't—"

"Selene."

The simplicity of it, the power of her name, stopped the flood of words, such as had never come out of her in all her life before. She stared at him.

He was not in awe of her, nor had he changed because of her confession. And yet she could see that he had believed it; that he was considering it: what it meant, what it had cost her to let it go.

She had let it go to a man. She had been away from the people too long. When had she last spoken to a woman? When had she even seen one outside of the markets?

Everything was slipping away from her. Her people; her memories. Her strength to resist the visions. With the queen's death, she had lost her hold on herself.

"Selene," Nabu-rimanni said again. As before, she went still.

He had great power, for a man. He was wise and quiet, and he was strong. Stronger than she, just then; unsullied by grief or thronging visions. They were all about her, hungry for blood, like the shades of the dead.

"If you let the visions come," he said, "and stop fighting them, you can master them."

"How do you know?" she demanded. "Are you cursed, too?"

"I suppose I am," he said, "in my way. I do think too much."

"If thinking were all it was," she said, "it would be the simplest thing in the world."

"Well then," said Nabu-rimanni, "I confess I've given you a horseman's advice. Resistance has gained you nothing. Maybe you should run with the visions instead."

"What, give in to them? Let them overwhelm and drown me?"

"Haven't they done that already?"

That reduced her to speechlessness. He brushed her lips with his fingers, so light and so free of pretension that it was a long moment before she realized what a liberty he had taken. "Lady," he said, "whatever your Goddess has laid on you, She must know that you can bear it."

"*I* don't know that I can."

"You don't trust Her?"

"No!"

He did not cry blasphemy. Of course not: She was no divinity of his.

Still, Selene knew better than to let that word hang in the air. "That was disrespectful. I shall do penance for it. But this gift, this curse—I never wanted it. I ran away. For years I escaped it, but in the end it found me. Now I can't get away from it."

Again he touched her softly, taking her hand and folding it in his. She stared at those long fingers, at the faint white line of a scar across them. They were a horseman's hands, callused with sword and spear, but there was a stain of ink on the right hand.

He was a thing that was not common anywhere she had lived: both warrior and scholar.

And yet, when she looked up into his eyes, there was nothing foreign about him. Male and Persian he might be, bred and born in a world altogether alien to hers, but the soul behind that face was—not sister, no. But kin.

"How can you understand me so well?" she asked him.

His lips twitched very slightly. His shoulder lifted in the half of a shrug. It was all very Persian and yet perfectly familiar.

The world was shifting under her feet. Kalanos' burning had cast her loose from whatever moorings she had had. All the old fears were gone or transmuted. Her convictions, her sureties— they were all broken. A little while longer, and she would no longer even be Selene.

No, she thought, tightening her fingers on Nabu-rimanni's. He would defend her against that. He knew her name, both the word that the world spoke and the truth that lay beneath it.

She had not felt this way since Ione left. She had never thought she could feel this for a man.

Men are for breeding. Women are for love.

The voice was fainter than it had ever been. Her belief was crumbling.

She had lived a hand of years among these people, but she had never been a part of them. She had drifted like a shadow, serving Etta, watching over her, guarding her. She had seen much, suffered not a little in the body, but her heart had been sleeping. She had drifted as in a dream, touching nothing, feeling little.

Now she was coming awake. Death on death had roused her, but not in any way she might have expected. She was alive. She lived and breathed. She had a heart and a spirit. This hand that held hers, these eyes watching her with grave patience, were intensely, painfully real.

She did not want to wake. If she clung to her dream, if she held to her distance, there would be no pain and no fear. The visions would fade away. She would not have to feel.

It was too late. The walls were cracking; the stones were tumbling down. Her queen was dead. Kalanos was dead. And she, Goddess help her, was alive.

"I don't know how to live," she said.

"It's simple," he said, "if never easy. Simply do it."

"I don't—"

He drew her toward him. She had no power in her to resist.

When he kissed her, she was not surprised at all. It was as inevitable as death, as birth; as the sun slanting through the high windows onto the tiled floor.

He seemed more startled than she, as if his body had acted without his will upon it. He began to draw away.

She held him, exerting little strength, but he made no move to escape. She had not held anyone in her arms who could return that embrace since she bade farewell to Ione. There had been no sense in her of absence, no regret, until she felt those arms close about her. What woke in her then was fierce, consuming— hunger of the body as well the spirit.

At first she feared he did not want her: his response was restrained, almost cold. Then he caught fire.

She gasped, then laughed. That gust of joy, that sudden dizzy delight, caught her off guard. To find that in the midst of grief— that was the Goddess' gift, and one that she could gladly accept.

SIXTEEN

The hill of Susa rose straight up out of its fertile plain, with the river winding around its feet. The famous lilies had not yet bloomed; it was still early spring, and although the sun was warm, the wind blew chill in the evenings.

Alexander had come there from Persepolis: four and twenty days on the road, in a revel that had not ended or even slowed since Kalanos' funeral.

"It's the king," Selene heard a man say in the market of Susa. "Ever since the army wouldn't follow him across India to the stream of Ocean, he's been odd."

"Drowning his sorrows in wine instead of Ocean," the man's companion said. They were Macedonians, speaking their language that was oddly like Selene's own. Macedonians were always outspoken, just as Persians were nearly always circumspect.

"Well," said the first man, "and now it's gone to his head. This latest fancy of his . . ." He trailed off in a growl.

"What, marrying off his officers to Persian women? What's

odd about that? We always take the women when we win a new country."

"Not in formal marriage," the first man said. "Not as if they were equals. And the king in that new getup of his—the gown and the hat—next you know, he'll come prancing out in trousers."

There was a general shudder in the wineshop at that. All the drinkers there were from Macedon: burly, leathery men with a grand show of scars. Selene had happened on an enclave of old Macedonians, troops who had marched with their king since he rode out of his own country.

They did not notice her. In Persian dress she was invisible. Even those who knew the king's Amazon stared blankly past her, seeing the coat and trousers and cap and glazing over the face.

These men had been out too long. They admitted it freely. The joy of adventure, the delights of conquest, the riches they had amassed in all their victories, had long since palled. The exotic had become commonplace; they had seen worlds their fathers never imagined—even if they had refused to travel the few more days, or weeks, or months, or years that would bring them to the edge of the world.

They were tired. They were sick with longing for their own country, their own language, their own customs. The food they ate, the wine they drank, were so foreign that they professed to have forgotten what a man ate and drank in Macedon. Their wives no longer remembered them, their sons had grown up without them. They were foreigners in their own lands.

Selene had not been away from her people for as long as they had, but she was just as sated with foreignness. She was bound here as they were by honor and duty, by commands that she could not disobey, however much she might chafe at them.

She had forgotten what she came to the market for. She turned blindly back toward the palace and Etta and—with a warm flush in her center—Nabu-rimanni.

He was her anchor in this world. Since Persepolis he had become something more. Neither of them was flaunting it, but Selene did not think it was a secret that they shared a bed at night—hers, for choice, because she had to stay within reach of Etta.

He had not been in that bed last night. The king had announced his grand plan yesterday: to give the conquered Persian princesses husbands at last after years of apparent forgetfulness; but none of those husbands would be Persian. All the royal daughters and sisters and cousins would be given to Macedonians of appropriate rank. At the same time he offered a handsome reward to the ordinary troopers who had taken Persian women into their tents.

Selene had not ventured the banquet that purported to celebrate this decree. Nabu-rimanni had gone as kinsman of the loftiest brides: the daughters and sisters of his brother the late Great King. He had not come back after, but Selene refused to fret. If he had been with a woman she would know it. This was a men's thing, a nightlong wallow in wine.

Sometimes even that one had to be a man. She relieved Petros of his guardianship over Etta and Arrhidaios, and settled to a long afternoon of keeping the king's brother entertained.

Etta was unusually still. She showed no interest in the play of colors from the bit of crystal that Petros had hung in the window; she did not try to escape and find a horse or a bow and go hunting. She simply sat where she had been when Selene came in, with her blank face and her empty eyes and little enough life in the rest of her.

At first it was restful, but after a while Selene began to grow uneasy. The flood of visions that had struck her in Persepolis had passed, leaving barely a memory. The sense of imminence she had had, the breaking down of barriers, had faded. Her fears had been for nothing. Kalanos' passing had shaken her defenses, but they had risen again. She was safe from the curse of foresight.

And yet, looking at Etta in her absolute stillness, Selene recognized the cold sensation in the pit of her stomach. It was the sight making itself known, since her eyes refused it.

She could continue to turn her back on it, but her guardianship of Etta was strong and set in her bones. Even while she played at knucklebones with Arrhidaios, who won more often than he lost, she kept a part of her awareness on Etta.

The long afternoon drew toward evening. Petros came back and took charge of Arrhidaios. Just as Selene reached for Etta's hand to lead her away, an exceedingly elegant but somewhat rumpled page in Persian livery burst through the door.

That had not been his intention. Selene heard the laughter of drunken soldiers outside.

Her glance crossed Petros'. He nodded slightly, left Arrhidaios to a last game with the bones, and strode through the door. A moment later, Selene heard his voice raised in a battlefield bellow.

Arrhidaios threw back his head and laughed. Etta was oblivious. The page curled in a tight knot at Selene's feet, shaking uncontrollably.

Petros came back looking none the worse for wear. The soldiers had fled. "Young sir," he said to the page with grave courtesy, in his usual quiet voice, "I beg your pardon. My countrymen have worshipped a little too diligently at the shrine of Dionysos."

Gradually the boy stopped shuddering and unfolded. His Greek was rote recitation and somewhat stiff, but it was clear enough. "Lady, if it would please you, her majesty the Queen Mother requests the honor of your presence."

Selene had not expected that at all. In spite of Nabu-rimanni's words years ago, that the two of them should meet, she had never met his mother. At first there never seemed to be occasion, then the Persian royal ladies were left behind in Susa while the king set out to conquer the rest of Asia.

It seemed that this was a time for settling old affairs. Selene could not think of anything to say but, "My lady must eat, then sleep. If her majesty could—"

"Lady," the page said, "her majesty asks—bids—commands."

That was clear enough. The page led the way out of the room. Selene followed, with Etta trailing blankly behind.

Petros had cleared the corridors of stray roisterers. No one was hanging about the queens' palace except the eunuch guards. These bowed at Selene's coming and admitted her to a world that she had, until now, been careful to avoid.

She knew somewhat of harems. She had seen one here and there in conquered cities, and been aware of those that followed many of the Persian lords even to war. They were rich with gilt and silks, perfumed with rare unguents, but nothing could disguise the fact that they were prisons. Women lived in them, shut away from the world, bound as chattel to a man.

Among the people, such a thing was unimaginable. Selene felt a shiver of old, cold horror as she passed those elaborately gilded doors and heard them boom shut behind her.

She brought herself sternly to order. No one would or could lock her in against her will. She made her eyes see this place as if it had been any other part of the palace. It was old and narrow and small and rather dark, but the courts were open to the sky, and there were windows, many of them open to sunlight and the warmth of spring.

She could not say she relaxed, but the first fit of the horrors

passed. She could walk steadily, following the page, with Etta
walking blank and mute beside her.

The Queen Mother of Persia was not where Selene would have
expected her to be, sitting inert on a throne in some heavily cur-
tained chamber. She was on her feet in a sunlit court, dressed
much as Selene herself was, shooting at targets with a bow. Nor
was she the doddering ancient that rumor made her. She was not
young, no, but she was vigorous, and remarkably fit and strong
for someone who had never been seen outside the confines of the
harem.

Watching her as she drew aim and loosed at the target, Selene
half shivered and half smiled. There was no doubt who this was:
her youngest son was her image. Nabu-rimanni had the same elegant bones, the same straight shoulders and firm chin, and the
same aquiline profile. If he had been a woman, this would have
been the face he wore.

The arrow thudded into the target, piercing the throat of the
snarling barbarian painted on the cloth. As the Queen Mother
turned, Selene saw that she was not, after all, identical to her son.
Nabu-rimanni was a gentle soul for all his warlike skills. There
was nothing gentle about his mother Sisygambis.

Those dark eyes pierced Selene, reading her as effortlessly as a
treatise on a scroll. There were people about, women and
eunuchs, but they were shadows. Only the Queen Mother seemed
real.

Sisygambis handed her bow and quiver to one of the shadowy
attendants. "You," she said to Selene, "come."

Selene was hardly inclined to refuse. She followed Sisygambis to a corner of the courtyard, where a canopy of silk was stretched from column to column. Under the canopy was a table, and on it a meal as simple as Selene had seen in Persia. It reminded her, in fact, of Alexander's fare on the march: bread, meat, a bowl of spring greens and another of stewed fruit, and water laced with wine only so far as to kill any sickness that might be lurking in it.

By the time Selene had seen Etta and herself fed, she had decided not to be surprised by anything Sisygambis might say or do. Certainly she could understand why Alexander respected the Queen Mother so highly, and why the Queen Mother had chosen to disown her son the Great King and call Alexander son in his place. This was as strong a spirit as Alexander's own, although it was less perilous to the body it inhabited. This was a spirit of earth, of deep and enduring calm; not a spirit of fire.

Among the people she would have been a great priestess. The Goddess was strong in her, whatever she might choose to call Her.

Selene was content to eat and drink in silence. She has never been one for casual conversation. Neither, it seemed, was Sisygambis; and Etta of course never spoke.

When the food was cleared away, the servant replaced the watered wine with a concoction of fruits and spices, sweet and tart at once. Selene sipped it suspiciously, and almost choked in astonishment; then drank a deep draft. "This is wonderful," she said.

Sisygambis smiled. It was a warm smile, startling in that stern and regal face. She looked altogether different when she smiled. "Is it not? My mother taught me the making of it, then I added a spice or two of my own. My son Alexander calls it the nectar of his gods. They drink it, he says, in their halls above the sky."

Selene blinked somewhat at the mention of Alexander. It was perfectly matter-of-fact. Sisygambis, it was said, had not spoken the name of her other royal son, the late and unlamented Great

King, since he fled for his life. He had left her behind with his wives and daughters, at the mercy of the conqueror. That conqueror, by the greatest good fortune, was Alexander, who had a philosophical objection to the rape and slaughter of women.

Sisygambis clearly had never forgotten or forgiven. She would be a bad enemy.

Still she did not seem hostile to Selene—even when she said, completely without warning, "My other son is completely besotted with you."

"Do you find that objectionable?" Selene asked coolly enough: the calm of the battlefield, watchful and still.

Nabu-rimanni's mother sipped the nectar that she had made, slowly, taking as much time as she needed. Selene endured the wait with well-trained patience.

That did not escape the Queen Mother. The corners of her eyes wrinkled: the beginning of a smile. "I object to little that my son may choose to do. He has always been a good son, though never so good that a mother would worry."

Selene's lips twitched. She had been braced for enmity, and this was anything but that. Still she was wary. "I am not anything that a mother in Persia would approve of," she said.

"You are not," said Sisygambis. "Nevertheless, both of my sons approve of you. And you have a good name among the men. Brave in war, they say, but circumspect, and never wanton."

"You would know what the men are saying?"

It was presumptuous, but the Queen Mother did not seem offended. "Child, I know everything."

That startled laughter out of Selene.

"They say you never laugh," said Sisygambis, "and seldom smile."

"Does your son say that?"

"My son Alexander says that you are not what you choose to

let others think. My son Nabu-rimanni tells me that I should mind my business and he will mind his."

"And by that you deduce that he's besotted?"

"Of course he is," said Sisygambis. "Have you wondered why a man of his age has no wife?"

"I would presume he does not want one," Selene said.

"Ah," said Sisygambis, "but there is no marriage among your people, is there? Men are put to stud, and women live their lives altogether apart from them."

"Isn't that how it is here?"

"But none of you owns a particular man or harem of men. No?"

"No," Selene said.

"Here a man has women. But not Nabu-rimanni."

"He had a wife," said Selene, "long ago. She died."

"She was a child," Sisygambis said, "and he was not much older. Her death prostrated him. He has a fair bit of my other son in him, does Nabu-rimanni: he loves to excess. But unlike my son Alexander, he gives that love sparingly."

"I can't promise not to hurt him," Selene said. "No honest person can. But I'll never mean to do it."

"A very honest answer," Sisygambis said. "Bear in mind, if I hear that you have broken or even lightly wounded his heart, I will hound you to the ends of the earth."

Selene bowed low and without mockery. "Of you, lady, I would expect no less."

"Good," said Sisygambis. "We understand each other. I hope you will understand my son, as well, when he asks of you what he intends to ask. Be gentle when you refuse. Promise me that."

Time was when Selene would not have known what Sisygambis was speaking of. But she had been living in this world for long enough, and seen enough of men who were not properly brought up, that she could well guess. "You think he'll ask to marry me."

"I know he will," Sisygambis said.

"And you expect me to refuse."

The dark eyes held steady upon her. "Would you accept?"

"I think," Selene said after a moment, "that I would prefer to answer him—if he should ask."

"That is fair enough," Sisygambis said.

"Would you approve," asked Selene, "if by chance I did accept?"

"No," Sisygambis said. "You are altogether unsuitable to be a wife, although as a concubine you are sufficiently exotic to be interesting."

"Then you want me to refuse."

"Not if you break his heart."

"My people are much simpler," Selene said.

"We are called a complicated nation," said Sisygambis. "I will trust you to choose as rightly as anyone can."

"If he asks."

"He will," said Sisygambis.

"Maybe," Selene said.

SEVENTEEN

If Nabu-rimanni intended to speak to Selene at all, let alone threaten her with marriage, he seemed in no hurry to do it. He did not come to Selene's bed after she returned from his mother's palace, nor did she see him anywhere that she went on that day or the next.

On the morning after the third lonely night, Selene went hunting for him. The city was whipping itself to a frenzy over the great festival that the king had ordained for three days hence. Close upon a hundred Macedonian noblemen would marry Persian princesses, with Alexander leading them all. He was to take two: each the daughter of a Great King.

They were building another city on the plain, a wall of silk and gold enclosing a hundred bridal chambers. Caravan after caravan streamed into Susa, bringing the wealth of the world to ornament the festival. Whole herds of cattle were being slaughtered; flocks of fowl, rivers of fish, were dying to feed the multitudes. It was extravagant beyond the comprehension of a simple warrior from the steppe.

Selene did not try to comprehend it. To find a single Persian among thousands—that was more within her reach. She tracked him through the guards and the servants, in and out of banqueting halls and council chambers and his mother's palace. He had gone from there to the stables and ridden out, but returned before dark the day before.

He was not in the library, which surprised her. Nor was he in the archery court or the riding court or among the Persian princes who had gathered to growl over the king's grand plan. Not one of them was pleased to welcome a Macedonian into the family.

When at last she found him, she was ready to give up the chase. He had circled back to the queen's palace, but entered by another way than Selene had used. The guards there knew her, which she found interesting. They let her pass without question, as if she had been expected.

He was in the sort of room in which she had expected to find Sisygambis: heavy with silken draperies, thick with cushions, and overseen by a flock of eunuchs. The two women with him were so like him that Selene had no doubt they were his brother's daughters, the royal princesses of Persia. Their height and grace recalled the Queen Mother, as did the beauty that by their people's standards was quite remarkable.

They did not have their grandmother's strength, nor, it seemed, did they share their uncle's intelligence. The taller of them was placid, even a little smug. The other, who was somewhat smaller and somewhat more delicately made, had dissolved in tears. She was by far the lovelier of the two, with skin that, when not blotched with crying, was as pure as ivory.

"Stateira," Nabu-rimanni was saying to her as Selene paused in the doorway. She knew that tone well: quiet, patient, and very gentle, but with iron beneath. "What need for tears? You know Alexander. You've loved him since you were a child."

"I do love him!" Stateira cried. "But I have to share him."

"All women have to share," her sister said with calm that must have been calculated to madden her. Selene would wager that this was Drypetis, who would be given to Hephaistion. They must be almost of a height, although Drypetis was probably the taller. "You're sharing him already with that fox-faced witch from Sogdiana."

Stateira's glare was murderous, even through her tears. For an instant Selene saw Sisygambis in her. "The bitch from Sogdiana is barely noble and never royal. Not like this one. Not at the same wedding. Not as if we were equals. My father was king after her father. I outrank her. Ploddy old cow. Why couldn't she have waited until my day was over before grabbing at hers?"

"It was not her choice," Nabu-rimanni said, "any more than it was yours. The Great King commands; we all must obey."

"If I am to be queen," said Stateira, "why must I obey?"

"Because the queen obeys the king," Drypetis said.

Selene bit her tongue. Anything she could say would worsen matters immeasurably. She considered a retreat, but Stateira had caught sight of her.

"You! Are you a messenger? Is there word from the king?"

Selene felt Nabu-rimanni's stare like a swift, sharp stroke. She declined to meet it, bowing instead to Stateira and saying politely, "Not that I know of, lady."

The princess' eyes went wide. "You're not a eunuch. You're a woman. Then you must be—"

"The king's Amazon," her sister said. "She visited Grandmother a day or two ago. I saw her through the screen. Grandmother likes her."

"Grandmother doesn't like anybody," Stateira said, "except Alexander."

"So," said Drypetis. "This is almost as rare a creature as Alexander himself."

"An Amazon," Stateira said as if to herself. Her eyes had narrowed. "They own men—men never own them. I should have been an Amazon."

"Then Alexander wouldn't want you for a wife," Drypetis said.

"Then I wouldn't have to share him," Stateira said with a toss of her head. She whirled on Selene. "I wouldn't, would I? Men would have to share *me*."

"Men would matter little to you at all," Selene said.

It was not a wise thing to have said, if matters stood with Nabu-rimanni as his mother had warned her. But she could not stop herself from telling the truth.

"What, not even a little?" Stateira asked.

Selene could only answer honestly; it was all she knew. "How much does a woman matter to a man in your world?"

"Very little," Stateira said. "Maybe not at all. Except to make sons."

"There now," said Nabu-rimanni. "That's hardly fair. We revere our mothers. We cherish our sisters. We love our wives."

"In your way I suppose you do," Stateira said. "It's imprisonment for us, and captivity against our will. Mostly we accept it. But some of us can think, and wonder. Some of us don't see that it's at all fair."

"Nothing in life is fair," her sister said primly.

"If I were an Amazon," Stateira said, "I would kill you."

"You would not," Selene said. "We do not kill our own. That's a great offense to the Goddess."

Stateira blinked. She was given to flights of fancy, that was clear enough. Selene was too flatly practical for her taste.

Selene had had enough of that princess and her sister. Whatever she had meant to say to Nabu-rimanni, she could say in another time and place.

She bowed and began her retreat. Nabu-rimanni rose in relief that Selene hoped was not as visible to his kinswomen as it was to her, and bowed likewise, murmuring words that he must have forgotten as soon as he spoke them. He was behind her as she withdrew. Neither of the princesses seemed inclined to stop them.

Selene walked as if she were alone, taking the straight way back to the rooms she shared with Etta. There were two rooms, inner and outer; the outer was much smaller, but it had a door that could be bolted, and that had been an advantage while Nabu-rimanni was still coming to Selene's bed. The rooms' advantage for Etta, insofar as she could be said to prefer anything, was that they were close to the king.

Etta was asleep when Selene looked in on her. The guard who had been watching over her saluted crisply and took his leave. He was one of the king's men, loyal and discreet, but the glance that slipped past Selene had a smile in it. Everyone thought he knew what she was doing with the Persian king's son.

She wished that she did. Nabu-rimanni stood just inside the door of her little room, leaning against it, looming rather large. He did not mean to threaten, she did not think, but he was a man. He could not help it.

She was not in patience with his kind tonight. She set about preparing for bed, not caring if he stayed or went.

When she lay down, he was still looming. His brows had drawn together. She turned her back on him, pulled the coverlet up over her ears, and squeezed her eyes shut.

"You were hunting me," he said, his voice only a little muffled through the quilting of silk and linen.

She buried herself deeper. She had nothing to say to him. The hunt was over. She had found him. Now, it seemed, she was not to be rid of him.

"You're angry," he said. "Why?"

She did not answer.

For so big a man, he was remarkably quiet on his feet. Still she felt the shift of air as he came to stand over her, and she caught the light scent of the herbs that his servants scattered in his clothing chest. He was not given to musk and heavy perfumes as so many of the Persians were, men and women alike. It was one of the small things she loved about him, but tonight even that made her skin prickle.

"My mother," he said, "wise as she is, does not command my heart. Nor does she speak for it."

He knelt beside her. If he had touched her, she would have knocked him flat. But he kept his hands to himself.

"If you would quarrel," he said, "at least let me do my own fighting. I've been tried, it seems, and sentenced, without a word from me at all."

That brought her about at last. "Yes! No word. You disappeared. Is that what a man does when he wants to claim a woman? Vanish and leave his mother to do the haggling?"

"Or his father." He met her glare with calm that made her want to slap him. "You missed me that badly?"

"I noticed that you were missing," she said, biting off the words.

He looked—Goddess, he looked smug. Guilty, too, directly after, but for the smugness she could have killed him.

Everything about him was turning her to thoughts of violence—and it was not even time for her courses. It was the mood of this place: the king's grand gesture of conquest, and the odd, discordant undertone in everything he had done since his army refused to follow him to the edge of the world. Susa itself fed that strangeness. It was an old city, ancient beyond memory and almost beyond understanding.

She could feel the sight pressing on her, willing her to open herself to it. In this city where the past lay so heavy, present and future demanded their share.

She could—so easily—have given way. To know what would become of them all, what this man would do, whether he would be any part of her after tonight—

The sight was not a tamed beast, even if she would have ridden it in that of all directions. It eluded her grasp and slipped away, for which she was more than grateful.

All the while her mind wandered, Nabu-rimanni stood watching her. He knew better than anyone how to wait, and how to be patient.

"What do you think of?" she demanded suddenly. "When you stand there like that, what is in your head? Anything at all?"

"Little enough," he said. "I was thinking how beautiful you are when you are angry, and how angry you would be if you knew, and that would only make you more beautiful."

"And men say women's logic is preposterous."

"Well: isn't it?"

"Men are not logical."

"Nothing human is," said Nabu-rimanni, "except the Greeks— and I have my doubts of them."

She bit her lip. He was tricking her into a smile. He could always do that, curse him.

"Promise," she said, "that you won't ask anything of me but what a man would ask of an equal."

"Have I ever done anything else?"

"Don't change," she said. "Promise."

For once she could not read him. He had gone opaque. If that was hurt, then so be it. He said after a distinct pause, "I promise."

"Good," she said. She turned her back on him again, drew up the coverlet once more, and let him make of it what he would.

He hung about for a long moment, but then he turned and retreated. That was what she had willed him to do. Still, as the door snicked shut behind him, she caught herself regretting it.

She crushed the regret with a hard heart. He must not think that he could buy her body with promises. When she was ready, she would summon him. Then she would see what came of it.

EIGHTEEN

The king's wedding feast went on for nine days. If the revelry before had seemed excessive, then there were no words for this. Selene had never seen so much gold or so much wine or so much feasting.

She hoped she would never see it again. It was too much. Even Etta seemed to feel it: she was odd, restless, unsettled. Selene had not had such difficulty with her since she was a child.

On the fifth day of the festival, Selene lost her. Petros and the guards who looked after her when Selene rested were not at fault. It was Selene herself who failed of her duty.

Etta had gone wandering as she sometimes did. Selene thought she might find herself a horse and go on the hunt, but she prowled the palace with no apparent purpose. Selene suspected that she was looking for the king.

Selene had had years to grow into vigilance that was like its own facet of the sight. She knew where Etta was, always—even when she was out of eyes' reach. It was a sense in the skin, just as she knew the whereabouts of her own body.

She lost it. She was caught in a swirl of revelers; her mind was elsewhere, pondering a certain large male person who had not intruded upon her since she sent him away. The reek of wine, the jostling of bodies, the drunken voices bellowing in her ear, dizzied and dismayed her, whirling her about until she hardly knew where she was.

When it had passed, she had stumbled against a wall in a colonnade she barely recognized, and Etta was gone. Altogether gone—from sight, from sense. Selene reeled. But for the wall, she would have fallen.

She could hunt a single Persian in a city full of them. It should be profoundly simple to find a young woman with a Greek face and a great amount of red-gold hair.

Selene could guess where Etta had gone. It was not easy to make her way there through the crowds, but she had crossed battlefields unscathed. She managed the breadth of Susa with a cut and a bruise or two.

The city of tents outside the walls was the core of the revelry. The brides must be cowering in the tents, dreading that the mob without would break down the fragile walls and overwhelm the bridal chambers. There were troops on guard, Macedonians and Persians from picked companies, with the king's Immortals of both nations, but too many of those had dipped into the wine.

They were inexhaustible. Selene had given up hope of finding anyone in this crush, even the king. She directed her path as best she could, let herself be borne in the current when it ran where she was minded to go, and did her utmost not to give way to the terror that was rising in her—that Etta would be lost; that she would never be found again.

Where Alexander was, there must Etta be, or as close as she could come. That was Selene's best hope and reassurance.

Two of the tents were higher and more splendid than the others. They were set side by side but not touching, with an aisle between. Some wise spirit had hung a curtain near the rear of the aisle, so that if the king was minded to cross from one to the other, he could do it without attracting the attention of the revelers in the center of the great square.

He had gone to Stateira first, people said, nodding and winking and adding jests that Selene did not find amusing at all. Most of them had to do with the king's rather notable lack of height and the bride's rather notable excess thereof. Selene, who was the king's height almost exactly, caught herself reflecting once again on Stateira's uncle, who was considerably taller than his niece.

It was this place and this world: it narrowed a woman's mind and degraded her intelligence. Selene thrust through a roaring mob of Macedonians, tipping one resistant soldier headfirst into the winejar and shooting such a glare at the rest that even those hardened veterans retreated in haste.

Alexander was not anywhere in the crowd. The bridegrooms were sequestered with the brides, or so Persian tradition required. She saw a number of them roistering with the rest, even so: lords of Macedon in badly rumpled Persian dress. One of them, whose name she did not recall offhand, had dispensed with the trousers and hacked off the sleeves of the coat, so that it more or less resembled a chiton.

Selene found opening after opening, darting through each, aiming as best she could toward the royal tents. Alexander would be in one or the other. And where Alexander was, she had to hope, there Etta would be.

The circle of guards around the tents was both stronger and more vigilant than Selene had expected. But she had been Ione's student even before she went to war with Alexander. She mounted a diversion. One drunken soldier, thrust from behind, stumbled into another; he fell athwart a third. When the brawl began, Selene darted through the gap it had opened in the wall of guards.

The bridal tent was a brighter prison than the harem in the palace. Light shone through the white silk of the walls. Everything within was gold: golden hangings, carpets woven of white and golden silk, golden furnishings, golden lamps—Selene's head ached from so much splendor.

She was standing in an anteroom. Curtains of silk concealed the inner room. There was movement beyond: whispers of air, the rustle of silk.

Selene was fearless in pursuit of her charge, but even she hesitated to cross that barrier—briefly, to be sure. She drew a breath and set hand to the curtain.

Whichever of the brides had been installed in this tent, she was not in evidence. Alexander was sitting cross-legged in the midst of an enormous bed. The bed was silk and gold, but the coverlets were hidden in heaps of parchment and Egyptian papyrus, maps and scrolls and blocks of ink, pens, wax tablets scribbled over in his fast inelegant hand. He had a map unrolled on his knees and was frowning at it, apparently oblivious to the incongruity of the time and place.

Etta lay at the bed's foot, half-buried in cushions. She watched him as always, rapt as if in contemplation of the sun.

Selene did not mean to disturb him, but his senses were too finely honed for that. He glanced up from his maps, frowning in annoyance at the interruption, but at sight of her he loosed his swift smile. "Oh, good! Someone intelligent. Come here, hold this down. Now look. Tell me what you think."

Selene had learned long ago not to be surprised by anything

Alexander took it into his head to do. This was a very odd thing to be doing in the middle of his wedding, but it was very like Alexander. She came as he asked, held down the edge of the map, and pondered it for a while. Then she said, "You're thinking of going west."

He nodded. He had been looking tired since he came out of Gedrosia—as if some of the fire had gone out of him. But here, in the midst of his maps and plans, he had something of his old eagerness back again. "Yes! Yes. I went as far east as my men would let me. But that's only half of the world. Maybe less than half. No one knows for certain how far south Africa goes, or how far north is the edge of Europe. I'm King of Asia. Now I'm thinking, why not be king of the rest?"

"I would ask why be king of the world," Selene said, "but I suppose there's no explaining it."

"It's easy enough," he said. "I'm called to it, just as you're called to be your queen's protector."

She looked from the map of the western world to his face. He was somewhat younger than she, but he was beginning to look older. There was a worn look to him, a raggedness about the edges. Naked as he was, she could see the scars, some of them pitted deep and imperfectly healed, and the ravages of long marches, starvation and thirst, and the months-long wallow in wine that had culminated in this vast outburst of a wedding.

At the moment he was perfectly sober. She could feel the sadness in him, the faint bitter edge that had followed him from India. On that day when his army refused to follow him, he had stood at the zenith of his life. Now he had begun the long descent.

"I will not," he said, answering her thought as Hippolyta had used to do. "I will not give way. I will never be conquered—not I. Not ever. The east is mine. So will the west be. Then, who knows? I'll find a few willing men—and women, too, maybe. I'll sail beyond the Pillars of Herakles, and find the world's end after all."

"You won't stay to rule what you've conquered?"

He looked a little startled, as if she had reminded him of something he had chosen to forget. But he said, "I'll leave strong regents behind me. Strong, and loyal. Hephaistion follows me because he loves me, but he's a homebody at heart. He's as tired as the rest of them, though he'd die before he admitted it."

"Is that why you gave him a wife? For an excuse to stop following you?"

"That won't stop him," Alexander said. "No; that's politics. We all need heirs—the more the better, with the empire we're building. There will be plenty for everyone by the time I'm done."

"I don't see you working particularly hard at it," Selene observed.

For a moment she thought she had miscalculated: that she had sparked his swift and, these days, increasingly dangerous temper. But then he laughed. "Oh yes! You caught me out. Stateira was bored. She doesn't read, you know, or think overmuch, though gods know she's easy on the eyes. I sent her to play with her sister, so I could work in peace." He regarded her with a bright and wicked eye. "Can you think of a better time or place to do it? They all think I'm doing my royal duty. Which, make no mistake, I have—but I can't do it for nine days straight. I'm Alexander, not the great god Zeus."

She had to smile at that. "If I'm intruding," she said, "only say so, and I'll go."

"No," he said. "No, stay. You aren't like the rest of them. My old master Aristotle used to say women are a lesser creation, a vessel made by the gods to contain a man's seed. I think the old man fell into one of the traps he used to deplore: the easy assumption, without sense or reason behind it. He never stopped to think that if you keep any creature in a cage and never let it out, never educate it or encourage it or give it any reason to use its intelligence, it will never grow to be wise."

"That is our belief," Selene said. "Keep it locked up and wrap it in silk and it grows soft and weak. It never learns to be strong." She paused, debating the wisdom of saying the rest. In the end she decided to take the risk. "Stateira is neither a child nor a fool. Her weakness is a ploy. She'll use it to get what she wants."

"Of course she will," said Alexander. "I'd be disappointed if she didn't. She's teachable—that's why I chose her. She'll make me a son, a king for Persia."

"But not for Macedon."

"No," he said without sign of offense. "Not for my own country, or my empire either. I have other plans for that."

She did not ask what they were. Her eyes had fallen again on the map, on the campaign that he was pondering, the great sweep westward with a renewed army and a strengthened empire.

She blinked. The edges had blurred, the writing faded. The names that took shape on the papyrus were not names she recognized. None of them had anything to do with Alexander.

"There will be an empire," she said, "from the Pillars of Herakles to the east of India, from the cataracts of the Nile to Ultima Thule. But—"

He did not hear that *but*. He bent over the map, eager again. "You see? You see how we'll begin? First we'll finish securing Persia. Then we'll turn westward—gathering the fleet, recruiting new armies. We'll take Arabia first. Then we'll sail past Greece toward Italy. There are kingdoms there, and cities ruled by something other than kings; and colonies of Greeks anywhere within reach of the sea. I'll win those over. *They* will follow me to the world's end."

She did not try to quench his excitement. The empire she saw, or felt in her bones, was not his. But he did not want or need to hear it.

NINETEEN

The world's foundations were shifting underfoot. Selene left Etta in the king's bridal tent, where she was as safe as she could be in this part of the world, and made her way back through the mob. She had found a refuge over the years, one that always welcomed her, however often or seldom she went there.

The chief of Alexander's cooks had established his kingdom in the palace kitchens. His name was Marsyas; he came from Corinth. He had been taken as a slave in one of the endless wars to which the Greeks were given, but Alexander had freed him and would have made him ridiculously rich, as he put it, if he had not reined the king in. He was content with his position, in which his rule was absolute, and with such share of the king's wealth as he would allow Alexander to give him.

He was a lean whipcord man who looked more like a stable-hand than a cook—and he was young, which strangers found startling. He had been born in the same year as Alexander.

He greeted Selene with a wide white grin. "Lady Artemis!" he said. That was his fancy, because she was an archer and a hunter and she bowed to no man. "Have you come to work magic again?"

"If you can spare a pot," she said, "and an herb here and there."

"At your disposal," said Marsyas, "as always."

As always, however busy the kitchens might be, there was a corner for Selene, and a pot over one of the fires, and anything that she might need for her meditations. A plucked fowl today, an onion, a handful of dried apricots, and a mingling of Indian spices. While they stewed in the pot, she came to a decision.

Most of the pot's contents went to the cooks, who knew her arts well, but she filled a bowl with the choicest bits, covered it, and sent it by one of the cooks' slaves, with a message that she made him repeat until he could deliver it perfectly.

Most likely the one she had summoned would not come at all. She was going to expect that he would. While she waited, she pondered another creation, this one of cream and honey, cinnamon and pepper, white flour and eggs and almonds ground fine. This was a delicate thing, a cake as light as she could make it.

Nabu-rimanni came while it was baking in its carefully chosen corner of an oven. Selene was half asleep, waiting for it and him.

He kissed her awake. That was bold enough to earn him a blow of the fist, but she stopped before the stroke found its target. Her lips warmed to his. He tasted of the spices in the gift she had sent him.

"It needs more cardamom," she said.

He sat beside her on the bench. The cooks were aware of them both, but there was courtesy here. No one stared or offered insolence.

"You are a sorceress with spices," Nabu-rimanni said.

Selene peered into the oven. The cake was not quite done. She sat back and carefully, deliberately, wove her fingers in his.

He had sense enough not to remark on it. He did not pull away, either.

"I see," she said, "that life is too short for foolish quarrels."

"Was it foolish?" he asked.

"You think it wasn't?"

He wisely refrained from answering that.

The cake was done. She retrieved it and set it to cool, waiting with him in silence, resting very lightly against him. There was comfort in it, a sense that in a strange way she had come home.

She almost recoiled, but she caught herself before he could have felt it. He would never truly understand how unthinkable this should have been, for a woman of the people to be so captivated by a man. That way lay slavery and worse, or so she had been raised to believe.

It was a kind of slavery, but one she did not wish to be free of. He was bound as well: she caught him watching her, trying not to be obvious about it. She kissed his hands one by one and pulled him to his feet.

He was not quite as docile as his silence might have indicated. He rose at her urging, but he did not follow her at once. "Do you mean this?" he asked her.

She scowled. "Do I—What do you mean?"

"Am I a convenience, or do I matter?"

Her teeth set. She had to answer, but it was not easy. Not at all. "You matter," she said.

Did a deep knot of tension go out of him? It was hard to tell. He followed her then, willingly, even with the hint of a smile.

Selene knew better than to hope that because she was happy, the rest of the world would follow suit. There was a certain quiver of guilt in the contentment of her spirit, when it was so clear that Alexander's grand exuberant game was playing itself out.

He left Susa in boats, riding on the rivers with a few of his chosen friends and his guard of foot soldiers. Hephaistion marched on land with the rest of the army and the royal women. The king was left to rest for a while, to be as much at ease as that restless spirit could ever be.

It was a mark of Alexander's exhaustion that he allowed it. Time was when he would have upbraided his friend for conspiring to make him rest. This spring and summer, he indulged it, insofar as Alexander ever could. There were armies to muster, kingdoms to rule, cataracts to demolish so that the Tigris flowed straight and broad from Opis to the sea.

He came to Opis in the full heat of summer. Selene was sailing in the king's boat, because Etta would not leave him. She clung as close as one of the dogs, sleeping at his feet and crouching in a corner during the day, watching, barely blinking, day after day.

Little by little as the voyage went on, Alexander's Macedonians had withdrawn to other boats in the fleet or gone off to join Hephaistion on the land march. A day's sail outside of Opis, all the mariners and the servants and companions were foreigners to Macedon—most from conquered nations, and most of those were Persian.

It was not intentional, Selene did not think, on either side. There was no conspiracy. Alexander had Marsyas to cook for him, and Selene when she was inclined. There were soft-voiced, soft-footed servants from the palace at Susa, waiting on him with invisible skill. The clerks who took dictation were Greek or Persian; the guards were strong young men from his new bodyguard, sons of Persian noble houses. He had called in musicians to play for him, some from Persia, some from India, weaving complex melodies on unfamiliar instruments, or singing strange and intricate songs in languages as far-flung as his conquests.

Nabu-rimanni had come in that morning, riding along the

riverbank with messages from the commanders in Opis. He was rather lofty a prince to be running errands for the king's generals, but he had been with the army and the Immortals for the past month. It had been a hard wait for him, it seemed.

For Selene the days had been full enough, but it had been lonely in the nights. She was deeply glad to see him.

Once he had delivered his dispatches, he settled by Selene near the bow of the boat, where she was taking her ease between breakfast and the daymeal. A light canopy kept off the worst of the sun; a breeze was blowing, lessening the weight of the summer heat. Many of the Macedonians in the other boats were naked, but Persians were prone to modesty. Even Alexander indulged it by keeping on a tunic of Egyptian gauze. Selene found the fashion comfortable enough, and the wisp of fabric cooled her rather well.

Nabu-rimanni had the full measure of Persian body-shyness— which was a shame, in her estimation, but there was no talking him out of it. Today he unbent so far as to take off his coat and shoes and twist his thick curling hair up off his neck. She lay with her head in his lap, sighing with pleasure as he combed her hair out of its plait.

He did love to play with her hair. There was no color like it in Persia: rich brown shot with gold, like shadowed bronze. It was never as glorious as Etta's or lost Hippolyta's, but as he did not tire of pointing out, it had its own splendors.

People were watching, but idly, without either lust or envy. It was too hot for either.

She drowsed in the heat and the lapping of water and the buzzing of insects outside the veils of gauze that hung from the canopy. The singers had fallen silent for a while. The king was asleep.

She slid from waking to the edge of dream. She knew she was asleep; she was aware that she dreamed. And yet it was as vivid as if she saw it with her waking eyes.

The king lay in a bed of purple, guarded by golden lions. His eyes were shut; his cheeks were pale. His breast was still.

She struggled away from the dream, but it followed her. She heard wailing; she heard the clash of weapons, and men shouting. It was a word in Greek: *Kratistos.* The strongest. "To the strongest! To the strongest, he said!"

The dream bore her back toward the bed. Alexander was dead. The soul was gone out of him. She looked down at his face, which was emptier even than Etta's. It was no older than the living face under the canopy, drifting toward Opis in the gilded boat.

She grasped at that, at the heat and sunlight and the rocking of waves. The dream had held no fear or foreboding, only a sense of imminence; but as she willed herself awake, the import of it struck her.

Her glance leaped toward Alexander. He was awake, sitting up, conferring with a pair of his clerks. The life in him was as strong as ever, but the flesh was losing its power to sustain it. For a moment she saw Kalanos' body on the pyre, wreathed in flames.

She squeezed her eyes shut. The peace that she had had, the lazy contentment, was gone. Yet again, the sight had ambushed her.

She turned for refuge to Nabu-rimanni's face. The light reflected from the water, diffused through gauze, gave it the quality of a painting on a wall: beautiful and still, and rather remote. She saw no death there, no more than was in any man.

Slowly the dream retreated. All that was left, as the sun touched noon and began to descend, was a distant unease, a sense of foreboding that would not leave her.

TWENTY

Alexander's army—all of it—was waiting for him when he came to Opis. Massed ranks lined the river, clashing spears and swords on shields, roaring his name.

And yet there was a hollow ring to all the shouting. In times past it would have gone on and on, irrepressible, irresistible, as he disembarked from the boat and rode into the city. Here, it followed him exuberantly enough, but in its wake was silence. Men lowered their weapons and shields and grounded them, and stood still until their commanders dismissed them.

Alexander seemed not to notice the falling off. He had embraced Hephaistion at the quay and greeted the rest of his generals with a fair measure of his old, high enthusiasm. As he mounted the horse that was waiting for him, a gleaming beauty from the studs of Nisaia, he managed to acknowledge the ovation even while he filled his friends' ears with the plans he had been pondering on the voyage. He was full of his western war, brimming over with it. He did not see the dark glances under Macedonian helmets, or hear the spreading stillness behind him.

Selene was far enough back to be well aware of it, riding with Nabu-rimanni and some of his kinsmen. When they passed through the Macedonian ranks, her hackles rose. A low growl followed them, a rumble underfoot. The eastern troops cheered gladly enough, but the veterans from Macedon set their teeth and refused.

Some of them spat. Nabu-rimanni's brother Oxyathres, who wore the livery of the king's Immortals, barely evaded a flung stone. Another, hurtled with better aim, clipped his horse's rump. The beast bucked and reared.

Oxyathres was a splendid horseman, as all the Persian princes were. He kept his seat and his dignity. But the message was clear.

"What does it matter?"

Alexander was dining with Macedonians tonight—no foreigners, even those dearest to him, had been invited. Some of the Persians had gathered in the hall of a house not far from the king's palace. Oxyathres was there, and Nabu-rimanni.

It was not the sort of gathering that in ordinary times would have welcomed Selene, but Nabu-rimanni had sent a page with a proper invitation to dinner. She had come expecting to find him alone. Instead he was there with his brother and two or three of his cousins, and a very noble guest indeed: the ancient and august prince Artabazos, who had known Alexander when the king was a child.

They greeted her courteously. She was careful not to show surprise or discomfort. A place was set for her at Nabu-rimanni's right hand, a place of honor. No one remarked on the fact that a woman did not dine with men in Persia.

They had eaten well in the Persian style: richer spices and notably more sweetness than the Greeks preferred, and soft conversation of trivialities until the plates and bowls were cleared away. When the wine came out, with a graceful young page to serve it, then the talk turned to the king and his army.

One of the cousins had drunk deeper than the others, demanding wine that was barely watered. "Does it matter?" he asked again. "Really? The Macedonians are barbarous by nature. But the king—he is civilized. He takes to our ways as if born to them. He makes himself truly a Great King. Let him send his veterans away. They're worn out; they're sick with longing for their sheepfolds and their brawny wives."

"It matters to the king," Oxyathres said. "These are his people. He was born among them; his ancestors ruled them. They've had enough of foreign ways. They want to go home."

"Then let them," his cousin said. "He's past needing them."

"Now there," Artabazos said, "you misunderstand both the king and his people. Alexander will always need Macedon. However fond he may be of us, however our ways may please him, at day's end, he remains a Macedonian."

"If that is so," Nabu-rimanni said, "and, my lord, I don't doubt it, then there is a lovers' quarrel brewing. The mood among the veterans is foul."

"Does Alexander notice?" the cousin asked. The wine in his cup was barely watered, and he was swaying gently where he sat. "I suppose he cares, but does he notice?"

"Alexander notices everything."

Selene had not meant to say it aloud. But since she had, and since they were all staring at her, she said, "He knows. That's why he's having a Macedonian night. He's working to win them over."

"The captains will be easier than the troops," Oxyathres said.

"They're a beginning," said Selene.

"But only a beginning," Oxyathres said.

"Were you proving a point?" Selene asked Nabu-rimanni.

The gathering had ended early, as such things went. Artabazos pleaded the weakness of old bones; the others retired out of respect. Selene did not think any of them believed in the old man's frailty. He was as strong as a man a fraction his age.

It was a useful pretext. Nabu-rimanni had taken rooms in the house, which were considerably more pleasant than the cupboard in the king's palace that she shared with Etta. She would have to go back to it before the night was out, but for a while she could stay.

She had taken him fiercely, startling him, but he laughed and welcomed the attack. They lay together after, breathless, slicked with sweat, while their breathing quieted and their hearts stopped hammering. When she could think again, she asked the question that had been niggling at her. "Were you flaunting me?"

"No," he said.

She lifted herself on her elbows, glaring down at him. "No? Then why, after all this time, was I invited to dinner with your noble relations?"

He did not try to evade her eyes. "I didn't invite you. Artabazos did. He was curious."

"Why now? I've been with Alexander since Zadrakarta."

"You've been with me since Susa."

"Ah," said Selene. Her glare had softened, if not entirely. "Are you going to tell him there's no marriage in the offing?"

"He knows," Nabu-rimanni said.

"I don't suppose he approves."

"You should ask him."

"Maybe I will," Selene said.

She was not surprised, as she left Nabu-rimanni half-asleep in his bed, to find the page waiting for her. She could have declined this new invitation—he made it clear that there was no compulsion—but she, like Artabazos, was curious. She followed the child down the passage and up a stair to rooms rather larger and more imposing than those she had left.

Artabazos was wide awake, fully dressed, and dictating letters to a pair of scribes who seemed as unperturbed by the lateness of the hour as their master was. He greeted Selene with a smile and a nod, and beckoned her to a chair. She sat and waited while he finished his letters.

It was peaceful, sitting there, listening to the rise and fall of his voice. It must have been deep when he was young: it was still imposing, with a strong cadence. It lulled her almost into sleep, but she was too wary to succumb. The sight was waiting on the other side of that dream, and in it was Alexander's death.

"Lady," he said. She snapped awake.

His clerks were gone. He was sitting with his gnarled hands folded, studying her with eyes that were in no way dimmed with age. "I beg your pardon, lady," he said. "I had forgotten how much sleep the young require. If the hour is too late, then perhaps another time—"

"I'm well enough," she said.

He nodded. Persians found her manners rough, but he was like Nabu-rimanni: he accepted her as she was. She supposed they were related. She had a fair enough mind for horses' pedigrees, but when it came to breeding men, she could never remember which sire was which.

"I have to ask your pardon again," he said, "for succumbing to curiosity, and using my kinsman to bring you where I might see you."

"Yes," she said. "He told me. He said to ask you why. Surely you've been curious about me since first I came to Persia. Why now?"

"Why indeed?" said Artabazos. "You were not, in a manner of speaking, family. And, I confess, I was reluctant. My memories are decades old. Maybe I should let them be forgotten. But seeing you with my young cousin, seeing how he is with you, woke old joys and old sorrows. It's been a long while since I spoke with one of your people."

She raised her brows. "You knew us before we came to Alexander?"

"I did," he said. "I've seen your hidden country. I'd ridden your hunting runs and spoken with your people."

That woke Selene fully. "You lived among us? A Persian?"

"Even so," he said smiling. "I was in exile then, before I went to Macedon—before I knew Alexander. I lived a year and more with the royal clan."

"Yes," Selene said in sudden understanding. "Yes, you did. Do you remember the woman who kept you with her?"

He sighed. "I do indeed. She was young, no more than a child, but beautiful—and wild; oh, by the Good God, she took my breath away. I've never met a boy, however headstrong, who was as reckless as she."

"Do you remember her name?"

"Ione," he said. "Her name was Ione."

Of course it was. There was a shape to the passage of time, and a pattern in the workings of the Goddess' will.

He was watching her intently, as if like Nabu-rimanni he could read her thoughts. "You know her."

"Yes," Selene said. "She's the queen's warleader." And more, but that was not for him to hear.

"She's done well," said Artabazos.

"Are you surprised?"

"Not in the slightest. She was a wonder of a woman." He paused. "I don't suppose she remembers me."

"She remembers your language," Selene said. "The rest she keeps to herself."

"Yes," he said somewhat ruefully. "She would do that. If I learned nothing else among the clan, I learned that a man is a far less significant thing than he might like to imagine."

"That's a hard lesson," Selene said.

"It is," he said. "But salutary. It served me well in the rest of my exile. I owe your people a debt, lady, for lessons well if not easily learned, and for hospitality above what I had any right to expect. Perhaps I owe them my life, when all is considered. I was a properly arrogant idiot when I came wandering into your queen's hunting runs. I left rather less arrogant and a fraction less of an idiot."

"We are death to a man's pretensions," she said.

He laughed. "And well you might be! Lady, I am glad that I gathered the courage to speak with you. May I do so again, now and then? You bring back memories—with remarkably little sadness. And maybe," he said, "it would do me good to recall my proper place in the scheme of things."

"We are all the Goddess' children," Selene said.

"So we are," said Artabazos.

That had been an odd meeting, Selene reflected as she made her way back to her own bed. The sense she had had since she knew the queen was dead, that the long quiet was ending, had grown so strong that it was almost unbearable. Time that had flowed like a slow deep stream was quickening to the flood. She was caught in it like flotsam. There was nothing she could do to resist it.

TWENTY-ONE

After Alexander's Macedonian dinner, after several days of audiences with his captains and his generals, Alexander ordered an assembly of troops. They gathered on the plain before the city walls, forces of all nations, from veterans to new recruits.

There was a great army of those: thirty thousand splendid young men with Persian faces, but armed and armored in the style of Macedon. They were glorious; they flashed in the sun. Their pride shone out of them.

The veterans had seen them march into Opis the day before, and were no happier about it today than yesterday. As the morning stretched and the heat rose, and Alexander did not come out to stand on the high dais that had been built under the wall, they began to grow restless. Time was long past when any Macedonian would collapse from heat, even in full armor, but they were not in comfort. Sweat streamed down their faces under the bronze helmets. Fists tightened on grounded spears—tightened and released, tightened and released.

There was going to be a battle here, if the king did not put in

an appearance. Selene, crowded onto the wall with a good part
of the populace of Opis, could see how the fight would go. The
phalanx of veterans would wheel and charge at the ranks of
newcomers, and hack them to pieces while they stood astonished.

She clung to the sun-heated stone of the parapet, dizzy with
the confusion of sight laid on sight. Her eyes saw the army standing still, glittering in the morning light. The inner eye saw the
battle that was brewing: swords clashing, spears stabbing, blood
springing.

When at long last the king came out, the roar that greeted him
partook less of adulation than of hostility. She could only see the
top of his head, the bright gold of his hair bound with purple, but
she knew as much from the sound of the Macedonians' growl as
from the glimpse she had from above, that he was dressed in his
variation on Persian royal fashion: the purple robe of the Great
King with its white striping, and the diadem. The Macedonian
cloak with which he finished it off only added insult to injury.

He stood perfectly still. Once the silence would have been
swift and absolute. Today it was some considerable while before
the army quieted enough for him to speak. His heralds would
have blown trumpets, and some of his captains did bellow for
silence, but he waited his men out.

There was still a distinct rumble from the crowd when the
high clear voice rang out over the ranks. He was speaking Macedonian, a dialect as rough and unpretentious as the farmers and
shepherds who had put on armor to march to the king's war.
"Men of Macedon! When you were in India you begged not
to march farther. You wanted to go home, you said. You'd had
enough. Never mind the bloody Ocean, you wanted the hills you
were born in. Well, men. Now's the time. I can't send all of you
back—I need my Macedonians. But you who've grown old serv-

ing kings, and you who've taken wounds in a hundred battles—now you can rest. I'm sending you home. You'll see your wives again, and see how your sons have grown. You'll rest in your own beds in your own country. You're going home."

It was a grand crescendo, meant to stir the heart. It stirred the army—indeed. But not in the way Alexander had intended.

Out of the babble of protest, one brazen voice came clear. "Tell us the truth, Alexander! You're tired of us—you're sending us away. Well and good, then. Sick, hale, old, young, raw recruit and worn-out veteran—if you don't want us, we'll make our own way home. You say your father wasn't old one-eyed gimpy-legged Philip—he was some god from Egypt. Let *him* be your army!"

Even what little Selene could see of Alexander had gone rigid. She could imagine his expression.

Another voice rose above the clamor. "*Alexander!* You can't toss us out like a worn-out sandal. We've followed you to Hades and gone. Why don't you want us any more?"

There was no logic in that outcry. Alexander was only doing what a wise commander did: culling the old and the sick and sending them home. It was compassionate as well as sensible. They should have known that, and understood it. Just as they should have remembered that they themselves had begged to be sent home—hectored and harangued Alexander until he gave way.

But now that he had, they did not want it at all. They were as contrary as children.

He stood utterly still while they roared against him. With a sudden, violent sweep of the hand, he sent his guards into the mob. Swiftly, mercilessly, they seized men who seemed to be ringleaders, and hacked them down.

The shock of that rippled through the mob. They backed away from the king's men with their swords and spears. Their shouting sank to a mutter, but a mutter it remained, a long low growl that would not stop even for the terror of death.

Alexander turned his back on them. He did not stop or even slow until he had reached the palace, which was halfway across Opis. Not one person in that city dared to get in his way.

Alexander shut himself in his rooms. His guards had orders to keep everyone out.

Everyone, that is, except Etta. Where Etta went, there was Selene—not gladly at this particular moment, but Etta was not to be stopped. As the gilded door opened for them, someone else slipped through. Selene saw without surprise that it was Hephaistion.

That great lord and general looked like a boy caught in a prank: breathless, furtive, and faintly guilty. He was not, however, repentant. He walked quietly behind Selene. Etta had darted ahead, but she knew where the girl was going. She took her time in getting there.

Alexander had thrown off his Persian finery and pulled on a linen tunic, which would have gratified his troops if they had known, and ordered his clerks out of their workroom. He sat there alone, glaring at the rolls of his armies.

Etta crouched at his feet, displacing the dogs that had been performing that duty. He did not turn or look up, but obviously he was aware that the others had come in.

Selene settled in the least obtrusive corner. Hephaistion hesitated just inside the door. After a while he came in softly and sat near Alexander. He reached for one of the rolls, opened it, and said in a perfectly casual tone, "If you're going to dismiss them all, you'd better let the commanders know."

A growl was the only answer he received. He had not been ordered out; Selene noticed that.

Of all Alexander's Companions, his oldest and most trusted friends, Hephaistion was the closest to him. They had been lovers when they were boys, people said, but if they still were, it was not a frequent thing. That they were friends, companions of the heart, she could well see. There was an ease between them that she could not mistake.

Alexander was not about to admit it, but she could feel his relief. He needed his friend here, demanding nothing of him, understanding why he had withdrawn to this place and what he had to do—both now and in front of his army. Hephaistion would pass no judgment.

They worked in silence for a long while. When Alexander spoke, the sound was a little startling. "People are unreasonable," he said. "That's the way of the world. I can excuse them for getting tired of following me. It's a long way for a man to go if there's no god calling him onward. But gods, what's got into them? I'm giving them what they want, and they've risen up in mutiny. What's happened to us? Why can't I keep them happy? It used to be easy. Now it's the hardest thing in the world."

"Well," said Hephaistion. "You know what your mother says. Love's a fine and splendid thing, but love gone cold is poison."

"To my mother it is," Alexander said. "She loves too much; she suffocates the one she loves. Then it turns to hate." He rounded on Hephaistion. "You know what I swore. I'd never be like her. I would keep love alive, and be faithful, no matter how long or how hard it might be."

Hephaistion did not move to touch his friend, but his glance said all that his hands could have done. "I know. I remember. You'll never have the edge she has—you know that. You're sane. Divinely obsessed, but sane."

"I would hope so," Alexander snapped. "But now I have an army in revolt. I've made my point with the edge of the blade. Now I'm going to give them what they want. I'll send them all away. Every cursed one of them."

"Alexander—" Hephaistion began.

"Don't start," said Alexander. "My mind is made up. If you insist on being here, help me get the rolls together. It will give me something to do while I wait for them to come crawling."

"And if they don't?"

"They will," said Alexander.

That far at least, Alexander knew his men. Well before sundown on the first day of his retreat into the palace, men came pounding on the gate, demanding to speak to the king. The king was indisposed, the guards told them. That deterred a few of them, but most squatted in the shade of the wall and refused to leave.

By nightfall there were a good thousand men camped in front of the gate. More straggled in through the night, and in the morning most of the rest had crowded into the square and overflowed into the streets and alleys near the palace. They were chanting the king's name: "Alexander! Alexander! Alexander!"

The gates of the palace remained obstinately shut. The king did not come out. No one who was not already in the palace was allowed in. Those few lords and servants from within who tried to leave were mobbed; they fled back into shelter, badly ruffled and white about the eyes.

Toward evening of the second day, the chanting died down. Spokesmen with strong voices were pushed through to the front, where they could cry out to the king. "Alexander! Come out and talk to us!"

But the king was not going to let them sway him. Not so soon. For a second night, his Macedonians bivouacked outside his door. With the coming of darkness, they fell silent. It was a glum silence. Torchlight revealed bowed shoulders and hangdog faces.

Alexander paced his rooms for most of that night. Selene, bedded down with Etta on one of the couches in the anteroom, heard him prowling. Once Hephaistion said sleepily from the great bed, where he had settled as if he belonged there, "Come and sleep. You're not doing yourself any good gnawing at your liver."

"It's my liver," Alexander snarled back. "I'll chew it up and spit it out if I want to."

"Idiot," said Hephaistion, but he was quiet after that. No one who knew Alexander would press him when he was minded to resist.

After some little while, Alexander stalked into the room and flung himself down on the bed. It was a vast bed; he was well out of Hephaistion's reach. But he was lying down. That was enough to go on with.

By morning the pounding on the gates had begun again. The men were yelling for Alexander to come out.

There was an edge of desperation in it. Not even when they refused to follow him to Ocean had he turned away from them as he had now. They were bereft.

The day ripened into blazing heat. Any sensible soldiers would have retreated to shade and what coolness they could find, but Alexander's Macedonians had long since forsaken either sense or reason. They were pounding spears on shields and stamping their feet, bellowing for the king to come out.

He made them wait until noon, and then somewhat after.

When at last the gates opened, a double rank of men marched out. They were all Persians in the armor of the king's Immortals, tallest and strongest of all the men in Persia, and every one of them of royal lineage.

The Macedonians gave way before them. They spread in a double rank before the walls, shields interlocked in a grim echo of the phalanx of Macedon. Alexander's veterans found themselves face to face with a shieldwall bristling with spears.

That did what nothing else had managed to do: it reduced them to silence. In that silence, Alexander ascended the wall and stood over the gate, looking down at the space his Immortals had cleared, and the massed faces beyond. They stared up at him with the blank entreaty of sheep.

He stared back with no expression at all. That in Alexander, who was nothing if not volatile, was terrifying.

When he spoke, there was no sound in that place, not even the buzzing of an insect. "I am not sure," he said, "that I dare say anything to any of you. I'm no king to you. You flout my authority. You fling rebellion in my face. You never even stop to ask why I made the decision I did. You haven't asked my advice, you haven't offered your opinions. I can't even tell what you want now. You say you want to go home. I told you I was sending you home. You say you want to stay. I told you I was keeping any of you who is young enough and hale enough to fight. But those who are going, who asked to go, are crying out that they want to stay. Those who are staying, who asked to stay, are crying out that they want to go home. What am I supposed to do? How am I supposed to satisfy you?"

He paused. His glare raked the lot of them. They stared up at him, mute. "I've given you everything," he said. "I gave you Greece. I gave you Persia. I gave you the whole of bloody Asia. Do you even remember what you were when I brought you out of

Macedon? By the gods, I do. You were half-naked savages. I clothed you in purple. Now you whine and moan for your filthy bearskins and your stinking hovels. You sneer at gold and silver. You moon over wooden bowls and shields of reeds and swords so thick with rust they crumble at a touch.

"You were paupers when I mustered you. The kingdom was mired in debt, and you were all drowning in it. Now every one of you is as rich as a king.

"But no," said Alexander with a twist of scorn. "That's not good enough for you. You want Macedon? You have it. You don't want it? Then suffer. I'm sending you all away, every last sniveling one of you. Let my father Ammon be my army, you said. So I will. The men of Asia will fight for me. You," he said, "are dismissed."

They gaped at him. Surely they must have expected this. All their gods knew, they had professed to want it. And yet they looked as if he had smitten them with the broadside of an axe.

"Report to your camps," Alexander said. "Your commanders are waiting. They'll muster you out. If you've squandered all your loot, they'll pay your passage home. Now go. Get out. Leave me to my father's army."

He did not wait to see if they responded. By the time anyone found the wits to speak, he was gone from the wall. They had nothing of him but the shieldwall in front of them and the spears lowered to prevent them from storming the palace.

These were Macedonians, with heads as hard as their native stone. They flung down their weapons and howled. Not one of them moved to obey the king's orders.

Alexander had not expected them to. He shut himself in the palace again, but this time he was not alone. He summoned the princes of Persia. They had to run a gauntlet of Macedonians in order to reach him, but none of them was a coward.

Selene cared little for the finer points of men's squabbles. She gathered that the king, having dismissed all the Macedonians except for his Companions, had set Persians in their places. The Persians were hardly inclined to contest their elevation. Some of them seemed rather smug about it; most of the rest accepted it as their due.

Meanwhile, outside the walls, the rebels had flung down their weapons. Great heaps of spears and swords rose before the gate. The men, disarmed, besieged the palace with entreaties.

There was no more talk of revolt. Sudden death of their ring-leaders had barely slowed them, but Alexander's visible anger struck them to the heart. They did still love him, Selene thought. They were still his men, although their youthful passion had gone cold.

Alexander was still angry, an anger that did not lessen over-much as the days passed. It was the anger of hurt, of the lover scorned. He let his Macedonians wait and suffer rather longer than perhaps he should have, but in the end he could not help himself. He had to relent.

On the fifth day after the mutiny began, he ordered the gate to be opened. His guards in the palace braced for the onslaught. Rather to their surprise, it was slow to come. The men in the square stood staring as if they could not believe that they had won their way at last. Then one by one, tentatively, they straggled toward the gate.

Some of them were muttering that it was a trap; that the king had gone mad and would shut them in and have them all cut down. But most still trusted Alexander, however far he might have gone toward the ways of the decadent east.

He was waiting for them in the largest of the halls, which was not nearly large enough for all of them. He was wearing a Macedonian tunic and a war-cloak that had been woven in Macedon and had been visibly and frequently mended. He looked like one of them, and he spoke their rough patois. He was still angry—still sharp with the edge of his tongue. "Well? Is there something you're wanting to tell me?"

They could not all press in toward him, though a good number of them tried. After some considerable confusion, which Alexander waited out with arms folded and face blank, they thrust one of their number to the front. He was as Macedonian as the rocks of Aigai, a grizzled, leathery, scarred old veteran with a voice reduced to a rasp by years of bellowing across battlefields.

He did not kneel, still less fling himself flat. He stood erect as a Macedonian did in front of any man, even his king. Prostrating oneself, his posture said, was for barbarians.

"Kallines," said Alexander. He knew all his men by name, it was said. Selene, watching from a shadowed corner, could believe he knew most of the captains, if not every trooper.

Kallines nodded briskly. He would expect to be recognized. "Alexander," he said. "I don't suppose we can end this foolishness now."

"That depends," said Alexander. "What do you have in mind?"

Kallines scratched his beard—like all the old guard, he would have nothing to do with the king's fashion of shaving the face. The fact that the Persians held to the same belief had not occurred to any of them. Macedonians as a nation were not subtle enough for irony.

"I was thinking," Kallines said, "that we'd apologize for doubting you. We thought you'd turned your back on us and gone over to the barbarians. Now you're going to send us away. We want to go home, Alexander, but not like this."

"How do you want it?" Alexander asked, still rather cold.

"Let us go," Kallines said, "the way you intended. But let us go as your loyal men, who followed you from the time you were a boy, and helped you to your victories."

It was not a grand speech and it was certainly not a long one, but it moved Alexander as nothing else had. The dam of coldness broke. He sprang down from the dais and pulled Kallines into an embrace so strong that even in armor the man grunted. "You *are* my loyal men," he said, "my kinsmen, my own blood and bone. No matter how many worlds I may conquer, no matter how many nations I may take for my own, you are still the first and best. You are mine as no other will ever be."

TWENTY-TWO

The quarrel was mended. Both sides had their way: half the Macedonians left for home, and the rest professed themselves happy to stay in the king's service. Alexander was their beloved again, and they were his.

Alexander had worked his particular magic. He drew strength from it, as if he fed on the love his people bore him.

Every night Selene dreamed, and that dream was always the same. The great bed with its golden lions. The king lying in it, lifeless and still. Nothing changed that dream. If she lay down, if she let sleep overtake her, it was there.

While she was in the dream, she knew no fear. When she woke from it, she lived with a strange sense of waiting. The word for it, when she took time to think, was *imminence*. Something was coming.

The men about her seemed to have no sense of it. What their women thought, she did not know. Alexander had sent them from Opis to Ecbatana, which was the summer palace of the Persian kings. He dallied along the way, pausing a full month in

Nisaia among the herds of horses. She reflected that his wives would be less concerned with sharing him with one another than with sharing him with his army.

Ecbatana was a mountain city, altogether unlike the cities of the plain. Its walls were sevenfold, and each wall was covered in gleaming tiles, blue and gold and green and red, black and white and silver. The palace was built to catch the breezes off the mountains, with wide windows and open courts and halls full of light and air.

For Selene, who was born to the steppe, this was both beautiful and inescapably strange. It melded with her dream somehow, so that she seemed to be living in a world outside the one she knew. In a peculiar way, she had gone to the high place as seers had for time out of mind—but not to die. There was no sense of her death here. What she had come to was a sort of birth.

On the road up from the fields and herds, something in her had shifted. An eye had opened; a wall had fallen. The higher she rode, the thinner and colder the air, the closer she came to accepting what she had refused since she was a child.

She did not hear the Goddess' voice. Her gift was to see. She saw the pellucid air of the heights and the gleam of snow on the highest of them, the flight of eagles and the swift passage of storms over the mountains.

With some difficulty, there in Ecbatana, she saw the lives that men led. They were as inconsequential as the flocking of birds. Beggars, kings—they were all the same in the eye of the Goddess.

Was this how Etta saw? There could be no babble of thought to confuse it. Maybe the Goddess used her eyes to look on the world.

It was difficult for Selene to come back inside her skin, to be a mortal creature again, with mortal understanding. Naburimanni, as always, was her anchor. The touch and smell of his

QUEEN OF THE AMAZONS

body, the feel of his hands, the taste of his kisses, made her real. When she was with him, she did not know how coherent she was, but he seemed to find nothing unusual in her words or actions. She must be moving and talking and acting as she always had.

Maybe everyone else was acting as oddly as she was. The king's revel was still going on. The Greeks and the remaining Macedonians called it "worshipping Dionysos." In the endless banquets that began at midday and went on until dawn, more often than not Alexander wore a leopardskin and a crown of vine leaves, as if he were the god himself.

Selene was not fond enough of wine to spend her days and nights swimming in it. When she was not looking after Etta, she was as far outside the walls as a horse would carry her, drinking in the emptiness of the sky.

One day soon after they all arrived in Ecbatana, she was escaping from the palace through one of the servants' corridors. There were always people passing back and forth, and people stopping to gossip as well. Two such had paused on a stair as she began a descent toward the stables. She would have edged past, but something one of them said made her pause.

". . . Hephaistion," he said. He had a bowl in his hands, covered with a cloth. "He fell over last night when he got up from dinner. Sick as a dog, he is."

"The Good God knows," the other servant said, "our new masters drink enough to rot anyone's vitals."

"They do, don't they?" said the first. "But this isn't the wine-god's fault. He's burning up with fever."

Selene's shoulderblades tightened. *It begins.* Where the words came from she did not know. The sense of imminence had grown.

She flattened against the wall as Hephaistion's servant finished his conversation and continued the ascent. After he had passed, she turned and followed him back the way she had come.

He was aware of her—she caught the flash of his glance—but he did not either speak or try to elude her. Servants knew what she was; they had known it long before she herself would admit it.

When they had left the stairway and gone down the corridor to Hephaistion's rooms, Selene heard an all too familiar voice. Alexander had come to look in on his friend.

He was not shouting; he did not sound angry. Even so, Selene heard him clearly from the passageway. "You are going to stay in bed. You are going to take your medicine. You are going to get well."

The answer was a growl.

"Yes, you *will* follow orders," Alexander said crisply. "Look, here's the man with your gruel. Drink it up and stop making faces. You know it's good for you."

The servant with the bowl disappeared into the room. Selene hung back. She had caught a glimpse of the man lying in the bed, lit by bars of sunlight. There were no lions and the man was not Alexander. Yet it had a strong flavor of her dream.

She would dearly have loved to ride away from this city and this vision, but she could not make herself go. The palace and the city were full of rumors and gossip as always. Hephaistion's illness, that first day, was a small part of their concern. By the third day it was larger, and by the fifth it had receded again, as he was seen outside of his bedchamber, looking wan but steady. Alexander chased him back to bed the moment he heard of the uprising, but everyone agreed that the king's constant favorite was in no danger of dying.

Selene was no physician. Healing was not her gift. The king's physician was assured—and publicly so—that if Hephaistion continued his simple diet and his regimen of rest and calm, another five days or a little longer would see him well enough to go out in the sun again.

The physician was Greek and very learned. If he had been as sensible as he was wise, he would have recalled that this was a Macedonian, and a young one at that.

On the seventh day of Hephaistion's illness, Alexander had gone to officiate at another of the interminable festivals of games that marked any Greek or Macedonian celebration. He had left Hephaistion firmly and apparently docilely tucked up in bed, with orders to stay there until Alexander came back.

"But I feel perfectly well," Hephaistion declared, "and I'm sick to death of milksops and gruel. Gods, what I'd give for a cup of good wine and a nice bit of fowl."

"I'll bring you both," Alexander said, "after the games, as soon as it's safe."

"But I want them now," said Hephaistion.

Alexander laughed and cuffed him, not lightly. "There— you're whining. Now I know you're getting better. Behave yourself, will you? I'll be back as soon as I can."

Hephaistion snarled but subsided. Selene happened to be there, because Etta was there, dogging Alexander as she so often did. Selene saw the rebellion in his eyes. Alexander did not: he had already turned away.

Etta followed Alexander, and Selene followed Etta. That was her duty. But she paused just before she passed the door, and looked back at Hephaistion. As light as the room was, awash with sun, he seemed wrapped in darkness.

She shivered, but she did not speak, either to him or to the king. She knew she should not have done that; but that much of her old resistance still lingered.

No one knew exactly what happened after Alexander left. The guards stood outside the door of his rooms, faithful to their duty of keeping people out and Hephaistion in. Somehow he got up from his bed, slipped out by an unwatched door, and made his way to the kitchens. Some cook there, either not recognizing the king's high commander or failing to recall that Hephaistion had been ill, gave him what he asked for: a jar of wine chilled with snow, and a boiled fowl.

The messenger came late in the day. Alexander was still engrossed in the games. Selene, who found them stupefying, had gone nearly as blank as Etta. The messenger's arrival, with his green-pale face and shaking hands, fit into that blankness as if she had been waiting for him.

He passed through to the king by virtue of his royal livery and a whispered word here and there. Alexander had been aware of him since he entered the stadium: his shoulders had tightened, his fist clenched.

The man was a Macedonian. He did not fling himself flat as a Persian would have done. He did drop to one knee, for ease in reaching the king, and leaned toward Alexander's ear.

Selene did not need to hear what he said. She knew. "It's Hephaistion, Alexander. He's worse."

Alexander did not stop to ask how much worse. He barely even stopped to hand the generalship of the games to the nearest notable before he was gone.

Etta darted in his wake. Her movements for the most part were slow, as if she drifted in a dream; she could stand or sit for long hours in absolute stillness. But when there was need, she was lightning-quick.

She caught Selene off guard, but there was no mistaking where she had gone. Selene followed as quickly as she could.

The king did not know the city as well as Selene did. He took the long way, the public way. People crowded it, and while they gave way before the king, they still prevented him from making as much speed as he liked.

Selene took the shorter, much less difficult way. She reached Hephaistion's rooms some time before Alexander. The guards were gone; the doors were open. She found them within, and the king's physician with them. His face when he raised it was the color of chalk.

He barely eased when he saw that she was not the king. She advanced into the room until she could see the man he tended.

Death was never beautiful, whatever the poets might say. Hephaistion had died vomiting blood. His face was stained with it. Someone had tried to compose his body, but there was no disguising either that he was dead, or that he had died in pain.

Someone hurtled into Selene from behind. She fell sprawling.

Alexander never even noticed that he had bowled her over. He had stopped short beside the bed. His back was rigid.

His voice when it came was soft and tight. "Get out," he said.

The guards glanced at one another. Servants and hangers-on were wiser: they beat a hasty retreat.

"Alexander," said the king's physician. "This is not—"

"I know," Alexander said. "Get out."

They all did—slowly at first, but then in such a crush that they got in one another's way. Alexander ignored them.

Selene did not leave, because Etta did not. Either they were forgotten or Alexander did not care. The room was empty, Selene thought—for what was either of them, after all, but the Goddess' instrument?

When all the rest were gone, Alexander crumpled. With a raw sound that bore no resemblance to a human word, he fell on the lifeless body.

TWENTY-THREE

For a night and a day Alexander lay on Hephaistion's body. Long after his voice was gone, his weeping went on.

There was no comforting him. A few bold spirits tried: Ptolemy, a succession of Companions, even a Persian satrap or two. He took no notice of any of them.

He would not eat or drink. Whatever needs his body had, he ignored them. His whole being, without exception, was mourning.

On the second day he came out. His face had aged years. His voice was cold and quiet. "That quack who killed him," he said to the guards at the door. "Crucify him. Then send men to the temple of Asklepios. Bid them raze it. Raze it to the ground."

The guards were young, not long out from Macedon, but they were not fools. They carried out his orders. There was no argument; no attempt to reason with the king. Even these raw boys could see that he was no longer sane by any measure they knew.

He gave other orders, orders that had a certain logic to them, if that logic were mad. There would be no flutes or lyres or any other music in the army. No one would laugh, no one would sing.

Everyone would mourn. "All," he said. "All of Asia. Everyone. See to it."

When he had done that, he turned back toward the room where Hephaistion had died. The body lay where he had left it, for he had not let the embalmers near it. It had not even been bathed or made seemly as civilized people tried to do for the dead.

While he was at the door, Etta had come out of the corner where she had crouched for those two days, and sat on the bed, and taken Hephaistion's head in her lap. It was the most like volition of anything Selene had ever seen her do. Her eyes as they met Alexander's were exactly like his: wide and fixed as if they stared directly into the sun, and perfectly empty of human feeling. She had no soul. His was seared to nothing by the immensity of his grief.

"He was the other half of me," he said to her. "I know what people thought of him—that he was beautiful, loyal, moderately competent, carelessly arrogant, and rather stupid. He was altogether my creature, with nothing of his own unless I gave it to him."

He bared his teeth. "None of them knew him. None of them cared. He was nothing to them. And now they'll come weeping and moaning, wailing with false grief, groveling and toadying and watching their backs because after all I am the king, and he is dead, and I have gone mad."

Etta's blank stare asking nothing of him, expected nothing, felt nothing. He must find it soothing while he braced himself to face the effusions of an empire.

"Maybe I'll kill them all," he said, "and make of them a holocaust. What do you think of that?"

Etta blinked slowly. She yawned and stretched, clambered off the bed, and turned her head from side to side, sniffing.

She was hungry. Selene rose softly from her station by the wall.

Alexander's eye caught the movement, darting toward Selene. She froze. His glare was burning cold.

It softened infinitesimally as he recognized her. "Lady," he said with a shadow of his old courtesy.

It was odd, thought Selene, how calm she was. This man was more dangerous than a tiger. But she did not see her death in his face, although there was death enough for anyone who crossed him.

"My queen is dead," she said. It was old news. She did not know why she said it.

His brow twitched; his head tilted. "You understand," he said.

She lifted a shoulder: half shrug, half assent.

"No one else understands," he said. "None of them shares a soul. I don't care what Aristotle said—if we were all divided in the time before time, precious few of us ever find the other half. But I did. I did, and now—"

He broke off. Selene could think of words to say, but he would hear them from far too many of his followers. She kept silent.

"Thank you," he said.

She inclined her head. After a pause she said, "Etta is hungry."

"Then she should eat," he said.

"Yes." Selene moved toward him. He shifted aside. She sought the servants' entrance through which Hephaistion had gone to find his death.

Etta stayed with Alexander. That did not trouble Selene. They would keep each other safe.

The palace was in chaos, but the kitchens were no more or less confused than they ever were. Marsyas ruled his kingdom with an iron hand.

He asked no questions of Selene, except one. "The king?"

"He doesn't know he's hungry," she said.

"Yet," said Marsyas.

She went back up laden with the makings of a feast, all but the wine. The jar was full of fruit nectar instead.

When she came to the room where Alexander was, the embalmers had come to take the body. They worked quickly, with eyes rolling white—and well they might. He was dangerously near to breaking again.

Selene laid down her burdens on the table beyond the bed. Etta barely waited for them to be uncovered before she had fallen on them with ravenous hunger.

Selene kept one bowl away from those eager fingers. Marsyas had prepared it especially for Alexander. There were bits of roast mutton, sliced thin, and salty goat cheese, and greens laced with oil and lemon: simple fare, such as Alexander loved best. She set the bowl in his hands and held them there, clasped about it, until he started as if from a dream. "I'm not—"

"Eat," she said. "You can't bury him if you're dead, too."

"I wish I were dead," he said.

She shivered inside her skin. "Not yet," she said.

He paused. His brows had gone up.

He did not ask what she meant. He sat on a camp-stool that somehow had found its way into the palace, and methodically, grimly, as if it were a duty and not a pleasure, ate every scrap of Marsyas' offering.

Alexander without Hephaistion was oddly incomplete. The two of them had not been together constantly; sometimes Hephaistion had gone off for months at a time on this or that command of Alexander's. And yet he was there in the world—alive, and young enough and strong enough that surely he would live to a great age.

Now he was gone. Not even Alexander could order him brought back from the dead.

The first madness of grief passed, but the immensity of it neither shrank nor faded. Alexander had Hephaistion's body embalmed by Egyptian priests, preserved for eternity. Then he sent it in processional to Babylon, where he would see it burned on a pyre so lofty, so splendid, so awesomely extravagant, that the world had never seen its like, nor ever would again.

In Babylon, the world would change. Selene felt it in the wind. Through that autumn of mourning, into a winter of war against a people of whom she knew little and cared less, she advanced from dream toward reality.

In the spring the waiting would end. What she waited for, she did not know. It was the Goddess' doing, whatever it happened to be.

TWENTY-FOUR

Babylon was a city of mud and water, girdled with marshes, squatting on the bank of its broad slow river. Its towers were low and broad, its temples massive, their feet firmly planted in earth. There were gardens everywhere, torrents of greenery pouring over ancient stones and tumbling down walls that had stood since the gods were children.

Hephaistion went to his pyre there, with a funeral that outdid anything Alexander had done before. It gave the king neither comfort nor peace, but it put an end to the excesses of public mourning and the displays of false grief. That suited him more than well enough.

The seers of Babylon, whom men called the Chaldeans, were famously wise. They had come out to Alexander as he marched toward the city, and warned him of disaster if he should pass the gate.

"Disaster to me?" he asked. "Or to my people?"

They conferred among themselves, with much wagging of

QUEEN of the AMAZONS 203

beards and shaking of heads. At length they answered, "To you, great king. To your people as a consequence, but—"

"Well then," Alexander said, "that's not so terrible. I don't suppose there's a way around it?"

For that they needed no lengthy debate. They said promptly, "Great king, if you would enter by any other gate but that of the east, and once you have entered, if you would restore great Marduk's temple as you swore to do when first you conquered us, then the stars permit—"

"I'll consider it," Alexander said.

He did consider it—and he went into Babylon regardless, by west gate, and came out again alive. But the Chaldeans' signs and portents had not changed.

Alexander was too circumspect to laugh at them, but he was as lighthearted as anyone had seen him since Hephaistion died. He had always been one to laugh at death. Now that it had walked as close to him as his heart, he had even less regard for it than before.

"All they want is a new temple," he said one morning as he sailed through the reed-choked marshes and stagnant fens that passed for a river in these parts. He was avoiding Babylon, to keep the Chaldeans quiet, and exploring the channels through which he hoped to bring his fleet on its way to Arabia.

They were all in the flat-bottomed boats that the people of this country favored for getting about in the marshes: a round score of them, with Alexander in the lead as usual. He shared his boat with several of the Companions, including Ptolemy, one or two of the king's squires, a small crew of sailors, and Etta and Arrhidaios with their keepers.

There were Chaldeans on the voyage, but they were well back among the boats. Even so, Ptolemy made a sign against evil and spat for good measure before he said, "Of course they want you to build them a temple, but that doesn't mean they're lying about what they see."

"I'm sure they believe it," Alexander said. "Look: I went in, I spent days in the city, I came out without so much as a scratch. If there was a curse waiting for me, it didn't bite."

"That doesn't mean it won't," Ptolemy said.

Alexander widened his eyes at him. "What, you of all people, fretting over eastern superstition?"

"The Chaldeans are famous for telling the truth," Ptolemy said. He was nothing if not stubborn.

"Only gods are never wrong," said Alexander, "and sometimes I have my doubts of those." He shrugged and smiled. "Never mind. Look! Is that it? Are these the old kings' tombs?"

"They are, sire," said the captain of the boat.

There was not a great deal to see. In among the reeds, rising up out of dark pools, were fingers of crumbling stone. Figures were carved on some of them, stiff old kings with muscular arms and massive curling beards.

Alexander leaned forward to see the nearest as they glided past. As he moved, a gust of wind caught his wide-brimmed hat with its purple ribbon and plucked it from his head. It whirled away across the water, fetching up against the tomb. It seemed that the king carved on it had caught it in his upraised hand. It had not touched the water at all.

Alexander went pale. This was an omen that even he could not ignore.

One of the boatmen dived from the prow and swam strongly across the stretch of water to the tomb. He grinned as he plucked the hat from its perch, and said in obvious delight, "Look, sire! It's still dry. Best not to get it wet, eh?"

"That doesn't matter," Alexander began to say, but the man was not listening. Just as he thrust off from the tomb, he clapped the hat on his head and began to swim back toward the boat.

"By the living gods!" Ptolemy burst out. He spoke for all who were in the boats, most of which had come to see why the king had paused.

Either the boatman was lacking in wits, or some god has possessed him. He swam quite happily to the king's boat and swung himself aboard, proudly brandishing the king's hat with its trailing ribbons. "See? Not even damp!" He presented it to Alexander with a flourish.

Alexander moved to take it, but Ptolemy struck it from the man's hand. It fell between them and lay like a dead thing. Ptolemy seized the boatman by the throat.

"No," said Alexander. "Don't kill him. He didn't know what he was doing. Give him a talent of gold for his service—and a flogging for the omen he's brought on me."

The man must be simple: he gaped at the guards who took him by the arms and removed him to another boat, which turned and struck off toward the camp. Both his gold and his flogging would be waiting for him there.

Alexander's boatmen prepared to turn back as well, but he stopped them. "No. We're not done here. We're going on." His eye fell on the hat, which was still lying where its rescuer had dropped it. No one had dared to touch it. "Take that," he said, "and burn it."

He went on with determined lightness of heart, but even the most hard-headed of his Companions—and Ptolemy was certainly such—were shaken out of all composure. Chaldeans foretelling disaster in Babylon were bad enough. This was the worst omen of all. The king's diadem had left him of its own accord and fallen on a tomb. Then it had passed to another bearer.

Dinner that evening was a small affair: those of the Companions who were in camp, a few favored Persians, and Etta settled in a corner with Arrhidaios. There was wine, but Alexander was drinking little of it. His great rite of Dionysos had ended the day Hephaistion died. He had not ordered that god's temple burned as he had that of Asklepios, but however much the healer god had failed Hephaistion, the god of wine and excess had been the instrument of that failure.

Conversation around the table went in fits and starts. Everyone was brooding over the omen. By the time the dinner had reached its middle course, they all gave up trying to talk about anything else.

Selene had been invited to sit beside Nabu-rimanni, who was there with his brother Oxyathres, but she did not want to be in the light, not just then. She retreated to the corner with Etta. Arrhidaios was in a garrulous mood, but it was harmless chatter, focused on nothing in particular, leaping from this whim to that. It was comforting in its way.

Up at the larger table, Ptolemy said what they were all thinking. "We've got to find a way to avert the omen."

"I don't think there is one," Alexander said.

"How do you know? Have you even looked?"

"The man has had both his reward and his sentence," Alexander said. "The hat is burned. What more can I do?"

"The soothsayers might know," said the Companion Perdikkas.

"No one's seen them in days," Ptolemy said. "Just when they

finally have a chance to make themselves useful, they disappear."

"They've said all they need to say," said Alexander.

"Selene hasn't."

Arrhidaios' voice was loud and unwontedly clear. It drew every eye to him. He grinned at them. "Selene sees things," he said. "She's better than the Chal—Chal—the soothsayers. Ask *her* what to do."

Selene would have been happy to melt into mist and vanish. Arrhidaios was as happy as the boatman had been that morning, and as completely unaware of what he had done. She had never told him what she was, and certainly Etta could not. Only Nabu-rimanni knew. And yet somehow Arrhidaios had discovered it.

Children and the simple were closest to the Goddess. Selene hardly needed to meet those eyes to see Her there. It was time, She was saying. She had been patient long enough. Now Selene would do as She willed.

"Is that true?" Alexander asked in Selene's silence. "Do you see what they see?"

"I'm not a diviner," Selene said. It was a surrender that she spoke at all. "All I have are visions, like memories of what's to come."

She kept her eyes on Alexander. She was aware of the others, and Nabu-rimanni most of all, but if she looked at him she would lose her resolve.

"Tell me what you see," he said.

She had never spoken a vision in public before. She struggled to be clear, so that no one would misunderstand. "I see you," she said, "lying in a bed with golden lions. You seem asleep, but the soul is gone from you."

"Lions?" he said. "As in Babylon?"

"As in Babylon," she said.

"Am I old? Am I grey?"

"You will never be old," she said.

"Then when?" he asked her. "When will it be?"

"I can't answer that," she said.

"Can't or won't?"

She set her lips together.

Alexander frowned. He was not angry, which rather surprised her. He was thinking—pondering what she had said and not said. "I don't suppose you see how I can get out of it."

"Sometimes fate can change," she said. "Sometimes, the harder we try to prevent it, the more we assure that it will happen."

"So I should do nothing? Not avoid it, not seek it?"

"I don't know," she said. "I can only tell you what I see."

"How long?" he asked. "How long have you known?"

"Since Kalanos died," she said.

His brows rose sharply. "That long? A year and more?"

"Would it have made a difference if I'd told you when I first saw it?"

"Probably not," he said.

"Why didn't you?" That was Ptolemy. He was not hostile as some of the others were; he honestly wanted to know.

This was her punishment for defying the Goddess. It was mild, she supposed, as such things went. She answered him because it was difficult; because she wanted to clamp her jaw tight and run away from them all. But that would only worsen matters.

It was a curse to see consequences as clearly as that. Every mistake had its echo, bounding back with doubled force.

"I didn't say anything," she said to Ptolemy, "because I didn't want to know what I knew. I never welcomed this gift. I left my own country to escape it. Now it's found me."

"It took its time," Alexander observed. "Will you let me know if you see anything else?"

"Yes," she said with a faint sigh.

"Good, then," he said. He sat back and reached for his cup, which his page had filled with heavily watered wine. "We're not going to talk about this now. I'm going back to Babylon. If my death is there, then so be it. I've never lost a battle yet. I'll defeat death, too. You'll see."

A shiver ran down Selene's spine. She had had no sudden rush of vision, and yet in his words she sensed . . . something.

"Are you well?"

Nabu-rimanni had left the banquet before Selene. She was not particularly surprised to find him in her room when she came there, waiting patiently while she undressed Etta and put her to bed.

Usually she went to him after Etta was settled, but she had not done that for a few nights. A week? Two weeks? A month? Time seemed to drag through the long torrid days, and yet it was flying toward some inevitable conclusion.

The last thing she had thought she wanted in this heat was the warmth of flesh on flesh, but when she moved, she moved toward him. They made love wordlessly, speaking the oldest language of all, the language of the body.

She had answered his question, after a fashion. He folded her in his arms and held her softly. She was oddly cold, a coldness of the heart. Even he could barely warm it.

"This is what it's like," she said, "when the sight is on me. I can't belong to anything else, or anyone else. It's not fair to you. Maybe you should—"

"I can wait," he said.

"Why?"

"Because I love you."

He said it perfectly matter-of-factly. She lifted herself on her elbow. His face in lamplight was calm. "Men don't share."

"Maybe not with another man," he said. "A Goddess . . . that's not so hard."

"You don't know what you're saying."

"You want to quarrel," he said, "and toss me out, so that you can be nobly and unnecessarily alone."

"A seer by her nature is alone."

"Why?"

Her own question, turned back on her. She could not answer it as easily as he had, at all. When she did, the words seemed weak and inadequate. "I've been ignoring you for how long? A month?"

"I've been away for most of that," he said, "mustering armies in Persia."

"But if you hadn't been—"

"If I hadn't been," he said, "I would have sought you out, or you would have come looking for me. You aren't made to be cut off from the world."

"A seer—"

"What did your predecessor tell you? What was her warning?"

She glared at him. "How do you know about that? I never told you."

The lids lowered over his eyes. He had long lashes, and thick. She could feel him watching her from beneath them. "She did warn you, didn't she? 'Don't let it consume you. Don't let yourself be driven apart. You can be what the Goddess meant you to be, without abandoning the world or the people in it.'"

"That's not what she said," Selene said.

"No?"

"Not exactly." She gripped his chin, winding fingers in his

beard, and held him fast when he would have turned his face away. "You can't know. You can't have seen—"

"Sometimes I can see," he said. "Other times I can imagine. You let slip things. Not often with words, and your face is very well guarded, but your eyes—"

She squeezed them shut. She could still see him. She suspected that he could still read her. "Yes," she said angrily. "Yes, she said something like it. She told me not to become what she became, a voice on the wind, empty even of a name."

"Selene," he said. "Your name is Selene. If you ever forget it, I will remember."

"What if I don't want you to?"

"Then I'll know it's most vital that I do."

"What if I don't love you?"

She held her breath. That had burst out of her, born purely of temper.

His kiss brushed her lips and then her eyelids. "One thing a man is good for," he said. "He'll stand his ground beyond sense or reason, and he'll fight to the death for what he believes. I believe in you. I'll hold you to the world when nothing else will."

Stubborn man. She should bloody his face for him instead of covering it with kisses, but her body had its own conception of what was proper.

The Goddess had given him to her, just as She had given the sight. Selene would have to ponder that, to understand what it meant. It was better than struggling to understand her visions, or dreading what she might discover.

TWENTY-FIVE

Once again Alexander entered Babylon and established himself in the palace there. He showed no sign of fear, no dread of whatever might be waiting for him.

His Companions wanted to double the guard and add a phalanx of tasters. At that he rebelled outright. "What's next? I'll not eat a bite that hasn't been chewed and swallowed first? You can't protect me from every minutest thing."

"We can try," Ptolemy said grimly. But he knew his king. He called off all but two of the tasters, and ordered somewhat fewer than half of the guard to stand down.

Alexander could see perfectly well that he was still more thoroughly protected than before, but he also knew his men. If it kept them happy, he would suffer it—and do his best to elude his protectors.

He did not trouble Selene. It was one of his gifts to know who could tolerate rank and honor, and who could not. What she wanted was not to be had in this part of the world. To be a hunter and warrior of her people—she had fled that. She had no desire to be named a seer here or anywhere.

He let her be. Sometimes when Etta was in his shadow and Selene was in Etta's, she felt his eye on her. She never met it, and he never spoke of what he was thinking.

She was waiting as they all were: every breath held, watching every shift in the wind. All but Alexander. His expedition into the west was nearly ready. The fleet was gathered, the land forces nearly all in order. Embassies had come already from the west, blustering or cajoling, sometimes offering belligerence, sometimes tribute. Alexander was gracious to them all, as he could afford to be. He would conquer them as he had conquered everyone else.

Already in late spring, the heat was a powerful thing. Not only Selene thought with longing of the cool heights of Ecbatana, but Alexander's eye and mind had long since turned away from mere comfort. He had a war to begin.

His spirit was as bright a blaze as ever, but after the omen on the river, he was determined to do as much as he could, as fast as he could, if his time was indeed to be cut short. He worked feverishly far into the night, then rose before dawn. His clerks, who knew him well, went to battle stations: taking watches like guards, shifting smoothly from one to the next. No one man could keep pace with him when he was in this mood.

"You'll burn yourself out," Ptolemy said with sorely strained patience.

"Maybe," said Alexander, "but I'd rather go like a star across the firmament than an ant across the floor."

"Then what?" Ptolemy demanded. "Have you thought about that?"

"I've thought about it," Alexander said.

"And?"

"I've thought about it."

That tone, even Ptolemy would not argue with. But he said, "You had better make a decision soon. If, all the gods forbid, you go without a clear choice of heir, you'll leave a free-for-all."

"I have no intention of leaving," Alexander said, "or dying, either, whatever the omens may say. I've defied them before. I will again."

"And if you don't?"

"I will," Alexander said.

Not long after Hephaistion died, Alexander had sent an embassy on the long journey into the desert of Egypt, to Siwah where was the shrine of Zeus Ammon. That god, Alexander believed, was his father. He had sent a question for the oracle, as simple as he could make it. "Is Hephaistion to be numbered among the gods?"

Now the embassy had returned, sunburned and desiccated still, but every man of it intact. The answer was not entirely as he would have wished, but it was not terribly disappointing, either. Hephaistion was not to be deified, but he had been elevated to the ranks of divine heroes. He was not a god, but he walked among them.

Or so the priests at Siwah said. Alexander professed himself satisfied. But in that satisfaction he let Dionysos in again. It began more or less innocently, as a proper Macedonian celebration, but once the wine-god had taken hold, he was not inclined to let go.

Alexander had not slept in days. Etta on the other hand had, sometimes so deeply that Selene had to assure herself that the girl still breathed. Alexander was up all night, every night, at this grand dinner or that, and out all day with the fleet on the river or the army on the plain.

The news from Siwah merited a long day's rite with sacrifices and a long night's revel. Alexander came in near dawn, wafting the scent of wine and the flowers that crowned him. He was steady enough on his feet; Macedonians could drink prodigious quantities before they toppled over.

He had not come in to sleep. He wanted a bath, then a change of clothes. He had been invited to another revel, one that looked to go on past sunup and well into the day.

Selene had been dozing in a corner of the king's bedchamber. She started awake at Alexander's coming. Etta, curled into a knot in the center of the bed, did not move at all, even when Alexander bent over her.

"She's well," Selene said. "It's a new thing; she sleeps with all that's in her."

Alexander looked up and sighed gustily. His face was flushed; his eyes were bright. "She looks dead," he said.

"I know," Selene said. "I was alarmed, too, the first time or ten. But there's nothing wrong with her. I hope you don't mind that she's here. I can carry her to her own room, but the last few times I've tried, she's sleepwalked back here."

"I don't mind," he said. He sighed again. His breath caught slightly; he swayed a very little.

Selene's eyes narrowed. "You're ill," she said. "You're running a fever."

He shook her off. "It's nothing. It's just bloody hot. I'll take another bath when I come back. Look after my friend here, will you?"

"Always," Selene said. "Alexander—"

He was already halfway to the door. She knew she might regret it later, but she forbore to run after him. He must know what she was going to say. He did not want to hear it.

She had said it herself: sometimes there was no stopping fate.

She settled in her corner again, drew up her knees and clasped them, and set herself to wait.

They brought him back at sunset. Men of his Companion cavalry were carrying him; Ptolemy paced behind. Alexander was conscious, but barely; just enough to insist that they take him to the bath. There in the shimmering chamber with its tiles of blue and green and gold, they lowered him into cool water.

"Fetch a physician," Ptolemy said to one of the guards.

"No." Alexander's voice was a shadow of itself, but there was no mistaking the fierce resistance in it. "No doctors. No doctors ever again."

"Alexander—" Ptolemy in almost the exact tone Selene had used the night before.

Just as with Selene, Alexander ignored him. "No doctors," he said as loudly as he could; the end of it broke in a fit of coughing.

Ptolemy cursed under his breath. He was afraid: a rarity in that tough old soldier.

Alexander groped until he caught his brother's hand. "Stop fretting," he said. "It's just a touch of the marsh fever. Go on, get to bed. I'll sleep here. It's cool."

"So it is," Ptolemy said. "Cooler than the rooms I'm in."

"Call for a bed, then," Alexander said. "I *am* going to sleep. See that you do the same."

He did sleep—better than Ptolemy. When he woke, he declared himself much improved, then insisted on getting up and being dressed and going off to perform the morning sacrifices.

Selene waited. Etta slept, woke only long enough to eat and drink a little, then went back to sleep again.

The air was breathless, the heat overwhelming. No one with sense would do anything but lie gasping in whatever shade she could find. Men of course had no sense, and were out marching and sailing boats and indulging in councils of war.

On the sixth day after he was brought in with fever, Alexander came back again in the arms of his guards. This time his voice was gone. His glare was murderous, but he could not say a word to keep the physicians out. The more sensible of them ordered cool compresses and baths in soothing herbs.

Etta woke as he lay there, crept up from the floor where she had been lying, and settled at his feet. Her eyes were open, clear and empty blue, fixed on his face.

The bed in which he lay was upheld on the backs of golden lions. Lions rose over the king's head, suspending the silken canopy. Its folds billowed softly in the breeze of a large fan wielded by a very small and sleepy page.

Selene watched as Etta did, in nearly the same perfect emptiness. The weight of earth had dropped away. She saw the people who came and watched or tended the king, then went away again, but their earthly substance had thinned to shadow. She saw the souls within, dim candles beside the blazing fire that was Alexander. Etta she could not see at all. In this world, she had no substance.

Alexander burned without measure or restraint. His consciousness hovered on the edge of dissolution.

He was nearly free of the flesh. It crumbled about his spirit, swollen with fever, racked with wounds, full of old pain.

The physicians gave up hope long after Selene knew that this fever would not pass. It was fear for their lives, she supposed, and a degree of wishful thinking. Many of them did love him; they wept as they did what little they could for him.

Hippolyta came to Selene in the night, after she had stopped reckoning time and merely lived from day into darkness. She had fed Etta when servants brought bread and possets that the king was too far gone to eat. Selene was empty even of hunger. When the queen came, she was waiting, standing guard over the gates of the dark.

Hippolyta was not as pale as Selene was then, nor as far removed from living consciousness as Alexander. She looked as she had in the prime of her life: young, strong, beautiful. She stood over Alexander, looking down at the wreck of him. Her face had the remoteness of a cloud, or of a god.

Selene did not move or speak, but Hippolyta turned to her. Through her Selene could see Etta sitting where she had been since Alexander was laid in the bed of lions, insubstantial as an image seen through water.

Hippolyta held out her hands. Selene knew better than to touch the dead, but she could meet the queen's eyes. They were dark and endlessly deep. "Help me," Hippolyta said.

Old vows, old dreams bound Selene. She had sworn oaths to this shade of a queen on behalf of her shadow of a daughter. Now they all came down upon her. She must see this thing done; she must bear witness to it when the time came, before the council and the women of the people.

Hippolyta laid her insubstantial hand on the husk that now

barely housed the spirit of Alexander. That spirit was more than human, more than mortal. What god had chosen to inhabit this flesh, Selene did not know, nor did it matter.

Moving slowly, with knowledge beyond thought or reason, she took Etta's limp cool hand in hers. Her free hand reached across the burning body of the king.

Never touch the dead. Her old teachers' voices echoed in her skull. They rose to a roar as her fingers closed about Hippolyta's.

The queen's hand was cold. It had substance, which Selene had not expected. Chill wind gusted through her; she caught the scent of graves, and glimpsed for an instant a light so bright it came near to blinding her.

Hippolyta tightened her grip until Selene gasped. The pain brought her back to this place and time, precisely balanced between the living and the dead. Warmth in her right hand, living but soulless; cold in her left, dead to earth yet living in a realm which Selene could barely comprehend.

Selene was the link and the joining. She was the bridge. Hippolyta opened the gate.

Alexander stepped out of his dying body as from an outworn garment. Selene saw once more the young king of Zadrakarta, naked without shame, with those remarkable eyes and that tilt of the head as he looked about him. He was as quick of wit as ever; his lips tightened as he stared down at the thing he had left, but Selene saw the understanding in him, and the refusal either to rage or be afraid.

He did not understand all that he thought he did. He took them in, the living and the dead and the one who was alive but empty of a soul. His eyes widened slightly. "What, no winged Hermes?"

"He comes for your people's dead," said Hippolyta.

"Indeed," said Alexander. "And what am I?"

"Dying," she said, "but with a choice. I bring it from my Goddess, king of men. Would you live? Would you look on the sun again?"

Selene saw the yearning in him, the longing that twisted his phantom heart with pain. Yet he said, "These things always have a price. What will I pay to be alive again?"

"Remarkably little," said Hippolyta, "all things considered."

"What, my wealth? My titles? Half my empire? All of it?"

"Everything," she said. "Even your name."

He lifted his chin. Selene had seen that look in battle. He was smiling, but his eye had the gleam of steel. "Then what will I be?"

Hippolyta swept her glance across Selene to the living shadow beyond. Etta had fixed her stare on Alexander. Even as bodiless spirit, he fascinated her.

Selene had understood some time since. It had a certain inevitability, and a certain monstrous tidiness, like one of the Greek plays Alexander was so fond of.

He laughed. If Selene could have killed him for it, she would have; but he was beyond any mortal harm.

He was not mocking her or any of them. He was laughing in incredulity. "*What* are you asking me to be?"

"Penthesilea," Hippolyta said. It was the great royal name of the people, and the queen's title.

Etta strained past Selene, stretching toward the shade that was Alexander. As unwise as it might prove to be, Selene let her go.

Alexander recoiled, but Etta was both swift and strong. He was but a shade; his body was sinking from the heat of fever into the cold of death. She was alive, if only as a flower is, mindless and soulless but fixed on the sun.

"When she was born," Hippolyta's voice said, sounding somewhat faint, as if it came from a little distance, "the Goddess gave her no soul. One was in the world for her, that was made clear to me, but it would not come until it had done its duty elsewhere."

"Impossible," said Alexander.

"For the Goddess, all things are possible." Hippolyta was fading; Selene's hand could not hold her, however tightly it clutched. "When first we met, we made a wager. I never asked for the prize that I had won. I ask it now. Will you take this gift that the Goddess has given you?"

He stiffened, then eased with an effort that Selene could see. "And if I refuse? If I call the wager void, because you died before it could be paid?"

"You die," Hippolyta said.

He looked down at himself, then up at Etta, as if she had not been as familiar as one of his dogs. But then, Selene thought, he had never imagined that this might be the flesh he wore when his own body had burned to ash.

He was a man like no other, but he was Greek enough to find women both alien and a little repellent. His mother should have been one of the people; she was never made for a life of meek submission. She had taught him both to love and loathe her sex.

Selene knew that he would refuse. He was Alexander; he was as near a god as a living man could be. But he could not take this gift, which he would see as a bitter sacrifice.

"I . . . will rule?" he asked after a stretching pause.

"You will rule," Hippolyta said. She was far away now, and faint.

"I will not be challenged?"

"You will be challenged," she said. "I'm too long dead to protect you."

"Have you allies?"

"Selene knows," she said, now so distant that Selene could barely hear her. "Trust her. Listen to her. Take her counsel."

"But I haven't—"

Hippolyta was gone. Alexander looked from Etta to Selene and back again. He looked long at the inert thing that had housed his spirit for nearly three and thirty years.

Selene said nothing. He spun back to her. "Tell me there's another choice. I'm not dead. I won't be dead. There's too much to do."

"There is always too much to do," Selene said. She did not know where the words came from, but they flowed as smoothly as if they had her will behind them. "Your life is ended, king of Macedon. The dogs have already begun to squabble over your bones. This—who knows? You could be immortal."

"I could come back," he said as if it had just dawned on him. "I could take—I could be—"

Selene waited for him to come to his senses. It did not take long. He knew better than she what the men of this world would say to such a thing. They would laugh. Then they would rise up in all their numbers, march against the people, and destroy them.

He fell silent. Then: "Will I remember? Once I wake up—will I still be myself? Or will it be like being born again?"

Selene spread her hands. "I don't know," she said. "It's never been done before. The Goddess has never set a body in the world while its soul still inhabits another. Why She did it—who knows why the gods do anything?"

"Maybe She was curious," he said. "Or maybe She needed two of me, and Macedon needed me first."

He had a fine sense of his own worth. But it was very likely true, what he said; Selene could hardly contest it. When she spoke, it was to say, "You must choose soon, before the fire goes out in the body. Or you will die, and there will be no returning."

He had no fear of death. But of leaving this life—yes, that he had. After all the grief and all the loss and all the pain of his wounds of both body and spirit, still he yearned to live.

"Better the lowest peasant in a living field," he said at last, echoing the words of his great hero Achilles, "than king among the dead." He sighed, although he had neither breath nor lungs for it. Without pause, without further word, he strode toward Etta.

With her mother's departure she had faded again, nearly to vanishing. Selene could barely see her, but it seemed that his eyes were as clear as her keeper's were clouded. As he drew nearer, she became more distinct. She was reflecting the light of him, the moon to his sun.

They stood face to face. Selene could have sworn that he was the living man and Etta the formless dead.

She raised her hand. He raised his to match her. They touched.

On the golden bed, the body gasped and convulsed. In the world between the living and the dead, Alexander blazed up like a beacon in the dark. As suddenly as he had caught fire, he winked out.

THREE

Queen of the Amazons

TWENTY-SIX

Selene fell headlong from world into world. The tiles of the floor were hard; they bruised her knees, and her hands that had broken her fall. She smelled the reek of sickness, and beneath it the sweet stench of death.

There was someone in the room, some strong presence. The skin prickled between her shoulderblades. She turned slowly.

It was only Etta. She had fallen from the bed and caught herself against one of its carved lions. She was breathing hard, as if she had been running. Her body trembled.

She lifted her head. Selene's breath caught. She had expected it, prayed for it, and yet to see it . . . it was astonishing. Terrifying. Splendid.

There was life in those eyes, expression in that face. Memory—it was there; all of it, as she turned to look on what she had left behind. Selene wondered if it was a blessing that Etta could remember; whether it would have been more merciful to veil her with forgetfulness and let her be born all new.

It was not Selene's place to judge the Goddess. She had done a great thing, as was well within Her power; a fearful thing, it might be, but as Selene met those clear blue eyes, she knew that she could serve this one whom the Goddess had made.

The young queen smiled at her, with a twist of wryness in it that Selene knew all too well, and a tilt of the head as she considered what she had chosen for herself. She moved carefully, as if she still had the scars from old battles, the deep sucking wound in the lung that had never properly healed, the leg, the shoulder . . .

Those were all left behind. This body was whole, pristine, without mark or scar. And young—as young as Alexander had been when he became king. It was a new life indeed, without the helplessness of infancy or the tedium of childhood.

Selene looked for regret. She saw none.

It had been so in all his wars when Alexander was alive. Once he had set his armies in motion, he never looked back. He fought the battle to its conclusion.

People were coming. The physicians had fled; the servants were gone. These could only be the wolves and jackals, come to gnaw the bones of his empire.

Etta—no, Selene should not call her that; she was queen now by right of blood and spirit, Penthesilea of the people. That was her name; that was the spirit that lived in her.

Penthesilea hesitated for a stretching moment. Old habits die hard, and she had never been a fool. She knew what must happen now: the wars of succession; the battles over the heirs; the struggle for rule of the empire her departed self had made.

Her face twisted in pain that must have been of the body as well as the spirit. Her hand went to her head; she dropped like a stone.

Selene's heart stopped. She leaped toward the crumpled figure.

A thunderous crash whipped her about. Whoever was outside had found the door barred, and set about breaking it down.

Penthesilea was deeply unconscious. Dear Goddess, Selene thought; if the spirit could not cling to the body after all, if it died in spite of itself, then it was all for nothing.

Penthesilea was breathing. Her face, even in a faint, had a subtle difference from the emptiness that had ruled it for so long. Selene heaved her up—not easily; she was tall and strongly built, well muscled with riding and hunting. Once she was up, she could move after a fashion, as if her body remembered how to manage itself without the encumbrance of a soul.

The invaders were breaking through. Selene quickened her pace as much as she could, aiming for the servants' door at the rear of the king's bedchamber.

She reached it none too soon. The wolves had closed in: the princes of Macedon, come to assure themselves that their king was dead.

They never noticed that the king's dog was missing, or his Amazon, either. Selene pressed on down the passage, with no clear sense of where she would go, only that she must be out and away.

She was aware of people passing—running in the same direction as she: out of the palace, she hoped, and away from the king's body. They darted past her.

Only once did she meet someone coming toward her. Her head was down, her body flagging. She stepped aside as best she could, as burdened as she was.

The man was very tall. He stood like a wall in front of her. Even as she realized who he was, he lifted Penthesilea in his arms and turned.

Selene was too tired to envy that easy strength. "I don't know where to go," she said.

"I do," said Nabu-rimanni. "I was coming to fetch you. It's not safe to be anywhere near the king now."

"The king is dead," Selene said.

"I . . . thought as much," said Nabu-rimanni. She watched him decide to grieve later, when there was time.

Now was not the moment to tell him the truth. She said, "We can't linger. There's going to be killing, and we're helpless."

"Not you," he said, but he wasted no further time in standing about. She had to trot to match his long stride.

Without Penthesilea's slack body dragging at her, she was remarkably light on her feet. She was barely winded when they came to the place he had found for them.

She would have chosen the stables. He had led her to the queens' palace. Word had reached it already, from the sound of it: weeping and wailing, and a shrill, blood-curdling ululation that Selene remembered all too well from the wilder regions of Alexander's long journey. His lowest-ranking wife was mourning her husband in the manner of her country.

The Persians were more seemly. The eunuchs wailed and tore their silken garments, but the women were silent as if with shock. Nabu-rimanni passed the guards without hindrance, striding straight toward rooms he knew well.

Sisygambis was there, and her granddaughters Drypetis and Stateira, and somewhat surprisingly, the lord Artabazos. There were no servants hovering about or whispering behind the curtains. One elderly eunuch, whom Selene knew to be deaf, dozed by the wall—the sole concession to the presence of a man who was not either husband or immediate kin.

Whatever council had engrossed them, it had fallen into silence before the newcomers arrived. Nabu-rimanni they greeted without surprise. Selene received an odd stare from Stateira, half resentful, half curious. It was a niece's stare, taking the measure of her uncle's lover.

None of them took notice of Penthesilea, except to think they understood why she lay unconscious in Nabu-rimanni's arms. "Is he—" Stateira began.

"Yes," her uncle said.

Tears welled in those beautiful eyes and slowly, exquisitely, overflowed. It interested Selene that Stateira was not screaming and beating her breast as the Sogdian wife was so audibly doing. Evidently her husband's death was less grievous than the prospect of sharing her wedding day.

Perhaps Selene was not being fair. She would allow the possibility.

Sisygambis had not moved, but something about her drew Selene's eye. She was perfectly still. Her face was a white mask, the eyes gouged deep in it. "My son is dead," she said. "My son—is—"

"No," Selene said. She was not sure until she said it, that she would or even should. Easier by far to escape while she could, before anyone guessed what soul had found its way to her lady's body.

But it was a long way to the people's lands, and Selene knew with absolute certainty that she must not pause until she came there. The waiting was over. The sense of urgency was almost beyond bearing.

"Your son is not dead," Selene said.

The Queen Mother frowned. "Are you making sport of me?"

"No," Selene said. "Never. Lady—"

She could not at once go on. Penthesilea had come rather abruptly to her senses. She twisted free of Nabu-rimanni's grip and fell hard. When he reached for her, startled and somewhat alarmed, she raised her head and glared through a tangle of bright curls. The vividness of life in her face, the fierce intensity of her eyes, rocked Nabu-rimanni back on his heels.

Sisygambis knew. One look at that face, those eyes, and she needed none of the explanations from which Selene struggled to choose.

The Queen Mother loosed a slow breath. Her hands were shaking; she clasped them together to steady them. "How?" she demanded of Selene.

The others did not understand. Nor, for the moment, did they matter. Selene answered as succinctly as she could. "The Goddess," she said.

"Obviously," said the Queen Mother. "But how? Or perhaps more to the point, why?"

"If I knew, Mother," Penthesilea said, "I'm not altogether sure I could tell you."

They were the first words she had spoken in that body, and the first Selene had ever heard from it. Her voice was rough, unused; but when she was more accustomed to it, it would settle to a deep sweetness. Rather more striking at the moment, her accent was distinctly Greek, with an equally distinct suggestion of Macedon.

It shocked the Persians profoundly. Nabu-rimanni looked as if he would faint.

"Incalculable are the ways of the gods," Sisygambis said after a slight but perceptible pause.

"But the ways of men are all too readily understood," said Selene before Penthesilea could open her mouth. "Lady, we need help in getting away from here, and we need it quickly. I know the smell of a war brewing."

Sisygambis' glance flicked toward Penthesilea. "You will not—"

"You know she can't," Selene said. "This choice puts an end to whatever life she lived before. Whatever happens here, this soul has truly gone beyond it."

"But not into death."

"By the Goddess' will," said Selene, "no."

The Queen Mother breathed deep. She was visibly shaken, but she mastered herself. "You will have horses, provisions, all that you need. My son will see to it. The couriers' stations will be open to you. But you must be swift. The Good God alone knows how badly the war will go before it is over."

"Come with us," Selene said. "There's death for you here— death for all of you."

Sisygambis did not flinch. Nor, somewhat to Selene's surprise, did her granddaughters.

"Maybe we will die," Stateira said with dignity that Selene would never have expected from her. "Maybe others will die and we will live. We are kings and children of kings. We will stand and fight, and if we win, we rule. If not . . ." She spread her hands. "That is with the Good God."

Penthesilea had gone rigid. Selene held her breath.

There was no eruption. Nabu-rimanni said, "Mother—"

"I will stay," his mother said. "You will go. This is your path, as it is hers. And—" Her glance took in Penthesilea, who had not moved or spoken. "This one will rule wherever she goes."

"But not here," said Stateira. "Of all the places in the world— not here."

"No," said Penthesilea, very quiet, very still. "Not here. I cannot be what I was. Never again."

Artabazos had been silent, watching, while the others spoke. His eyes never left Penthesilea's face. When the rest had been said, he spoke. "The couriers' stations will get you to Zadrakarta. Past that, what will you do?"

"Find horses," she said. "Get over the mountains. Claim a kingdom. Conquer it if I have to."

"Not a kingdom," Selene said. And when they rounded on her: "No kings. Queens always. Until the moon fades."

"Queens," said Artabazos, smiling as if at a memory. "Indeed. There is little any of us can do once you pass the mountains, but to cross them—with that, we can help. I have certain arrangements with the tribes near Zadrakarta. Those will gain you guides, assistance, and as much loyalty as can be had in that part of the world."

"It will be more than welcome," said Penthesilea.

"It's no more than you're worth," Artabazos said in quite serviceable Macedonian. "We'll not meet again in this world, any of us. But in the next . . . who knows? Even you might choose to rest a while among the blessed dead."

"I might," Penthesilea said.

"But first," said Artabazos, "there are worlds to conquer. Maybe even, in the end, the stream of Ocean."

"Maybe," she said. She moved forward, clumsy in this body, and hesitated.

He pulled her into a strong embrace. It held for a stretching moment, then let go.

She turned from him and faced the one who had been even more to her old self than Artabazos. Sisygambis sat perfectly still. "Mother?" Penthesilea said, as diffident as Selene had ever known that royal spirit to be.

Sisygambis shivered visibly at the title and stretched out her hands. Penthesilea took them. "May I have your blessing, Mother?"

Sisygambis bowed her head. "May the Good God go with you," she said steadily, "and the Goddess of the Amazons."

TWENTY-SEVEN

The sun was still barely up, but the fighting had already begun. Faction battled faction; the streets were stained with blood.

Artabazos' bodyguards escorted the three of them through the less traveled ways of the city. Selene knew a fair number of those, but Penthesilea had never seen anything but the grand avenues and the processional ways. It would be a new world for her, all of this; one that she had never expected to live in.

She was almost as quiet as the old Etta had been. Her steps had steadied before she left the palace; she had learned to balance herself, although she stumbled now and then. Then would come the only sound she made: the growl of a curse in gutter Macedonian.

They were nearly across the city when they met an insurmountable obstacle: a battle that raged through a succession of squares and down every street and alley. Half of the combatants were screaming the name of Peukestas. The others, as far as Selene could tell, were fighting to protect their houses and shops.

Penthesilea caught her arm. "Up," she said. "We have to go up."

Up to the roofs, she meant. Selene exchanged glances with Nabu-rimanni. The guards in their armor opened their mouths to protest, but Penthesilea stopped them with a word. "You've done well, but this is as far as you can safely take us. Wait here if you can—look for a signal from the wall yonder. When you get that, go back to your lord and tell him we're safely out of Babylon."

"But—" the captain began.

"Do it," said Penthesilea with such a crack of command that the man snapped to attention. She softened slightly. "You're too obvious, captain. You'll give us away. Don't worry—we'll take it from here. I'm not in any hurry to shake off this body now I've got it."

The man could not have understood that last, but the rest would be clear enough. He gave way, unwilling but in the end obedient.

Alexander always had known how to get his way with soldiers. This being that he had become, this wonder of a woman, ran lightly up a stair to the broad flat roof of a house. People were up there, watching the fighting below. None tried to stop the three of them as they crossed the roof and sprang across the gap to the next.

Babylon's walls were enormous, not only high but vastly broad. The guards who usually patrolled them were scattered today, putting down sudden flares of fighting. Here and there, guards were fighting guards, bellowing the name of this or that claimant to the all too vacant throne.

Penthesilea's face was terrible. Selene tensed, certain that she would break from her resolve and bolt back to the palace.

But the spirit inside her was stronger than that. She held on.

When a gap presented itself, she ran with the rest of them, aiming for one of the gate-towers.

The top of it was clear, but the bottom was clotted with combatants. Nabu-rimanni hunted about in the tower and came out with a rope. It was not long enough once they had lashed it round a crenel, but it would have to do.

The fighting had not yet spilled out of the gates. It was all focused inward toward the palace. Soon enough it would spread, raging like a wildfire through the empire, but today it confined itself within the walls of Babylon.

Three figures armed only with swords and knives and dressed as Persians were not worth a glance when there were armored soldiers to fight. Selene sent Penthesilea down the rope first, which suited her well enough, but Nabu-rimanni was more of a difficulty. She was ready to kick him headlong off the wall before he stopped arguing and went down ahead of her.

She waited until he was down—not so long a drop for a man of his height—before she began the descent. Even as she went over the parapet, a shout warned her that she had been seen. Some of the guards were still at their posts after all; or else these were looters, avid for any prey.

She was halfway down when the rope began jerkily to go up. She tilted her head back. Men's faces grinned down. They were Macedonian. She could smell wine even at that distance.

She spun in space a dizzying distance above the ground. The men above were laughing and laying wagers on whether she was woman or eunuch, and how quickly they could all make use of her. She breathed a prayer to the Goddess and let go.

For a long, beautiful, terrible moment she hung between earth and sky. Then she was aware that she was falling. She made herself limp, in hopes of a softer fall.

It was soft—after a fashion. It grunted on two notes, low and high. Nabu-rimanni and Penthesilea lay in a tangle under her.

She was intact. So were they, except for a bruise here and there. They scrambled themselves up and set off on foot toward the place to which Artabazos had directed them. It was, he had said, an hour outside of Babylon; but being Persian, he meant an hour's ride. Afoot on a road crowded with people fleeing the city, in heavy humid heat and a buzzing and stinging of flies, it was much longer.

Penthesilea trudged in front. What she was thinking or feeling, Selene could not imagine. Maybe nothing. She had a look Selene had seen too often on long marches: as if her mind had gone elsewhere while her body focused itself on setting one foot in front of the other.

First they must have horses. Then they must ride. The sooner they were out of this crumbling wreck of an empire, the better. Without Alexander it would shake itself to pieces.

That was not Alexander plodding ahead of her, head down and shoulders hunched. This was a new being and a new destiny. What they would find when they came over the mountains, Selene could not see. The sight was not to be forced; it gave her only darkness with a faint glimmer of stars.

She almost laughed. How like this gift and curse of hers: when she did not want it, it tormented her without ceasing. Now she wanted and needed it, it was gone. Nothing that she did could bring it back.

It would come back when she least wanted it. That was the way of it.

Artabazos had sent them not to a couriers' station—that was just outside of Babylon itself, and as much in disarray as the rest of the city—but to one of his estates. The man who looked after it was one of his grandsons, a reserved and quiet person who read the letter his grandfather had sent with them, examined the token that would grant them passage through the couriers' stations, and supplied them with horses, clothing, and provisions for a long, fast journey.

He asked no questions. He knew Nabu-rimanni; they were much of the same age. But he was not a convivial sort, and Nabu-rimanni was in no mood for it, either. He had gone as silent as Penthesilea.

None of them had much to say, when it came down to it. It was past noon when they mounted; Selene reckoned to ride as far as the next station, which would take them until somewhat after sunset. Urgency was pressing at her.

Even in her eagerness to be out of this country, she kept watch over Penthesilea. The spirit in her had gone farther than any that Selene knew of, by a stranger road. No wonder Etta had slept so long and hard through Alexander's illness: the Goddess had known what she must do, and had prepared her as best She could.

But Alexander had not been prepared, and it was his awareness in that body now, his memories, his dreams and, for all she knew, his regrets. She would never know how much pain he felt at abandoning everything he had ever been; at accepting this life at the cost of all that had been his.

He, now she, might be going to nothing more or less than death. It had been a year and more since Hippolyta died. Who ruled the people now, in what state the clans were left by her refusal to name another and more acceptable heir, none of them could know until they came there. The war of Alexander's succession was a vivid reminder of what could be.

The people did not fight among themselves as these men did. But when it came to the passage of power, women were not remarkably more reasonable than men. They could only ride as fast as they could, and trust that the Goddess knew what She was doing.

They came to the first couriers' station north of Babylon an hour and more after sunset. Selene did not want to stop, but Nabu-rimanni insisted on it. When she opened her mouth to argue, he tilted his head toward Penthesilea and said, "We stay."

Penthesilea was still on her horse, head bowed, hands locked on the reins. Selene caught her breath. She had been thinking too much, too hard, of what was to come; she had lost sight of what was in front of her. She thrust aside the groom who was moving to take the horse, and closed her fingers over Penthesilea's. Gently but firmly, she coaxed them to open.

Penthesilea sighed. With no more warning than that, she slid from the saddle, falling limply into Selene's arms.

This time, whatever it took, Selene was not about to let anyone take Penthesilea, not even Nabu-rimanni. She carried her lady, her queen, into the station, nor would she lay her down until the stationmaster had shown them a room and a bed.

The bed was clean. That was a blessing. There was water for washing, and watered wine, and bread and cheese and a bowl of honeyed dates.

Nabu-rimanni had not followed them. Selene was glad of that, for the moment.

When she had undressed the body she knew so well, she felt those eyes on her, with the spirit behind them that she also knew well, but not in this form. Penthesilea raised her hand and turned it, flexing the fingers, frowning slightly as if she could not even yet believe that they were hers.

Selene reached for the basin and the cloths and began to wash her. She shivered at Selene's touch, but did not drive her away. Selene bathed her carefully, alert for any sign of rejection. There was none. When Penthesilea was clean, as Selene dried her with equal care, she said, "It feels strange."

"It's a new body," Selene said.

"All new," she said. She shivered again. "I'm taller than I was. I think I may be stronger. That's more than strange. Some things . . . I didn't expect."

Selene was not inclined to ask what they were.

"I know," Penthesilea said. "I'm being ridiculous. Yesterday I was someone completely different. Today I don't know what I am. I'm all confused. And I keep falling over."

"You'd be more confused if you were dead."

That startled laughter out of her, but it passed as quickly as it had come. "I'm afraid to sleep," she said. "What if, when I fall asleep, it all goes away?"

"That's not likely," Selene said. "This isn't some charm you bought from a charlatan in the bazaar. This is the work of the Goddess. She'll have made sure you're anchored as firmly as any mortal thing can be."

"I know that," Penthesilea said, "but my heart doesn't. It doesn't beat the same. It's slower, a little, even when it's fretting. I think I'm supposed to be a calmer person. Or is that because I'm not—"

"Because you're a woman?"

She winced. "I'm sorry. I can't help it."

"Regrets?"

"No," she said promptly enough that Selene believed her. "Confusion, that's all. Shock. I knew I was dying. I knew I'd left everything undone and half-done. When they asked me who should rule, I couldn't get it out. They heard what they wanted to hear."

Selene had heard it, such as it was. The word that ran through the Companions had been no name at all. "The strongest," they had said. "He said, 'To the strongest.'"

"What did you mean to say?" she asked Penthesilea.

"Krateros," she said. "I meant Krateros. We had our moments, mind you, but there wasn't anybody else who could hold it together so well."

"It's past," Selene said after a pause. "You know that. You have to let it go."

"I know." Penthesilea raised her hands to her face, pressing them to her cheeks. Her fingers clawed; she lowered them carefully. "I'll be better once I'm away—really away. Over the mountains, in a country I've never seen before."

"Soon," Selene said.

"Gods willing," said Penthesilea.

"Goddess willing," Selene corrected her.

"Ah," she said. "I have a new religion now."

"A true one."

"True enough," she said.

TWENTY-EIGHT

The farther Penthesilea rode from Babylon, the more easily she seemed to let it go. That strong will and ardent spirit could focus with intensity that Selene had seen in no one else. Now they focused away from the life that was gone and toward the one that she had chosen.

They ascended from the steaming plain toward the blessed cool of the mountains. Mostly they rode in silence. Selene could not remember when last Nabu-rimanni had spoken a word. They had not shared a bed since before Alexander died. When they stopped to sleep, the women were given a room apart. He slept in the greater room with the couriers and travelers who, like him, carried the royal token.

Zadrakarta was the last station at which they would pause. There they must find horses and mules to take them over the mountains. They had come to the edge of the world: the meeting of land and sea, mountains and sky. On the other side of the mountains was home.

"But not for you." She had caught Nabu-rimanni between dinner and sleep, between the dining hall and the room where the men slept. He regarded her unsmiling. He might have been a stranger.

"We're going home," she said, "but for you it will be exile. You don't have to go. We'll be safe: Artabazos' allies will guide us until we come over the mountains. Beyond that I know the way."

"No," he said.

She frowned. "Of course I know it. I—"

"No," he said again. "I'm not turning back. I'm going with you."

"You don't have to."

"I want to."

"Do you?"

He drew a breath as if to speak, but words eluded him. He took her face in his hands and bent, and kissed her long and deep.

She was too startled at first to push him away. Then she had no desire to do any such thing.

When she came up for air, she held him tightly, drawing in the scent of him. "I missed you," she said, "but I can't keep you with me. You are what you are. Where we're going, there's nothing for you."

"There is you."

"Will that be enough?" she asked him. "Can it? In a world of women, where a man is nothing but an instrument for making daughters, will you come to resent everything that I am?"

"Maybe," he said, "but maybe not. You heard my mother. She's prescient, too. She said that this is my path."

"Do you believe it? Really? In your heart?"

"In my heart," he said as he had before, "I believe in you."

"What if I'm not worth believing in?"

"You have your religion," he said. "Leave me mine."

Her teeth clicked together. She could not decide whether to slap him or kiss him again. In the end she chose the latter. It was sweeter, and he was too perfectly unreasonable to argue with.

Nevertheless, after they had found what they needed in the bazaar and the horse-market but before they mounted to ride, Selene stopped him again. He was saddling one of the mares that they had chosen, no Nisaian at all but a sturdy mountain pony. Selene held the saddlecloth out of his reach until he turned and stared at her. "You can still turn back," she said.

"I know," he said.

"Then why don't you?"

"I told you why."

"You are not being sensible."

"No," he said.

"You'll hate me," she said, "for tempting you into this."

"Never." He paused. "Are you trying to tell me that you don't want me?"

"Not in this world," she said. "But—"

"I'm going with you," he said.

He was not to be moved. It was a profoundly foolish thing for a royal Persian male to do, but it was his choice. Selene could hardly deny that she wanted him, or that her life, even among the people, would be lonely without him. Long before she understood what was happening, he had become a part of her.

She hoped that would be enough for him. If it was not, he would come to hate her—and that would be unbearable.

They left Zadrakarta in the morning. Penthesilea, who usually led them, lagged behind. When they passed the place where games were held, she stopped.

The others turned back lest they lose her. As they came up

beside her, she said to Selene, "I met you first in this place. This that I am—I first saw it here."

Selene nodded. Her memory was vivid of that day in the sun, when Hippolyta fought hand to hand with the young Alexander.

Now they had come back where it began. Selene watched Penthesilea closely, only half aware that she was holding her breath. This was the crux, she thought. This memory, this place, would not let go. Penthesilea would weaken in her resolve, turn and run back toward the life she had forsaken.

But she was stronger than her memories. She straightened her back, drew a long breath, and went on past the arena. She had an air as she went of someone shaking the dust of the place from her feet. She was leaving that life behind, wholly and unmistakably. Her face turned toward the new life before her.

They rode out of Zadrakarta, away from the sea and up into the mountains. Nabu-rimanni never looked back. Selene did, in what was not quite regret. She felt as if she had lived a long dream and now was waking from it. She would remember where she had been and what she had seen, but in her heart she was going home.

As they ascended into the mountains, the sight began to come back. At first it was so subtle that she was not even aware of it, but one night under the bitter brightness of stars, as they camped at the summit of a high pass, she looked into the fire and saw world upon world.

The guides to whom Artabazos had sent them were as villainous-looking a crew as she had seen, but they had proven to be soft-spoken, polite, and almost fawningly respectful of the women. The chief of their tribe was their mother, a matriarch of great power and respect in this country. Maybe her ancestors had come from the people long ago, or maybe they had found the Goddess on their own.

Selene saw the guides in the fire, leading their charges over the mountains. She saw herself, dwarfed under the immensity of the sky, and Penthesilea, and Nabu-rimanni towering over them. At the same time she saw them in the camp: Nabu-rimanni stretched out, not quite asleep, and Penthesilea sitting up clasping her knees, with her eyes full of firelight.

Those eyes became the world. Selene saw as an eagle sees, skimming the jagged peaks of mountains, then soaring above the long roll of the high grass, the wide and windswept lands of the people.

As she thought of her own clan and kin, she descended; the world came up to meet her. She saw the camps at the meetings of rivers, in the high places, near the fields and bits of forest where the game gathered. She saw the people in the camps, living as they had lived since the dawn time: women together, men in villages, and nothing between them but the rites of breeding in the spring.

That was a distraction. Selene wrenched herself away from it. The clans were moving in ways that made her hackles rise. She saw swords, spears, bows strung and ready. She saw angry faces. She saw Ione among the elders of the royal clan, looking little older than she had when Selene last saw her—a familiarity like pain. She saw priestesses in the temples and riders on the steppe.

She saw a face that had aged far more than Ione had, but still she knew it. The exile rode at the head of an army. They were men and women both: men of the east, women of the people and women whose faces were strange.

It was almost a relief to see this of all visions. The circle was closing. The game was playing out at last.

But there was still time. There must be. The Goddess did not deal in false hope.

Selene opened her eyes to Penthesilea's face. "Time is short," she said. "The war is beginning."

"War?" That brought the conqueror's spirit to the alert.

"You were made for this," Selene said.

"Yes." Penthesilea leaned toward her. "Tell me. How do I win?"

Selene almost laughed at the pure and exhilarating arrogance of that. But she had to tell the truth. "I don't see you winning. I only see what you'll have to fight. The whole of the people will rise up—and not to follow you."

"Why not?"

"Because," said Selene, "they'll remember what you were, and how your mother forced them to accept you as heir against all wisdom or sense. The priestesses turned away from her then. They'll be offering a queen of their own. So will various of the clans. And there is the one who was sent away: she's coming back with an army."

None of that dismayed Penthesilea in the slightest. She grinned and applauded as if at one of the Greeks' plays. "Splendid! Glorious. Three of us against an entire nation. We'll need a Homer to sing our glory when we're done."

"Whether we win or lose," Selene conceded, "they'll not forget us."

"So tell me," Penthesilea said. "Tell me everything I need to know. Who are the clans, and who is likely to be for me—or at least not against me. Where we should go, how you think we should begin. I need to know it all."

"I'll tell you what I know," said Selene, "but not all of it tonight."

For a moment Penthesilea glared, affronted; then she laughed. "No; there's time, isn't there? Days still before we come out of the mountains and go down to the plains. Gods! that we had wings, and could fly."

"We'll ride as quickly as we can," Selene said, "and pray we're quick enough. But now, if we're wise, we should sleep."

Nabu-rimanni's arms were warm and strong in the chill of the mountain night. She had grown so used to his silence that she was startled when he said, "You see us dead. Don't you?"

"No," Selene said, "I don't. I see fighting; I see blood. We could die, that's true enough. But I'm not seeing it."

"Then we'll live."

"I don't know. I'm not a goddess; I can't see everything that will come. Only what She chooses to show me."

"You've accepted it."

"Have I any choice?"

He kissed her hair softly. "I suppose not. We're all the gods' playthings, the Greeks say. The Greeks are wise, in their prolix and contentious way."

Selene smiled in spite of herself, remembering the flocks of philosophers who had followed Alexander about, chattering incessantly and providing far more amusement than they would have been pleased to know. There would be none of those now, and no priestesses, either—all those had left Hippolyta over her choice of heir. What they would say to the one who returned, Selene hardly needed the sight to guess.

She was worn out with fighting it, then with letting it in. And yet she could not sleep. The stars were bright and hard overhead. Nabu-rimanni was a warm and familiar presence. She could hear Penthesilea breathing softly across the fire, and the guides at theirs, and the horses on their tether. The earth itself breathed in a slow, vast rhythm.

The life she had led on the other side of the mountains was

fading fast. All that was left of it was the man in whose arms she lay, the clothes she wore, and the spirit that Hippolyta's daughter had gone to find. She found she missed it a little. The world had been very wide while she was roving about it in the conqueror's train.

She was going home. She could be going to her death—Naburimanni had the right of that. And yet she was not afraid. All her life had been a long waiting time, waiting for this. Now it was coming, and she was glad. She would welcome it, whatever it happened to be.

TWENTY-NINE

They came down from the mountains in midsummer, riding out into the tall grass where the wind blew unimpeded from the world's edge. After the chill clarity of the heights, the steppe was warm and richly scented, full of living things. Penthesilea forged ahead, eyes wide and nostrils flared, like a young mare turned out to pasture in the spring.

Selene was aware of the murmur of war, a rumble in the earth and a singing in the air, but the sight as always was a capricious thing. It showed her nothing that she could use. The three of them had to travel as blind as any other mortals, keeping watch over their camps at night and riding warily by day.

Penthesilea was in her element, riding all but alone into the teeth of war. She needed armies to follow her, but she had no doubt that those would be waiting. In the meantime she was as free as she had ever been.

They were remarkably happy, all three of them; Nabu-rimanni, too, in his quiet way. Those sunlit days, those nights full of starlight, would be all too brief. There was pain at the end of

their journey, sorrow and fear, and probably death. But for a
while they were the Goddess' darlings.

Selene had been expecting for some time to come on a camp of
the people. They had found trampled circles and burnt remnants
of campfires, but all the signs were of a migration eastward. The
west was empty and unnaturally still.

Near the heart of summer, when thunder gathered along the
horizon and sudden blasts of storm roared across the plain, they
came to the place where the people had gathered for time out of
mind. There was the great camp on the bend of a broad slow
river, under the loom of a broken crag. The travelers hid themselves on the ridge to the west of it, tethering their horses and
mule below the summit and concealing themselves in the tall
grass.

Selene lay in the grass between Penthesilea and Nabu-
rimanni. There was a strangeness inside her, half excitement, half
terror. These were her people—at last. Would they know her?
Would they find her impossibly foreign?

She made herself focus on the camp. There was something odd
about it, that she had not been wanting to see.

The circles of tents spread far along the river and onto the
plain, each with its banner or standard: horsetail, oxtail, stag's
horn, sow's head, skin of lion or tiger or bear. They were all there,
as far as she could see; all the clans. In the center where the royal
standard should be, the white mare's tail streaming in the wind,
was a spear raised up above the tallest tent, and on it a blank
shield.

Selene's belly clenched. She had been young when the last
queen died, but she remembered how it had been at the gather-

ing: how the mare's tail had come down and been laid away in the Goddess' shrine, and the shield had gone up, round and white and empty. That it was here, a year after Hippolyta was gone, should reassure her at least somewhat that all was well; that the people were waiting for their new queen to come home.

And yet something was wrong. It was almost too subtle to sense: a niggle at the back of her mind, a faint prickle between her shoulderblades. The people moving about seemed ordinary enough, but as she peered closer, she saw men's faces. Most of them gathered near the center, strolling here and there, or standing at apparent ease; but something about them made her think of palace guards.

They were not men of the people, a few of whom might be there in the usual way of things. They were too dark, too small, too foreign of feature. And there were too many of them.

The exile was here. As soon as Selene thought it, she knew that it was so. Worse: the exile was in the center, where the royal clan should be.

No, Selene thought a little wildly. She was deluded. She would have foreseen it. This was the camp of the gathering in the absence of a queen. Ione must be serving as regent until the new queen's return. What these foreigners were doing there, Selene did not know. But they were not there because the exile had brought them.

Penthesilea stirred beside her. "That's not a small camp," she said. "What's the number? Six thousand? Eight? And most of fighting age. I don't see any children. Is that as it should be? And the men—there must be a thousand of them. I thought you didn't keep them in your camps."

"We don't," Selene said.

Penthesilea nodded. Her eyes had narrowed in a way Selene remembered well. That quick mind would be far ahead of her.

"That's odd, then. We need to get in closer. If we can get all the way in—can we do that? Would they know us, do you think?"

"Hard to say," Selene said. "You were rather younger when you left. Me, they might remember."

Penthesilea looked her up and down. "They might. You look just the same as you did the first time I saw you. Good bones, you know, and the gods' blessing."

"Goddess," Selene said as she always did.

The flash of a grin told her that Penthesilea knew that perfectly well. She was in a splendid mood. Three of them against eight thousand of the people would strike her as delightful odds.

"I think we should investigate," she said. "If it's as mixed a camp as it looks to be, we won't attract any attention, as long as we keep our heads down."

"That's mad," Selene said.

To her surprise, it was Nabu-rimanni who said, "It's good generalship. If we had spies to send ahead, we'd do that. As it is, it's best we stay together."

"I'll go," said Selene. "We can't risk the queen before she's even had a chance to claim her people. And you . . . beloved, you are a thing of beauty, but you stand out like a tree on the steppe. No one will forget us once they see you."

He did not like that at all, but he had sense enough to recognize that while there might be men in the camp, they were all easterners. There was no Persian among them. "I'll stay with the horses," he said, resigned. "If you're not back by sunset, no matter what comes of it, I'll go after you."

"Make it sunrise," she said. "I might learn more if I wander around the campfires after dark."

"Sunrise," he said with a sigh.

She took his face in her hands and kissed him. It was very hard to let go.

As she rose to slip away down the hill, Penthesilea followed her. Selene stopped short. "Stay with him," she said.

Penthesilea met her glare with a bland and imperturbable stare. "I want to see what I'm dealing with."

"You may want it, but you don't need it."

"I do." Penthesilea slipped past her, ghosting down the hill as she had been able to do before there was a soul in that body. Selene had little choice but to follow.

It was almost physically painful to enter the camp of the gathering as a stranger. There were sentries on the fringes, and women farther out than that, watching over the herds of horses and cattle, goats and sheep. But Penthesilea was a hunter in both her lives, and Selene had not forgotten the skills she learned among the people. They came as a rustle in the high grass, no more noticeable than a breath of wind.

As they emerged from the grass into the western edge of the camp, they saw that everyone was moving in the same direction: inward to the center. The horn of gathering was blowing, long and sweet.

Selene and Penthesilea vanished into the crowd. No one spared them a glance. They were all intent on whatever was calling them—something expected, from what Selene could gather, and something that roused them to a strange excitement.

The center of the camp was already full of people, but Penthesilea slithered and slid and lifted obstacles bodily out of the way, until she had taken a place within easy reach of the front. There the crush of people had left a space clear about the Goddess' shrine. Priestesses surrounded it; the high priestess of the gathered clans sounded the horn that had brought the people in.

The shrine was empty of power. The Goddess' stone was not there. There was an image of Her, but it was new and raw and not yet imbued with the faith of the people.

The queen's tent should have been as empty as the shrine, its flap sealed, waiting for the new queen to claim it. But someone was living in it: the flap was closed but not sealed, and the fire in front of it was burning brightly. A tripod stood over the fire and a pot hung from it, sending forth a savory scent.

It was almost too homely a thing; it made Selene's skin crawl. The one and only queen of the people stood beside her, unknown and unacknowledged. Whoever dared inhabit that tent was an impostor. The shrine empty that should be singing with power, the tent inhabited that should be forsaken—it was all wrong; all turned inside out.

It seemed a long while before the horn ceased its singing. The high priestess lowered it with hieratic grace, and waited in spreading silence.

When the only sound was the breathing of several thousand people overlaid with the wind that had begun to blow, the tent-flap drew back. A figure stepped out into the fitful sunlight.

Selene's hand locked on Penthesilea's wrist. It was not to keep the young queen from betraying herself—the spirit that was in her would not know who this was—but to keep her own impulses in check.

The years that had lain heavy on the exile when she was cast out seemed lighter now. She had grown no younger, but a fierce, almost painful beauty had come back to her. There was a winter glory on her, and a strength that knew neither age nor mortal frailty.

Many might call it the hand of the Goddess upon her. For the first time Selene wondered whether the Persians' belief—that there was a Good God and an Evil One, and the Evil One existed to destroy all that was of the good—might after all be true. The exile was like a dark image of the Goddess, radiating oblivion where She radiated light.

None of the people who surrounded Selene could see it. They were rapt, captivated by the false light of the exile's eyes.

Her voice was smooth and sweet. "I have seen," she said. "The Goddess has spoken, and my eyes have been opened. She has shown me the way."

The people breathed a long sigh. The exile smiled. "My people," she said tenderly. "I see glory; I see slaughter. I see the false ones slain and the true people victorious. They who proclaim the queen-ship of an abomination, a thing without a soul—they shall be conquered. There will be a new clan, a royal clan, a lineage of queens."

Selene's teeth ground together. Her grip on Penthesilea's arm must have been excruciating: Penthesilea twisted sharply free and stood rubbing it, with her eyes fixed firmly on her feet.

Selene had forgotten to keep her head down. Belatedly she lowered it. The exile's eyes were full of her own invented vision; she was not seeing faces in the crowd. And yet Selene was cold under her skin. This was a hideously dangerous place to be—and even more so for Penthesilea.

There was no quick escape. They were too far forward and the crowd too closely pressed together. The exile was still standing in the midst of them, still smiling. "We have driven the false ones from among us," she said, "but yet they live. Is this right and just? Is it in accordance with the Goddess' will?"

No, the crowd answered, chillingly soft. It would have been better if they had been screaming for blood. Hot passion cooled; calmer heads could prevail. This cold conviction was more dangerous by far.

A hand tugged at Selene. She knew without looking that it was Penthesilea's. It felt like the only clean thing in that place.

She followed blindly. The loathing that she had always felt for the exile had swelled to fill the world. As the nameless one was the dark face of the Goddess, so was this hatred the opposite of the adoration that so obviously possessed the people.

It was the sight—true sight, not the lie that the exile had imposed upon them all. Because it was true, it bound Selene to silence as Penthesilea extricated them from the mob of spell-bound fools.

Whether Selene wanted the gift or no, she knew pure and visceral revulsion at this perversion of the sight. She staggered with the force of it, stumbling across the path of yet another of the people. The face was a blur, but the voice—

"Selene?" It was shrill with surprise. "Selene, is that you?"

Penthesilea plucked her away sharply enough to snap her head on her neck. The voice faded behind her. No one raised the pursuit. They were safe—for a while.

THIRTY

Nabu-rimanni had the horses ready to ride. Selene had had occasion before to observe his gift of foresight; she was glad of it now.

They rode east, where the lie of the land concealed them from the gathering. None of them spoke until they were far away, with their shadows stretching long before them. Midway between noon and sunset they had crossed the track of a hunting party, but they managed to elude it.

They had not conferred, not in words, but they had all agreed to ride on into the dark. There was a moon; the sea of grass was silver-bright, etched with deep shadow.

Far into the night, they paused to rest the horses and let them graze. None of them was inclined to sleep. They sat together under the westering moon, leaning on one another, taking comfort in the warmth.

"The royal clan has been driven out," Selene said. "But I don't understand how—or why—"

"I'll wager they got out ahead of that woman's troops," Penthesilea said. "She'll go after them, you can be sure of it. That was a muster back there, though I've never seen one as subdued as that. It isn't the usual way, is it?"

"Not at all," Selene said. "She's laid a spell on them. She was always capable of that, but since she was cast out, she's learned new arts. She's grown strong."

"Charisma," said Penthesilea. "That's what the Greeks call it. Power and presence. Ability to rule." It was difficult to see her face in the wan moonlight, but her tone was wry. "She's good. Maybe not as good as I am, but good. An empty throne, a clan already weakened by its late queen's choices—no wonder she's got in as far as she has. But she's not a seer. She hasn't seen me."

Someone in the camp had seen Selene. She bit her tongue, knowing she should speak of it, but strangely reluctant. It was nothing, she told herself. There was nothing to tell.

"Would you know where the royal clan has gone?"

Nabu-rimanni was even less readable in that light than Penthesilea: a glint of eyes, a faint pale sheen of nose and cheek-bones, and the rest of it shadowed in beard. In that image of shadow and faint light, she saw the answer to his question. "East," she said, "and north, to the barren lands—away from the hunting runs and the villages with their fields and harvests. They'll starve to death if the exile doesn't slaughter them first."

"Well, and so will we," Penthesilea said. "We can't run as fast as we need to and still hunt and forage. We'll have to risk a village, if there is one anywhere near the way we need to go."

"There are one or two," Selene said, "but I don't think—"

"I think we can call ourselves desperate," said Penthesilea. "We have to risk it."

Nabu-rimanni sighed. "I think we do. We're no good to any-one if we're starving."

"We can't slow down," Selene said, "or Goddess forbid, stop. The sooner we find the royal clan, the better."

"Then we will," said Penthesilea. "We'll sleep a little now, then ride. How far to the village?"

"Two days, I think," Selene said. "Three at most."

"We'll make it two."

Selene caught herself smiling in the darkness. Even as troubled as she was, that bright fierce spirit made her heart lighter.

It was not much more than two days before they came down a long hillside to a village that Selene knew rather too well. She had spent her month there more than once, trying and failing to conceive a daughter for the clan.

It would have been better if they had found another village, where she was a stranger. But there was none within easy reach. Their provisions would be gone before they came to any of the others, and they would have wandered days out of their way.

They had to trust in luck and the Goddess. She had protected them in the camp of the gathering. Surely She could do the same in a village of men.

They approached Dryas village warily. All seemed as it should be. Men and boys were in the fields, tending the rows of green and gold and brown. Sheep and goats grazed peacefully on the hillsides. In the village itself, men and a few women went about their business. There was a market, and what seemed a thriving trade.

There were very few women. All those of childbearing age were at the gathering. Here were older women who had settled in the village, and girls too young to fight, and what was most remarkable: a great flock of children.

They were not visible at first, but as the travelers made their way into the village, they saw that every street and alley was alive with children's voices. There were packs of them roving about, but most had gathered in circles here and there, chanting the songs of the people, practicing at weaponry, or spinning or weaving or making themselves otherwise useful.

Penthesilea's brows rose as she counted them. "So," she said. "This is where they all are. All in one place—not the wisest decision a general could make."

"Indeed," Nabu-rimanni said.

He had argued all too persuasively in favor of the lot of them entering the village. He was a man, as he pointed out, and this was a village of men; and if he was rather exotic in this country, well then, could he not be a simple traveler and wanderer from the west? A number of those had come to the villages over the years, Artabazos not the least of them.

Selene would have held firm, but Penthesilea had listened all too gullibly. "No one knows me," he had said. "I'm in less danger here than either of you."

"That is true," Penthesilea had said. "Would anyone here even think to ask whether a Persian might be connected with the royal heir? If he were a woman, maybe they would. But a man?"

Even Selene had had to admit that there was merit in that, however small it might be. The craven part of her was not sorry that they would all be together, horses and mule and human people. She had given way, because she could not honestly prophesy that they would die just then.

Nabu-rimanni attracted stares as he rode through the fields toward Dryas village. Most were appreciative; none seemed suspicious. Some of the children trailed after him, remarking on his attributes in clear and carrying voices.

Maybe he was wishing that he had not learned the people's language. They were quite explicit in their speculations as to what was under the coat and, in particular, the trousers.

Certainly he drew attention from the women who rode with him. They were profoundly ordinary in comparison.

The market was not as well supplied with foodstuffs as they would have liked, but they could make do. While the others filled mule-packs and saddlebags with such necessities as they could find, Selene wandered somewhat apart from them.

It was easy to keep them in sight: Nabu-rimanni towered over everyone there. Selene settled into a semblance she had not worn since she last walked in this village, ambling easily, casting an eye on this man or that. She was careful not to return any man's glance. She did not want to invite recognition, still less stumble into an assignation.

She had wandered farther than she intended before she thought to turn back. The market was behind her. She had been listening to voices, catching odd bits of gossip, idle talk, and now and then a grain of substance.

They were calling the exile *seer*. One of the older women, sunning herself on a doorstep with a grandchild on her knee, said to the young man who sat beside her, "And to think she was exiled—and she the seer of the people. Not to speak ill of the dead, but the old queen was mad: obsessed with that abomination she gave birth to, blind to the Goddess' will and the priestess' anger—then vanishing over the mountains."

"She came back," the young man said. He was very like her; Selene supposed he was her son. "The daughter never did. She died out there, no matter what her clan is saying."

"The royal clan." His mother sighed. "They're cursed stubborn, keeping the queen-right and refusing to let it go."

"Well, but so is the seer, refusing to take the title until the clan surrenders it. She could change the law, but she won't."

"A queen lives more within the law than any of us."

Indeed, thought Selene. And by law and custom, a seer could not be queen. That, they had all conveniently forgotten.

"So what is the queen-right?" Penthesilea asked.

They had escaped Dryas unrecognized, and with laden mule and full saddlebags, forayed back onto the steppe. For the sake of peace of mind, they had gone west and then south for a while, to throw off any pursuit. Now they had turned north and east again.

It had been some time since Selene had told the others what she heard. Penthesilea had seemed to make little of it, until suddenly, out of nowhere in particular, she had asked her question.

"The queen-right comes from the Goddess," Selene answered her, "and is passed down from one queen to the next. Your mother received it from her sister, who had passed over her daughter. It's yours now and has been since you were newborn. It can't pass unless you pass it—but no one knows either that you live or that you've come into yourself."

"Then why would a woman on a doorstep think the royal clan is keeping it?"

"I think," said Selene, "that the outcast has spread another lie. The queen-right isn't a thing that can be held in the hand, but she may be telling the people that it is."

"But why? She's a queen's daughter. Obviously people think

the last queen was reft of her wits. As far as anyone knows, she's the last blood heir."

"Revenge," said Nabu-rimanni. He met their stares. "She was exiled by the royal clan, yes? It's her clan—her family. If her claim were legitimate, the clan would stand behind her, whatever it thought of the late queen's decrees. But it repudiated her. She doesn't want simply to destroy it—she wants to suck the marrow from its bones."

"Yes," Selene said. She should stop being surprised that he understood so much. "Mind you there are things that mark the queen, that the royal clan must be keeping: the chair in which she sits, the image of the Goddess that should be in the shrine, and the queen mare who will only allow the true queen on her back. It's a sign of her power to blind the spirit that she can claim to be queen, and none of these things has come to her. She will try to claim them—you can lay wagers on it. Pray the Goddess she doesn't come there before us."

"She'll be mustering an army," Penthesilea said. "That takes time, even if you're the gods' own general—and that, she certainly is not. Sending all the children to a small and unwalled village with no army to defend them is the act of an idiot."

"She knows her people," said Selene. "None of us will kill a child."

Penthesilea arched a brow. "No?"

"If the child has a soul," Selene said, "no."

"Then we had better hope they all do."

Selene drew a breath. She had been about to rebuke Penthesilea for being too much of that other, harsher world, but the memory of the exile's face rose like a wall between them.

The exile too had gone away. What she had learned in those years of bitterness, Selene could too well guess. Selene had brought a man back, a man who was both friend and lover—two things that she once would have deemed unthinkable. The exile had brought an army of men. How much farther might she have gone toward the inconceivable?

"She'll eat her own clan alive," Selene said.

"Of course she will," said Penthesilea. "It wounded her to the soul. She'll never forget or forgive—even after there's nothing left to destroy."

"Unless we get there first," Selene said.

"Yes," said Penthesilea. "The lies she's telling—we're the truth. When she comes to take the queen-right, or whatever she's pretending that it is, she'll find us sitting on it."

They grinned at one another, struck with sudden wildness. Penthesilea kicked her mare into a gallop, but not before the others had done the same. Even the mule followed without its usual bray of protest.

THIRTY-ONE

The royal clan had retreated far into a wilderness of stone. The land seemed bleak and barren, the bones of the earth jutting out of the sea of grass, stripped bare by wind and hard rain.

And yet it was not altogether a wasteland. There was a place where two knife-sharp ridges came together, where the wind was less fierce and the rain did not scour the rock clean. There, a richer green had taken hold; even, far up in a fold of the land, a wood of trees. The valley's entrace was a narrow pass overlooked by promontories of rock. Its center opened into a rolling green level.

The clan had camped at the southern end of the valley, almost under the eaves of the wood. The meeting of ridges formed a rampart behind them, sheer and inaccessible. The only way in was down the valley's center in full view of the camp.

Penthesilea approved. "They've got their backs to a wall," she said, "but in a war like this, where they're so badly outnumbered, they're better off risking a siege than a battle on open ground."

"Some of us have some small talent in war," Selene said dryly.

"Did I say you didn't?" Penthesilea did not look back to see what Selene might have said to that. She was riding ahead as usual, alert but in no way fearful.

When the ring of warriors rose up out of the grass to surround them, Penthesilea grinned in honest delight. The circle of spears closing in dismayed her not at all.

The three of them were careful to keep their hands well away from their weapons. The spears halted just short of pricking the horses' hides. If one of them had shied or veered, the spearheads would have drawn blood.

There were no faces to see, only the featureless bronze of helmets. And yet Selene recognized the curve of a chin, the angle of a head on a neck, the slope of a shoulder. None of them was Ione, but she knew a fair few of them.

She turned her eyes on the one nearest. "Tanis," she said. And just past her: "Callista. All's well? Is Ione in camp?"

There were no glad cries, no effusions of greeting. No one called Penthesilea by her old stutter of a name. The spears lifted just enough to point them toward the camp.

Selene took that as encouragement. They had not been killed or driven off, and they were being admitted into what was clearly a well-guarded place. The guards were wary, dutiful, and forbiddingly silent. It was well, she thought, all things considered.

As they began to ride toward the camp, the guards closed in behind Selene, leaving Nabu-rimanni on the other side of the wall of spears. He halted and sat very still.

Selene wheeled her mare and plunged back through the wall. Either the spears swung aside or she struck them out of her way, until she came to a rearing halt beside Nabu-rimanni. "He comes with us," she said.

"No," said Tanis.

Penthesilea had turned back as well and come to his other side. "Yes," she said, sharp as the crack of a whip. "He comes, or none of us does."

That was a clear choice. Selene spoke quickly before Tanis could call the bluff. "Let Ione judge. She is still regent. Yes?"

Tanis did not answer, but the wall of spears opened once more. It did not close again until they were all on their way, riding close together with Nabu-rimanni in the middle.

Selene did not give way to relief. Not yet. There were spears behind her and armed warriors ahead, and no friendly air about any of them. She caught the flash of glances in the helmets, flicking upon her and Nabu-rimanni, but pausing most often on Penthesilea. They knew who she must be; she had changed little enough since she was last in this country, except to grow taller and broader and to become more of a woman. But the spirit in her, the soul that animated that face, transformed her completely.

They rode into a camp of war, where even the children went armed, and strangers were met with guarded stares. It saddened Selene a little to see her own clan gone so hard and wary, but in this grim year, gentleness would have been the death of them.

Penthesilea made no secret of her fascination. Her quick eyes darted, taking in everything. No smallest thing escaped her.

There was no memory in that body; nothing here would be familiar to the spirit that now inhabited it. And yet, Selene saw a

certain settling, an easing of tension down the spine, as if Penthesilea felt that she had come where she belonged.

Ione was where she had always loved to be: out in the field in
front of the wood, training a company of young women in hand-
to-hand combat. She took no apparent notice of the arrivals, but
Selene had no doubt that she had seen and recognized them.

Most of their guards had withdrawn on entering the camp and
gone back to their stations. Half a dozen were still with them,
Tanis and Callista among them.

Penthesilea ignored them, intent on the exercises. After a little
while she sprang down from her horse, stripped off her coat, and
waded in. "Set your feet farther apart," she said to the woman
nearest, "and come in lower—like this, look."

She had a way about her: whatever she was or might have
been, she won instant obedience. In a little while, a good half of
the recruits were taking instruction from her, learning ways of
fighting that Alexander had brought from Macedon.

Selene dismounted and turned her mare loose to roll and
graze and drink from the stream that bubbled into a pool by the
wood's edge. After a considered pause, Nabu-rimanni did the
same. He was Persian to the bone: he felt safer on a horse than on
his feet.

What he must be thinking, the only man in a world of women,
Selene could barely imagine. It was not quite the same as being
the only woman in a world of men. She saw how he made himself
stand at ease, watching Penthesilea take this clan to herself.

Little by little Ione let her take the rest, drawing back until she
stood on the field's edge not far from Selene, arms folded. Selene
thought about the distance between them and what it might sig-
nify. Maybe everything. Maybe nothing.

She moved toward Ione. She felt the guards' eyes on her back,
but none of them stopped her. She took a stance just out of reach

and waited, watching as Ione watched. Penthesilea had them all in ranks now, two by two, performing a dance of combat. It was graceful, that unison, and beautifully deadly.

"That's who I think it is," Ione said suddenly. "Isn't it?"

"Are you surprised?"

"Not very," Ione said. "How did he take it? Waking in that body?"

"Better than I might have expected," Selene answered. "There have been moments—but they've been few. This was meant from the beginning. She feels it. So do I."

Ione was silent. The dance had come to an abrupt and ringing halt, with all of them in ranks and Penthesilea in front of them, arms wide, embracing them all. "Well done!" she cried. She spun on her heel and grinned at Ione. "You've done wonders. These are better than any pack of recruits I've seen."

"They're middling fair," Ione said. She nodded sharply, signaling the end of the lesson.

The ranks broke. They should have scattered, but they were too curious. Word ran swiftly from one to the next: "It's Etta. It *is.*" Some did not believe it; Etta had been worse than an idiot, and this was anything but that. But they all knew that face, although they had been children when they last saw it.

"It was Etta," Selene said, making no effort to raise her voice. They heard her; she meant that they should. "Now it is Penthesilea."

Ione raised a brow at that. "Not half claiming what's hers, is she?"

Penthesilea was close enough to hear that. "What, that isn't the name that goes with the body?"

"The body was never given a name," Ione said. "Penthesilea is a title. It belongs to the queen."

"It's a name, too," Selene said. "The first queen's name. And now hers."

"You don't think this is—" Ione broke off. "You'd better come with me. This isn't an argument we should be having in the middle of a field."

"There is no argument," Selene said. "There is only what is. You're ready for war, I see. Are you ready to accept a queen?"

"We'll see," Ione said. "Now come."

She meant all of them—Nabu-rimanni, too. However little Tanis liked that, she was not about to contest Ione's will. They went back into the camp with a small army in their wake, all the recruits following, still rapt on Penthesilea.

Armies always had followed that one. Ione led them all to the camp's center, where the space was wide enough for everyone who had been drawn into the procession.

It reminded Selene rather pointedly of their entry into the camp of the gathering, but this gathering was significantly smaller—and the shrine beside the queen's empty tent contained a thing of true and potent strength. The Goddess' image was there as it had been for time out of mind. No priestesses guarded it, but the elders and the warriors of the clan stood about it.

Here was the truth. Here was the queen-right, in this clan, in this place, before this shrine.

Ione went to stand in front of it. She cast no spell, but she needed none. Her firm and practical voice rang across the circle. "Good, you're all here. We won't waste time. It seems the queen has come home. She's been training recruits up by the wood. Now it's time she showed herself to the rest of you."

A grand speech it was not, but Selene was glad of it. The truth was a simple thing, and clean. Only lies needed elaborate structures of words.

Penthesilea needed no prompting to come forward. She stood

beside Ione, running her eyes over the crowd, marking each face and committing it to memory. The names would come later; those too she would remember.

She took her time. Everyone had opportunity to recall what she had been and to see what she was now. None of them could fail to see the light in her, the power and presence that had passed intact from the King of Asia to the young queen of the people.

She smiled at them. Many smiled back. Others remained expressionless or scowled, refusing to be taken in so easily.

"I've come a long way," she said, "to take what I'm told is mine. Now I see it, and it's worth the taking. I know you've suffered much for my sake, not even knowing if I would be able to come to you, let alone rule once I was here. Now that you see and hear me, are you still with me? Will you follow me?"

"Tell us who you are." That was Callista, standing in front of the rest, fists on hips. She had always been rebellious; years and maturity had not mellowed her in the slightest. "I know what face you wear, but who were you? *What* were you?"

Ione answered before Penthesilea could speak. "This is the one she went to find: the great soul, the royal spirit, that would come to save the people."

"Well, of course," Callista said. "That's what I would expect. I want to know who it is."

Penthesilea tilted her head. The gesture was so familiar that Selene's heart clenched. "I was King of Asia," she said.

"You were—" That robbed even Callista of words, though not for more than a moment. "I don't believe you."

"I do." Ione's voice was flat, with no doubt in it. "That's what drew you westward, wasn't it? You were a moth to the flame—an empty vessel to the soul that would fill it. When his body failed, you were waiting. What killed it? Arrow? Spear? Poison?"

"Fever," Penthesilea said. "I have no memory of what this body was before. It was empty when I came to it. What I was, where my soul was—I remember every moment. This face I wear, I saw at my knee, day after day. I know every line of it. Though if you had told me that one day I'd wear it, I'd have called you mad."

"You were a man," Callista said. Her face twisted; she spat. "All this we've been through, for a man?"

Penthesilea looked down at herself, thoroughly, then up into that scowling face. "Is that what I look like to you? Because I've lived in a man's body, and believe me, this is nothing like it."

"The soul has no gender," Selene said. "This is a great general, a commander of armies, a ruler of nations. Those nations are bereft of that ruler now, by the Goddess' will, so that we may have a queen. By that, you know She loves us—because thousands will die in that other world while we in this know Her blessing."

"How do you know this?" Callista demanded.

"I see it," Selene answered.

She felt rather than saw how Ione drew to attention. No one else did, apart from the two who had come with her. They knew what she was doing, and what it would cost her.

It was too late to stop it. The time for running away was long past. The people needed her as badly as they needed Penthesilea—and if that was arrogance, then so be it.

Knowledge was power, the Greeks said. The Greeks had a saying for everything. She looked straight at Callista and said, "I see war. I see blood and death. I see false prophecies and perversions of the Goddess' will. And yet I also see a queen who will rule as none has before her; who having lived a life of war and come through war to her queenship, learns to cultivate the arts of peace. She will do that, if she lives. That is true. I've seen it."

"You said, 'if she lives.' " Ione clearly did not like to say it, but it had to be said. "You're not sure of that?"

"Nothing mortal is certain," Selene said. "The exile is coming.

All the warriors of the people, the priestesses and the elders of the clans, are following her. There is a battle coming that we will be hard put to win. But if anyone can win it, our queen can."

"How close is she?" Ione asked.

"Close," Selene said. "Four days, five, six—it will end soon, for good or ill."

A murmur ran through the gathering, a shiver of alarm. Surely they had known this would come, but they were mortal; they had all prayed that it would not be so soon.

Selene was as mortal as they, and as given to foolish hope. But the sight was merciless. "Call the war-council," she said. "Call it now. This is not a battle to win by waiting and hoping. It needs strength and swift action."

"We have the strength," Ione said, "if not the numbers."

"I can see that," said Penthesilea. "While we wait for the council, you can tell me what I need to know. How many fighters we have, what weapons, how you've been planning to make use of them, everything. I have a thought or two, but I need your knowledge. If, of course, you're willing to give it."

For answer Ione knelt and kissed Penthesilea's hands. It was a rare gesture, a depth of homage more commonly given to the Goddess. It had the effect she intended: another murmur ran through the crowd.

Selene did not recognize the woman who pushed forward even as Ione rose, then knelt as she had done and did the same. Others followed—not all of the clan, but a jostling throng of them.

This was meat and drink to the spirit within Penthesilea. Selene had seen it over and over beyond the mountains, how people hungered to be near Alexander, to touch him, to attract his notice, to bask in his presence. Now in this new life and form, it was no different.

All this would end in the acclamation of a queen. Which it would be, whether Penthesilea or the outcast, Selene could not be certain. But here, on this day, the royal clan acknowledged their queen.

THIRTY-TWO

The young queen kept the war-council in session until long after sunset. When she finally let them go, the tent to which she was taken was the queen's tent.

She understood the meaning of that. Selene saw how she paused before she broke the seal—but only for a moment. The gesture when she made it was crisp, clean, and perfectly sure of itself.

That spirit would rule wherever it was. It could do no other.

She slipped beneath the flap and vanished into the tent. No one followed her. Whatever waited within, it was hers alone to face.

Selene could see it if she turned her mind to it. She chose not to, not tonight. Her eyes were blurred with exhaustion, but sleep was nowhere within reach.

There was a tent for her to share with Nabu-rimanni. She sent him to it with a murmured word: "You sleep. I'll come in a little while."

He looked as if he might have spoken, but he set a kiss on her forehead and went to his rest.

Selene stayed by the council fire. It had burned low; she fed it just enough to keep it alive. There were patterns in the embers, and visions in the flames.

Ione settled beside her. Selene could not say she had been expecting it, but hoping for it—maybe.

"That's a fine figure of a man," Ione said.

"He should be. He's Sisygambis' child."

"He's your lover."

The word she used was not the word for a man with whom one bred daughters, but that for a woman whom one loved. Selene drew a long sigh. "I didn't mean it to happen."

"One never does." Ione's tone was wry. "It's lucky for you, you know, that the seer can do whatever she pleases."

"Can she?"

"None but the Goddess can command her. Only the sight can rule her. She can live alone on a hilltop or in a crowd at the gathering. She can take a lover as her heart urges her."

"Even if that lover is a man?"

"Even then," Ione said. "Seers and queens pay a high price for the power that's given them. They earn the right to be odd."

"I'm a perfectly ordinary seer," Selene said, "though I don't think there's ever been an odder queen."

"She is remarkable," Ione said. "More than remarkable. Astonishing. It should have been obvious, the way the soulless one flew like a moth to the flame—but who would ever have imagined that the flame was her soul?"

Selene nodded. She was very tired suddenly, and empty of words. Her eyes were full of visions.

She heard Ione's breathing close by her, even and slow. It

brought back memories of other nights, years ago, and warm strong arms and long, lingering kisses.

Ione made no move to touch her, nor did Selene close the space between them. There was a strange contentment in it. This more than any was Selene's homecoming.

When Selene rose, Ione caught her hand and held it briefly to her cheek. She let go before Selene could draw it away.

Nabu-rimanni was not quite asleep. He lay on his side facing the tent wall; he did not turn at the sound of her coming. She stretched out on the blanket, front against his back, arm about his middle. Her cheek, still carrying the memory of Ione's touch, settled in the broad plane of his shoulders.

She could feel the tension in him. When her hand shifted downward, he pressed his own against it, stopping it. "Tell me she didn't send you away."

"She didn't." Selene twisted free of him, pushing him onto his back. He lay in the nightlamp's glow, face stiff, eyes flat. "You're jealous!"

"Not jealous," he said. "That's more than a rival. That's your heart."

"You are my heart," she said. "I love her; I always will. Nothing will change that. But she sleeps there, and I sleep here."

"For pity. Because I insisted on following you so far, and now I'm alone. You don't need to pity me. I've come to my senses. When this matter of warring queens is settled, I'll go."

"If you do that," she said perfectly calmly, "I'll track you down and truss you up and haul you back."

"To what? To be your lapdog?"

She knelt astride him and glared down. "Are you trying to make me drive you out?"

"I'm trying to make you follow your heart, not your duty."

"If I followed my duty," she said, "I would have tied you up before we came down from the mountains and had the guides pack you off to Persia. You are an outrage here, a scandal, and a thing all but unheard of. And I don't care. I want you here—unless you find it so unbearable that you'll go mad. I won't force you to stay if it's more than you can stand."

"I can stand it," he said, stubborn and irrational male that he was, "if I'm not second best."

She sat down hard on his middle. He grunted and wheezed. "Serves you right," she said, "for acting like an idiot of a man."

"But I *am* a—"

She stopped his mouth with her hand. "Tell me the truth," she said. "Is this unbearable? If you can stand it now, will you want to run in a day or a month? Can you really live in this world?"

She reclaimed her hand. Even with that, he did not answer at once. After a while he said, "I don't know. I want to think I can. I know I can live with you, but whether you can—"

"I can," she said. "Before today I thought so. Tonight I know so."

"Even though I'm an idiot of a man?"

He had found his humor again: his eyes were glinting. She kissed him quickly, though they both would have been glad of more. "I love you in spite of yourself," she said.

"But if that ever fades—"

"Not tonight," she said. "Tonight and for all the nights I can foresee, it doesn't fade. It grows deeper."

He sighed—not an easy feat with her sitting on his belly—and loosed the tension in his body. He had been holding it, from the look of him, since they left Babylon.

Selene had little sympathy for him. He should have trusted her, and himself.

She slithered out of her trousers and freed him from the drawers that his Persian modesty insisted he sleep in. He did not often let her linger to take in the sight of him, but tonight he must know that she needed it. He kept his blushes at bay and restrained the ingrained impulse to cover himself.

The Greeks worshipped male beauty. Her own people preferred the female. She had learned to see the virtue in both.

She spanned the breadth of his shoulders and chest and the narrowness of his hips. His skin quivered under her touch. Without the daily ministrations of servants, he had gone what the Macedonians would call a little rough: black curling hair sprouting on arms and legs, breast and belly. He was a lovely thing, like a stallion in the spring—still heavy with winter coat, but showing the sheen of summer beauty beneath.

His hair had worked out of the tight knot at his nape. She finished freeing it, combing it out with her fingers. It sprang into thick curls, coiling on those wide shoulders. She drew in the scent of it, horses and herbs and the musk that was a man. He did not reek as most men did; it was pleasant to be near him.

It was more than pleasant by the dim lamplight, while he lay as he had never allowed himself to do before, and let her see the whole of him. She kissed him from brow to toes, lingering where he quivered in pleasure, then from toes back to lips. His body by then was almost too hot to touch.

She raised herself above him. His heart was beating hard, but no harder than her own. She lowered herself upon him and began the slow rocking dance. She could feel the effort with which he kept himself in check. Little by little she let him let go, until the world was afire, and they had dissolved in it.

Nabu-rimanni was deep asleep. Selene swam out of dreamless
peace into a kind of dreamlike waking. The sweat of their wild
ride had dried. She itched in odd places.

She rose softly. The water in the skin that hung from the tent-
pole was cool; it felt lovely on her salt-streaked skin. She washed
herself without haste.

It was near dawn. The nightlamp burned low. Nabu-rimanni
was a shape of shadow and shimmer: tumbled black hair, bare
olive-smooth shoulders. He was not like some men; his back was
a clean smooth sweep, unmarred by the matting of hair.

She was terribly tempted to touch those shoulders, to know
again the silken pleasure of that skin. But she had not roused to
indulge in loving. While the rest of her gave itself up to the body's
pleasure, the thing deep inside her, from which the sight came,
had come to a decision.

On every path that she could see, there was blood and death.
On every path, one or more of them died: Penthesilea, Nabu-
rimanni, Selene, the royal clan. And, in every vision, Ione.

She could see no hope even with Penthesilea among the royal
clan. At best, they died less quickly. The enemy was coming,
rolling like a wave across the steppe, and there was nothing that
could stop her.

And yet Selene had not given way to despair. Not all paths
were visible to her. Some were hidden in shadow. One led from
this moment, as she dressed in silence and gathered what she
needed and slipped out.

The camp's defenses were transparent to the eyes of a seer. She
chose a horse from among the herds, a nondescript brown mare
blessed with both endurance and speed. She did not trouble with
bridle or saddle: the mare knew what she was doing, and was

amenable. Selene swung onto the broad warm back and slipped away through the circles of guards and sentries.

The enemy was much closer than Selene had foreseen—only two days' journey from the royal clan. Already Ione's scouts were running toward the camp, bearing the message that would rouse it to action.

The exile's scouts knew of them but let them go. It would amuse their false queen to let the quarry run for a while before she leaped to bring it down.

Selene rode most of the way with her eyes shut. Daylight was a distraction. In the shelter of her eyelids, she could see more clearly. The world shone with its own light: light of the spirits that were in living things, and the Goddess Who was in all that She had created. The paths of time and fate ran like roads of light through that shimmering world.

Small wonder that the seer had not cared that her eyes were blind. This was a clearer sight than any of the body.

The season of summer storms was drawing to a close, but that was when they were at their strongest. Selene rode through lightning and the lashing of rain, barely slowed by it, following the path she had chosen. She could not see what was at the end of it. It faded into darkness, which she chose to perceive as infinite possibility.

Late in the second day she rode toward the enemy's camp under a blue-black sky gashed with lightning. Thunder walked the ridges, but the camp was quiet, washed with the light of the westering sun. The air was preternaturally clear. The wind smelled of rain.

Selene made no effort to conceal herself. She had ridden

beyond the edge of her foresight. What would come of this, she knew no more than any woman.

The enemy's guards accosted her beyond the outermost circle of the camp. They could see that she was unarmed, and that she carried nothing more than a skin of water. She had not eaten since the night before she left the royal clan.

She felt no hunger. She had barely touched the water. She was all clean, all empty.

The guards surrounded her, intending to take her prisoner. She looked each one in the face. For each, a name came to her. She spoke it.

It was a simple thing, with no magic in it, but it cowed them remarkably. When she rode forward, they gave way, closing in behind her. They followed her into the camp.

The wind had begun to blow, flattening the high grass. It carried her into the circle of tents. She felt it on her back like a hand, although she hardly needed its urging. The center was waiting with its empty shrine and its false seer.

Not only the guards were following her. She had been recognized: she heard her name racing ahead of her.

The outcast was in the center. She had been sitting to her dinner: there was a loaf of bread in her hand, half-eaten. There were others with her, priestesses, elders, clan-chieftains, and men in strange armor who carried themselves with an air Selene too well remembered. They expected to rule here, once the weak women were subdued.

The mare halted before the shrine and spun neatly on her haunches. The priestesses who guarded that nothingness moved as if to interfere, but the wind struck like a blow and sent them reeling back. A moment later, the lightning fell.

The shrine burst asunder. None of the burning fragments

touched Selene or the mare: the wind spun them aside, swirling them into the queen's tent.

One of the chieftains, quicker of wit than the rest, stripped off her coat and beat out the flames. The shrine was gone, but the queen's tent was saved.

"An omen!" the exile cried. "The queen-right is taken—her shrine is defiled, and thus destroyed. But the queen has been preserved. I foresee—"

"You see nothing," Selene said.

She had silenced the exile. She looked down from the mare's back into that blank and startled face.

"You are not a seer," Selene said. "The gift you claim is a lie. The Goddess grants no favor to you or any who follows you."

"Indeed?" said the outcast. She had mustered her wits. "Have you a message, then? Are the rebels ready to surrender?"

"The queen has come," Selene said, "and taken what is hers. Those clans that go to her will be forgiven their rebellion. Those that stay will pay the price of false allegiance."

The exile raised a brow. "The queen? That mindless thing? Have you found a way to play it like a puppet?"

"Not mindless now," said Selene, "nor soulless, either. She is a great one, blessed of the Goddess."

"Lies," the exile said.

"Truth," said Selene.

She swept her gaze across the gathered people, realizing only after she had done it that her eyes had been shut; that she was seeing with the sight of the spirit. "Take yourselves now," she said, "and go to the queen, and she will forgive you."

"Even me?" asked the exile with an arch of the brow.

"If you beg for it," Selene said, "she well might."

The exile laughed, a fierce, almost feral sound. "Here I stand, queen of the people, and you tell me that I should grovel to a pretender. Are you mad? Have you come looking for your death?"

"I come to tell you what I see," Selene said.

"Then tell us," said the exile.

"You saw the lightning fall," Selene said.

"I see that no one died," said the exile, "and no one was hurt. The Goddess blessed us and protected us. Surely She would have struck me down if I had been false."

"She may yet," Selene said.

That was mere wishing, and the exile knew it as well as Selene. The exile smiled with deceptive good humor and said, "Come, sit with me. Tell me of your visions."

The guards were closing in. However great the power that had brought Selene here, in this camp the exile was stronger than she.

The wind had died; the lightning had drawn away to the eastward. It was very still in that place in the last of the light. The exile's face and the faces of the people were stained with blood.

"Blood," Selene said. "Slaughter. There is death in the wind." She met the outcast's stare. "You followed us. You knew we would lead you to the clan. My fault; I will pay. But so will you, and many who follow you. Unless," she said, "you end this. Go to the queen. Trust to her mercy."

"I am queen," the exile said. "My mother's error, her sister's madness—all gone now. All ended."

"Not ended," said Selene, "while Penthesilea lives. She is queen by the Goddess' will."

"Queen through a lie," said the exile. She nodded to the guards.

The mare was swifter to respond than Selene. She gathered her haunches beneath her. Even as the guards closed in, she sprang.

THIRTY-THREE

The exile's guards were on foot and unprepared; they toppled. Selene clung blindly as the mare darted and veered through the camp.

The exile's voice rose shrill and furious behind her. Even before the mare had come to the edge of the camp, hoofbeats pounded in her wake.

The outcast herself had joined the pursuit, attended by a pack of easterners—all men, and all supplied with remounts. Selene was entirely in the mare's power. Whatever plan she had had, it was no use now. She could only try to guide the mare away from the royal clan onto the sea of grass.

Night had fallen, but that did not matter to the mare. Selene was seeing blind again, without need for mortal light. The steppe without stars or moon was still luminous, still clear, every hill and hollow as sharp as if limned in full sunlight.

Death was all around her. She felt its cold breath on her neck. But stronger than that was the heat of the exile's rage. Selene had torn aside the mask of sanity from the raw ambition and the profound bitterness.

The mare could not run forever. In time even her great endurance would be forced to slow and eventually to stop, if she was not to burst her heart in the Goddess' service.

The pursuers had settled to a steady pace. They had a considerable advantage: they could change horses as their mounts flagged. They had only to keep the quarry in sight, and wait her out.

If Selene had had the wits to come armed, she could have made a stand. As it was, she could only run, and hope she led the enemy away from her clan.

Soon enough the mare slowed. So too did the pursuers. Selene breathed a little easier, for the mare's sake. She had no reasonable hope for her own. When they finished their game, they would kill her.

It would be an ugly death. She could see it if she chose, down the paths of possibility.

There was so much that she could see, but not the exile's death or defeat. There must be a path for it, though why it was hidden from her, she did not know.

The sun was coming. She felt it in her bones that ached from riding for so long. The mare was barely cantering now. The pursuers had dropped to a walk.

As the first light of dawn touched the horizon, Selene saw with a shock to the belly that she had come round in a wide circle. The enemy had herded her within a day's ride of the royal clan.

She was a fool, and soon she would die. What good it would do, she could not imagine. But she had begun this game; she had to end it.

The mare stumbled, nearly pitching Selene over her head. Selene brought her to a halt and slid to the ground. This was as good a place as any to make a stand. They had entered the wilderness of stones; the land was rising. There was a tumbled mass of stone just ahead, against which Selene could set her back. It even offered weapons: a scatter of broken rock and sharp-edged scree.

The pursuers, seeing her afoot, had quickened their pace. She could go no faster. If they caught her in the open, so be it.

The mare, who had been walking somewhat ahead, stopped short. Her head swung up; her nostrils flared. She took no notice of the riders behind, who had come well within bowshot.

A second company of riders rode headlong down the slope, boiling up out of the stones. There seemed to be hundreds of them, but there could only have been a dozen, or two at the most. Nabu-rimanni led the charge, with Ione close behind him.

Their horses were fresh and eager to run. The riders were picked archers of the clan, armed with strong bows. They caught Selene's pursuers completely by surprise. None of them had a bow strung: they had been coming on with spears and knives, to pick her off at their leisure.

The exile took the measure of the fight. The attackers were outnumbered, but not by much; and they were better armed. Her riders were falling.

She kicked her mount up beside one of the remounts, pulled herself across the space between them, and let her first mount go, straight into the path of the arrow meant for her. She hauled the remount bodily about and sent it bolting back the way she had come.

With their false queen gone, the queen's guards had no further reason to risk their lives in the fight. Those who were still mounted and unwounded flung down their weapons and spread their hands in surrender.

Ione's riders lowered their bows, but Nabu-rimanni kept his up and strung, with an arrow nocked and aimed at the man who seemed to command the guards. He was older than the others, with a scarred and weathered face; there was a ring of gold in his ear. He grinned gap-toothed at Nabu-rimanni and said fluently, albeit in a barbarous accent, "Don't kill us. We're done with this fight."

"Suppose," said Ione, coming up beside Nabu-rimanni, "you tell us why we shouldn't cut down every last one of you."

The easterner stabbed his chin toward Selene. "She's not hurt. We never touched her."

"Nor did they," Selene said. "Take their weapons. Make them swear by their fathers' bones that they'll go back to their own country and make no further war on any of the people. Then let them go."

Ione and Nabu-rimanni exchanged glances. They had reached an understanding, it seemed, while Selene was running after visions. "I don't trust them," Ione said.

Nabu-rimanni shrugged. "If they turn on us, we'll cut them down. If we find them fighting against us, we kill them. I don't take them for fools. Let them go."

"Well enough," Ione said, not happily, but it seemed her doubts were not strong enough to feed an argument.

Nabu-rimanni extracted the oath from them, with his height and obvious strength and his deep drumbeat of a voice. They seemed properly cowed and thoroughly inclined to ride off eastward without stopping until they came to their own country. They took their dead and wounded with them, but none of the remounts. Those were the price they paid for their freedom.

Long before they had vanished over the eastern horizon, Ione led her company away from the place of the fight. Selene rode one of the remounts while the brown mare rested. They were not riding swiftly; their horses were tired, and none of them had slept. Some of the riders to the rear were muttering about stopping to camp and coming back to the clan in the morning.

Selene was exhausted beyond sense. Her eyes were open, but she saw as she did at night and blind: strange light, blurs of motion and instants of sudden clarity. The one thing that neither blurred nor changed was Nabu-rimanni, riding before and sometimes beside her. He was his solid self, with a light in his eyes that she saw often enough in the waking world.

She found it interesting that he had known where to come and what he would find. His gift was strong, although he would not lay claim to the title of seer.

Her gift had worn itself out. She slid from dream into doze, rocked by the movement of the horse and surrounded by the protection of her own people.

There was no warning. They were riding against the wind, which was blowing strongly, deafening even the horses. The attack came up from behind, swift and hard.

These were women of the clans, armed with bows and swords. The outcast laughed as she led them.

Selene clawed her way to full consciousness. The others had come alive with gratifying speed: bows strung, arrows nocked, spears and swords ready to hand.

The attackers swarmed around and over them as they closed in a tight and bristling circle. Selene had a bow in her hand—it had been on the remount's saddle with a brace of hunting spears and a long knife. It was shorter and more massive than the bows of the people, but not quite as heavy as the Persian bow. She had strung it and fitted an arrow to the string with no conscious

292 Judith Tarr

awareness of doing it. A figure galloped toward her; an arrow flew past, so close to her ear that she felt the wind of its passing.

She took her time returning the shot. The other had drawn an arrow from her quiver and was lowering it just as Selene loosed. It was a difficult shot against the wind, but the distance was short, and for an instant there was a lull. The arrow flew true. It struck the rider's shoulder and spun her about, flinging her from her horse's back.

Selene had not waited to see if the arrow found its target. She had already found the next. She was aware in her body of Nabu-rimanni on one side of her and Ione on the other, arrows aimed, ready to loose. There would be no more shots after this one: the enemy was too close. They would have to shift to spear and sword.

Again Selene's arrow struck home. So did Nabu-rimanni's. Ione's was aimed true, but a flurry of wind buffeted it aside.

She wasted no time in regret, but slung the bow and limbered her spear. The charge was upon them.

Their arrows had cut a swath through the attackers, but not enough. There were still two for every defender. Easy odds, Alexander would have said. He was not there, in that life or this, nor would there be a second rescue.

They could only stand and fight. There was no retreat: they were surrounded. Nabu-rimanni with his size and strength could easily hold his own, but one bit of weakness came near to crippling him: that he was fighting women. He struck to stun but not to maim or kill. They had no such compunction.

They were all crippled, they of the royal clan, in not wanting to kill. Selene felt it in herself, slowing her arm and softening her blows.

The exile's voice sounded suddenly, as sharp as if it spoke in her ear. "That one—the man. I want him. Keep him alive, and don't maim him."

Selene looked about wildly. She could not see the exile anywhere.

The moment of distraction nearly was the end of her. Her eye caught the flash of a blade. She twisted away from it, but it was falling too straight, too fast.

Another blade blocked it. Bronze rang on bronze. Ione beat the enemy back. The enemy gave way before the ferocity of the attack, but she was younger, stronger, and fresher. Just as Ione began to slow, she struck Ione's sword aside and drove her own blade home.

Selene saw the blow as it began. She shortened one of the hunting spears, stabbing at the enemy. It was too little, too late. Ione's blood sprayed her as if with molten metal. Ione fell, cloven half in two.

Selene reeled in the saddle. A raw sound rose up from the heart of her. She saw the sword falling from Ione's slackened hand; she caught it and whirled it about her head. With no thought for life or limb or simple sanity, she charged against the attackers.

Nabu-rimanni was behind her. The rest of the circle uncoiled in a skein and surged after. They broke the circle of attackers, hacked and clove and killed, until the world dissolved in a spray of bloody mist.

For the second time that day, the exile fled the field, leaving her followers to the slaughter. She was no longer laughing. If Selene could have caught her, she would have died.

But there were too many bodies between, and too many

swords and spears. These women were not like the men: they fought to the death. And death they won for themselves, every one of them. Ione went to the Goddess in the old way, the warrior way, with an army of fallen enemies to escort her.

THIRTY-FOUR

They made a pyre of the dead where they had fallen, rebel and clanswoman together, for after all they had been of the same people. All but Ione. Her they wrapped in her war-cloak and brought back to the clan, to be burned before the Goddess and the people, under the eyes of the queen for whom she had died.

The smoke of the pyre was visible far out over the steppe. Even from the edges of the royal camp they could see it burning itself out, tended by a handful of warriors who would stay until the rain quenched it. They would gather the bones then and bring them back to the people, and leave the ashes to scatter in the wind of heaven.

The camp was much changed. What had been an open circle of tents was now walled with a palisade of sharpened stakes. Grass had been cleared to the length of a long bowshot, and the ground sown even more thickly with stones than it had been before. Women were still clearing grass and scattering cartloads of stones around the edges as the riders came down off the sea of grass, late the day after both of the outcast's battles.

It was difficult going, as worn as they were, and some of them wounded. Selene did not care. She had carried Ione's body from the place of the pyre, glaring down anyone who tried to relieve her of the burden. Her arms were numb, but she barely noticed. Her eyes were wide and burning dry.

She was aware of the mare picking her way through the sharp stones, and the others following, moving slowly. Faces appeared above the palisade; the gate opened to let them in. She rode through it into the camp.

The tents were as they had been before. The wood beyond was lighter, culled of its lesser trees, although the older, greater ones still stood. In the camp's center, the Goddess' shrine rose beside the queen's tent.

Selene laid Ione's shrouded body in front of the shrine. She knelt for a long while beside it, as the shadows lengthened and people came, stared, murmured, left again.

"Selene."

Penthesilea knelt beside her. The queen had come and gone more than once, but this was the first time she had spoken.

"Selene, it's time to lay her on the pyre."

Selene closed her eyes and ears and set her lips tight shut.

"You know what she would say to this," Penthesilea said. "She'd call it wallowing, and order you to stop."

So she would. That did not matter. "I caused this," Selene said. "It's my fault she's dead. I tried to stop it and made it inevitable. I knew the law that binds the sight—that if all paths lead to one end, all efforts to change it will assure that it happens. I knew, and I did it regardless. And now she's gone."

"She'd be gone if you'd done nothing," Penthesilea said, "and then you'd be racking yourself with guilt for that. She'd lay you flat for it, either way. Now let her go."

"I can't."

"You will."

At last Selene looked up. Penthesilea's face was in shadow, her hair a halo of ruddy gold against the sunset sky. "No one can command me," Selene said. "I'm the seer of the people. I serve the Goddess' will, and no other."

"You know what She says to this. She says it in Ione's voice. Listen to Her."

Selene shook her head, tossing it. She did not want to hear it. Even for her queen she would not do it.

The blow lifted her bodily and flung her sprawling. She lay with her head reeling and her jaw throbbing, too winded to kill the one who had done it. Penthesilea shook a hand that must have been aching fiercely. "Now get up. You can wallow after this war is over."

"No," Selene said. "I can't. None of us will be alive. There's no hope. Do you understand? None. We can't win."

"I've never lost a battle," Penthesilea said. "I don't intend to begin now."

"Hubris," Selene said. "Isn't that what your Greeks call it?"

"Only if it's false." Penthesilea reached down and pulled Selene to her feet. "You bought us time. Maybe not what you intended, and at a higher price than any of us wanted to pay, but it might tip the balance in our favor. Now I need you to help with the rest of it. If I can't command you, then I'm asking. Will you help me?"

"The people don't want you," Selene said.

"They don't know me."

Selene opened her mouth, but no words came out. She was perilously close to laughter, or was it tears? "You can't stop, can you? You go on and on. That's why you came to us. Because we need relentless hope and unbending determination."

"Because I'm too stubborn to know when to stop." She grinned at Selene. "And so are you. We deserve each other. Now will you help? I need you. We all need you."

This was a master of persuasion. She could play the heart like a lyre, striking every poignant note. And yet, even knowing that, Selene's resistance was wearing thin. She did not want, in the end, to despair. She wanted to hope—whether it was useless or no.

She let go with a sharp hiss of breath, turning her back on the shrouded figure. When people came to take it, she clenched her fists and set her jaw against the rush of refusal. Ione's spirit should rest. It had fought hard and long; it had earned its passage to the Goddess' country.

It was a full five days before outriders brought the word the royal clan had been expecting: that an army was marching on the valley. In that time, Ione had her pyre, and the palisade and clearing were finished. Penthesilea set in train the rest of the plan that her quick mind had conceived.

The sight showed Selene nothing useful. She better served the people fletching arrows and carrying stones, and taking a hand with the cookpots in the mornings and evenings. Those were all worthy labors, and simple. Simplicity was welcome. She could almost let herself forget what was coming, that none of them could stop.

On the seventh day after Ione's body came back to the clan, the army of the people camped in front of the palisade. They were thousands strong, against a bare three hundred.

Even after her double defeat, the exile was sure that she would win the war. She sent a priestess to stand in front of the gate, crying out her message in a clear high voice: "Come out, false one, and face the truth. Your resistance will destroy you and all who look to you. Surrender yourself, confess your deception, and I will spare you. You may go back wherever you came from."

Penthesilea had climbed to the broad rail that rimmed the palisade and leaned over the top, smiling down at the messenger. "I come from here," she said, "from this clan. I was named heir in front of the one who calls herself queen. She must remember. She was rather put out at the time."

The priestess was no child; her rank was high and her bearing august. She regarded the face above her with an expression almost of pity. "You do closely resemble the thing that vanished on the steppe," she said, "but your possession of wit and voice betrays the lie. We are not gullible or fools, to believe that a soul may occupy a body long after its birth."

"It is preposterous, isn't it?" Penthesilea said amiably. "If you're blind to the truth, if you're blinded by falsehood, your only resort is common logic. And that tells you I shouldn't exist. Have you thought to ask your Goddess what it pleased Her to do?"

The priestess' face had gone stiff. Those who proclaimed themselves the gods' servants, in Selene's observation, were often blind and deaf to the gods they served. She had learned that first from the priesthood of her own people; and nothing had changed since she went over the mountains.

"You will be destroyed," the priestess said, "you and all who persist in following you."

"I would hope not," Penthesilea said. "Are you offering terms?"

She could be awesomely provoking when she was in this mood. Selene suspected that if the priestess had been armed, she would have shot Penthesilea off the wall. As it was, she could only spit venom with her voice. "To you we offer nothing but the safety of a grave. To your rebels we say, 'Come down, accept the true queen, and live. Continue in this madness and you will die.'"

"Ah," said Penthesilea. "We agree, then, as to what each will offer the other. Tell your mistress that she's a gifted liar, but the truth will find her out."

"What would you know of truth?" The priestess spun her mare about and sent her plunging back toward the line of the army, heedless of the danger to the beast's hooves.

Penthesilea's jaw clenched at that. She could never abide cruelty, thoughtless or otherwise. She swung down off the palisade and said, "Now. Let's go."

Everything was ready; they all had their orders. Selene, who was not to be ordered about, chose to follow the queen. They moved quickly, each to her separate place.

Penthesilea caught Tanis just before they had to part. "Remember," she said. "No heroics. You'll keep them occupied—well enough. But try not to die doing it."

Tanis grinned at her. Of all those who had known Etta before she was Penthesilea, Tanis seemed most at ease with the transformation. "I'm not planning to die. I want to see what you do to our cousin when you catch her."

"So do I," Penthesilea said, grinning back. They embraced quickly and parted at the run. The day was fading fast; there was no time to lose.

Nabu-rimanni had left four days before, having barely taken time to rest from the battles with the exile before he rode out again. Selene had been too busy to fret over him, but as she gathered near the wood with the half-hundred warriors who would follow the queen, she caught herself missing him with sudden intensity.

Fear stabbed. She sought within her for the roots of the sight, but it gave her nothing. If he was in danger, she was not to know it.

There was nothing she could do, not from this place. She shouldered her pack and fell into line with the rest, slipping through the trees as night began to fall.

They had a long way to go before sunrise, and a great deal to do. The night was starlit, but there was no moon. Selene led because she could see in the dark. Penthesilea was close behind her. The others followed one by one.

They made their way quickly through the trees, having scouted the land well before, and marked out paths even while they cut down young trees for the palisade. The land sloped as they went on, gently at first, then more steeply. The escarpment rose over-head, seeming sheer, but intrepid scouts professed to have found a way up.

By starlight, with no time to waste, it was no simple climb. The scouts led. The others went in pairs, roped together for safety.

They were children of the steppe, not mountaineers, but they had acquired what skill they could in what time they had. Penthe-silea had scaled peaks enough in both of her lives; Selene had seen more of mountains than she wanted ever to see again. They brought up the rear, to catch those who faltered.

Time stretched into an infinity of sheer rock, handholds and toeholds, and moments of breathless terror when someone above slipped or lost her grip. There was a path of sorts: a line of ledges running slantwise up the cliff. At times it was no more than a fin-gernail's width; too occasionally it was broad enough to stand on, to rest and breathe before the next teeth-gritted ascent.

Selene had lost track of time when a gasp and slither above and somewhat to the side roused instinct, flattening her to the cliff-face. She felt rather than saw the bodies falling: two bound together, grimly silent until they struck rock far below.

With a wrenching effort she unlocked her fingers from their handhold and forced herself to press on. All too soon she found the place where the others had fallen: handholds shrank to nail-holds, perilously far apart. Her fingers were raw; her jaw ached from clenching. She must not waver, must not give way to exhaustion or fear. Above all, she must not press forward too quickly. Carelessness was death.

Somehow she crossed the gap. Beyond was easier: there were more handholds, and the slope was a fraction less sheer. She reached the end of it in a kind of numb surprise, groping for the next handhold and finding nothing, only a stony level and a wuthering of wind.

They were all there but the two who had fallen. There was the summit to cross, and a descent considerably less steep than the way they had come up. They had no time to stop or to mourn, and barely time to breathe. It was past midnight by the turning of the stars; by dawn they must be on the sea of grass.

The horses were waiting in the hollow below the escarpment, with a pair of young warriors to guard them. One was a grey, glimmering in the gloom. As Penthesilea moved to mount the bay that she had chosen from the herds, she found a grey wall between.

The queen mare had come, soft in the night, to claim her own. There was no ceremony in it, and no time to remark on it. They all mounted in silence, found their places in the line, and set off. It was rough going through tumbled country; they could not risk speed for fear of losing horses in the darkness.

Selene, who could see by the strange light behind her eyelids, was no more inclined to run than the rest. Her mount slipped and scrambled on slopes of jagged rock and struggled through thorny scrub. She could only cling to mane and sides and try not to unbalance the mare. Her body ached from the climb; the mare's movement loosened muscles cramped into knots, but woke new pain elsewhere.

Clouds ran to cover the stars. A chill wind began to blow. She smelled the rain before it came. It was cold rain, a foretaste of autumn.

They wrapped themselves in cloaks and made sure their weapons were covered and pressed on. The rain was a gift, if they could find their way without stars to guide them: it would keep hunters at home and deter scouts from wandering too far afield.

It would not last the day. That was a gift, too. They needed not to be found, but they also needed the enemy to be on the field, attacking the palisade, when they came where they were going.

The Goddess would provide, if it pleased Her. Meanwhile, as Penthesilea had observed when they began, they would do their part, and hope that She would be there when they needed Her.

THIRTY-FIVE

The rain blew away at midday. Under a rapidly clearing sky, the riders came round to the rear of the army. The camp was pitched just outside the narrow entrance of the valley, and it was barely guarded. The herds of horses, the flocks of goats and sheep, foraged on the sea of grass, all but unattended. Nearly every human creature was in the valley, and most of them were on foot, sparing their horses' hooves on the stony ground.

Penthesilea shook her head as she paused just below an outcropping, peering over it to take in the field before her. "People never think," she said.

"That's to our advantage," Selene pointed out.

"And that's why I always win," said Penthesilea. "The rest of the world thinks to the first contingency. I think to the second and the third."

So she had. The valley was shaped like a Greek amphora: wider in the middle, narrow at either end. One end was the wood and the palisade, backed up against the supposedly insurmountable cliff. The other was a narrow entry between two steep, tumbled hills. A little distance within was the beginning of the grass, a fan of level ground, not too stony. There was the command post, a canopy of white leather pitched under a jut of rock.

No one in either the camp or the army was expecting an attack from outside the valley, still less from the sheer walls above it. All their defenses, their sentries, and their scouts turned inward toward the palisade.

The women of the clans, with the exile's eastern men goading them on, had taken the field in front of the wall, barraging it with arrows and throwing spears. The more enterprising of them were hacking at the palisade from below, with shields over their heads to protect them from the hail of arrows and stones.

Tanis' garrison was doing its best to seem several times more numerous than it was. Many of the helmets that gleamed above the palisade were empty, shifted here and there by people from below. The deception might not last for more than a day, but with luck it would not have to.

Penthesilea's forces were in place. The ground was prepared.

But she did not give the signal. One thing was missing, one element in her plan that had not yet come.

They made camp up on the hillside, hidden in a tumble of stones. They lit no fires, pitched no tents, but found what comfort they could under the sky. The horses had fodder prepared for them in a hollow near the summit, fenced in with cairns of stones and a gate of woven cords.

They waited and watched. The attack on the palisade flagged after a while. The enemy halted in the field. Runners ran back and forth from the canopy, just below Penthesilea's watching post.

The exile was there. Selene could feel that presence, that power of empty lies and devoted deception. The fighters nearest the canopy were all men: the outcast's guard, as watchful as all the rest were—inward, but not outward or upward.

The army held its position as the shadows lengthened. It seemed they would not be returning to camp tonight: they lit cookfires and ate the daymeal there, spread across the field.

Siege warfare was not something the people knew. Maybe the men from the east had some skill in it; if so, they were not making use of that knowledge. There were no siege-engines, no rams. The exile had come prepared for the end of a hunt, with the quarry brought to bay and the hounds ready to rend it.

Near sunset there was a flurry, a wave of movement through the ranks. Torches sprang to life, dim in the daylight. While they were lit, the front ranks heaved up skins and vats of what must be oil and splashed them along the base of the palisade. The torches passed down in waves and were flung toward the wall.

Wood that was green and wet with rain burned badly, but here and there the oil fed a smoky blaze. Archers on the wall picked off some of those with torches, shooting by firelight as the daylight waned.

Up on the hillside, the watchers held their position. Penthesilea had sent out a pair of scouts before she made camp. They had not come back.

Waiting was the hardest part of war. Even knowing that the fighters within the palisade were there of their own will, fighting off assaults they had fully expected, still it was bitter to sit above them and do nothing.

Penthesilea watched until full dark had fallen. She ate then, downing bread and cheese and dried meat with good appetite. When she had eaten, she said, "Wake me when the scouts come back," rolled herself in her cloak, and went to sleep.

The others were gaping. "It's always been so with that one," Selene said. "Everything is in order. All plans are laid. There's nothing else to do but get a good night's sleep and come fresh to the battle."

"Amazing," Callista said. She lay down as Penthesilea had, and shut her eyes tight.

So did they all, except those who had drawn the first watch of the night. It was a sensible enough thing to do. Any sleep they could find would serve them well in the morning.

Selene dozed fitfully. Her heart persisted in waking her every time she slid into sleep, groping toward the memory of Naburimanni. The sight was blind to him. She only had glimpses of fire and shouting, and the exile's face contorted with either rage or elation.

In the end she gave up the fight. Young Chryse was nodding at her post. Selene sent her to bed and took the watch, gazing down the valley at the smoldering ember that was the fire in the palisade. It had not spread, but neither had it died.

At dawn she was still awake, yet not weary at all. The scouts were still gone. Penthesilea woke at first light and said at once, even before her eyes were fully open, "If they're not back by sunup, we'll carry on."

They ate their cold breakfast and broke what camp there was, and went to their places: some on this side of the gap, some on the other. Selene stayed close by Penthesilea.

Slowly the light grew. It would be a bright day, warm and clear. The waves of storms had blown away.

The exile's army was still in the field, still trying to bring down the palisade. They were not watching their backs at all. Even the guards on the camp had wandered inward. There were only a handful of priestesses and a few fighters who had been arrowshot or burned.

The signal was the sun's rising a fist's breadth above the horizon. Just before it touched that point, everyone on the hillsides set levers to the heaps of stone and loose scree that rose up on either side. If the enemy's scouts had done their duty, they would have recognized that those were not natural outcroppings. But they, like all the rest, had been intent on the encampment up by the wood.

For a long, terrible moment the attackers knew that Penthesilea's engineering had failed: that the hillsides would not fall. Then with a sound like a long sigh, both gave way at once.

They all scrambled as fast as they could, making for solid ground. Perched on promontories of rock, they watched the gate into the valley vanish, buried in masses of earth and shattered stone. On the one side was the camp with all their tents, their belongings, their flocks and herds, their stores of food and drink. On the other, with only what they had brought for a day's use, was the whole of the army.

They reeled about, taken absolutely by surprise. The explosion of air from the fall of stone had blown away the exile's canopy, but not the exile herself or the priestesses and the men with her. Selene regretted that almost as much as she regretted the deaths of the wounded in the camp.

As the dust settled and a long silence fell, Penthesilea rose from concealment and stood on the promontory, looking straight down into the outcast's face. "Good morning," she said. "Are you enjoying your siege?"

"If you could get out," said the exile, "so can we."

"Not before you starve," Penthesilea said. "Surrender now and we'll get you out of there. Refuse and see how long you'll last."

"You'll let us out," the exile said. "This, I believe, is yours." She nodded to the men with her, who had been sitting on a roll of carpets.

They stripped the wrappings from it. There was no mistaking the tumbled black hair or the curling extravagance of beard.

He was alive and conscious: as they hauled him up, he reeled, but he stood on his own feet. He tilted his head back, squinting against the sudden dazzle of light after hours in darkness, and said clearly, "Don't."

"We found this wandering the steppe," the exile said. "I was inclined to keep it—geld it, maybe, the way the outlanders do with inconvenient males—but it's fine currency, don't you think, for our freedom?"

"No," said Nabu-rimanni. "Don't let her use me against you."

Selene's heart had shrunk tight and small. Somehow she could still think. That he was alone. That the exile had not spoken of others with him. That the attack had been an obvious surprise.

He had not betrayed them. She could not tell if he had been tortured. He was standing upright, and steady now that he had found his balance. There were no visible marks on him.

Penthesilea's mind had leaped far ahead of Selene's. She said, "We are fond of him, but not in return for an entire nation. Mind you, if you kill him, I won't be answerable for what my people will do—particularly our seer. I hear she brought lightning down in your camp. Who knows what she could do if she were in an honest temper?"

"I'm not afraid of either of you," the exile said.

"Maybe," said a new voice that rang from cliff to cliff, "but are you afraid of this?"

Under cover of the fall of the hillsides, then while they were all distracted by the bandying of words, women had come up along the ridge. They held children in their arms or led them by the hand.

A low cry ran through the army. These, if Callista and the rest had fulfilled their promise, were the daughters and heirs of the chieftains and warleaders of the clans.

All together, at no visible signal, Penthesilea's warriors pulled their captives close and held knives to their throats. The children seemed unafraid: none cried, even the youngest.

Their mothers were another matter. Penthesilea addressed them in a cool, dispassionate tone, not at all strained by the art and effort of causing it to echo from the cliffs and reverberate through the valley. "If my soul had been born and raised here, you would know there was no danger. The people do not kill the people. But I was born a man in a world of men. I have killed with my own hand and through the hands of others. I have slain my kin in hot anger and in cold calculation. If the deed had not been done for me, I'm sure in time I would have killed my father—because by the gods of Macedon, that was a man to drive his offspring mad. I will do what I must do to end this war of lies and false visions. If you will not believe in me, in the queen who made me her heir and in the Goddess who sent me to you, then believe in the truth that you see above you. Grant me your fealty, and you and your children will live. Refuse, and you will both die—they as quickly as a knife across the throat, you as slowly as starvation and thirst."

The army was seething. The exile cried out above their clamor: "Don't believe them! We're thousands against their few score. We'll get out of this trap while they're still working up courage to act on their threats. And," she said, "I will have acted on mine." Her hand slashed toward Nabu-rimanni.

Selene had not even been aware that she was in motion. She was not walking; she thought she was flying. The rope that had served her so well in the escape from the royal camp was fastened above somehow, and she swung over the outcast's head. She was dimly aware of arrows singing past her: the exile's easterners had their wits about them.

So did Nabu-rimanni. He had shaken off his wrappings. There were cords about his wrists, but their knots were undone. As Selene swung above him, he leaped.

If he had been a smaller man, he would have fallen short. Even as it was, he barely caught her ankles. She gasped at the doubled pain of his considerable weight and his fierce grip.

People scrambled below. He heaved his legs up, an effort that nearly wrenched Selene in two, and locked them about her middle. The agony in her ankles gave way to a lesser strain as he twisted like an acrobat and surged up past her to seize the rope above her head.

Just as he secured his hold, they began to rise in jerky motion. An arrow passed so close it stung Selene's cheek.

They were forever on that ascent. There was no sound to be heard but the song of arrows winging relentlessly upward, until a sharp voice cried, "Stop!"

It was not the exile's voice. It came from farther away. The arrows lessened in number, though they did not stop entirely.

The ascent slowed to a halt. She felt Nabu-rimanni climbing up the rope, until all at once he was gone. Hands reached down to draw her up, pulling her over a ledge of rough stone onto a sun-warmed level.

She was blind with the light. She lay simply breathing, while the voice that had commanded the archers echoed through the rock under her body. "I surrender. I want my daughter back. Whether I'll accept you as queen—that depends. You're lucky, I grant you that. You're impossibly clever. What else are you?"

"Come up and see," said Penthesilea.

"Dun Cow," someone said to the queen. "That's Dun Cow."

Dun Cow was a large clan and powerful. It hunted the lands around the lakes in the south, and its chief village was also one of the nine temples.

There were other voices now, voices of chieftains and warleaders and lesser women of the people. The exile's voice rose above them. "Lies! You give way to lies."

"That's my daughter up there," said Dun Cow chieftain. Selene was seeing again without eyes, through the burning glass of the sun. She saw the woman standing in the circle of her kin, a tall and sturdy figure who looked younger than she sounded. This must be the heir whom Selene had known vaguely years ago; the chieftain then had been much older.

The exile had seen her, too—and far more easily. She snatched a bow from someone's hand, nocked, aimed, loosed.

The arrow pierced the chieftain's throat, cutting off what more she would have said. The exile did not pause to watch her fall. "If I have to kill you all," she cried, "I will! Cowards, fools, weaklings! Don't you see—"

"We see," said Penthesilea. She nodded to the company that waited with climbing ropes.

They swung down the cliff-face, ready to leap on the priestesses and, Goddess willing, the outcast. The exile's guards moved to close in, but the clanswomen closest had found their courage. They fell on the easterners with startling ferocity.

The easterners fought back hard. The melee blocked the ranks beyond, even if they would have come to the false queen's rescue.

Penthesilea's fighters came to earth, not all gracefully: some fell and rolled, others staggered. But they recovered quickly and were up and running, seizing priestesses. Some of them went limp, but most fought back.

The exile had a sword in her hand, warding herself with the flashing bronze. Selene heard Penthesilea mutter something in Macedonian—a quite filthy curse—and felt rather than saw her go down off the rock.

Selene's senses were coming back. Nabu-rimanni was holding her. He was like a part of her: as close as that, and as beloved.

She was furious with him: that he would use himself as a

decoy, that he would let himself be captured, that he would risk death or worse so that the others could win through to Dryas village and seize the heirs of the clans. It was a hero's act. It had very likely assured the victory. And it was absolutely stupid.

She wrenched away from him. Before he could catch her, she had gone back over the ledge, back down into the valley. In her fierce fit of temper, she was as light on her feet as a cat. She landed easily and set herself at her queen's back while Penthesilea stood face to face with the false queen.

THIRTY-SIX

The battle in the field had spread through the whole army. The priestesses were all taken captive; they were rising out of the valley even as the queens faced one another.

The exile had stopped her swordplay. She was utterly alone, with no one left to stand beside her. Her guards were far out of reach, fighting for their lives against their former allies.

Selene was caught in a trance of the sight. Her body was on guard, sword and spear at the ready, poised to defend her queen. Her spirit reeled among a myriad of outcomes, nearly all of which showed Penthesilea dead and the exile triumphant over her. In most of those visions, the outcast died on Selene's spear—but too late. Too terribly late.

Single combat was an ancient and honored way of settling royal succession. Penthesilea was grinning, delighted. This was thoroughly to her liking.

It was going to be the death of her. Selene made a choice, just in that moment, that could damn her in those eyes forever.

The rival queens were face to face, sword to sword. The exile was laughing, taunting her enemy. Penthesilea was silent.

She had never been noisy in a fight. She left that to lesser mortals.

The spear in Selene's hand was a hunting spear: short, broad-bladed, strong enough to stop a boar. It was too heavy to throw. She would have only one chance; then they would both turn on her, the true queen as fiercely as the false one.

Selene said no prayer, asked no favors of the One Who had cursed her with prescience. She gripped the spear-butt, sighted along it, and sprang.

The exile went down in a spray of blood, her head half cloven from her neck. Selene nearly went down with her, skewered on Penthesilea's sword.

Penthesilea stopped the blow just before it fell. Her face was terrible, her eyes blazing. Selene's death was in them.

Selene met them calmly. The exile was dead. Penthesilea was not. Nothing else mattered.

That calm could have maddened the queen, but through luck or the Goddess' intervention, it gave her pause. Slowly Penthesilea lowered her sword. "I will never thank you for this," she said in a still, cold voice.

"I don't care," said Selene. "You're alive and untainted; you'll not be branded kinslayer. You were going to die. In every vision, in every possibility, you were dead. Now we've moved past visions. We're in a world I never saw before. I can't tell you what will happen—except that you'll be here to see it."

"As queen?"

"I don't know," Selene said. "All I can see is your face."

"You're mad." The anger was fading. Forgiveness might never take its place, but Selene would not grieve for that.

It seemed she was not to be cast out quite yet. Penthesilea said, "Stay close. I have an army to settle."

But first she stooped down and finished what Selene had begun: hacked the exile's head from the remnant of its neck and thrust it on the blade of the spear that had killed her. With that for a standard, Penthesilea waded into the battle.

Stillness spread in ripples, as if the outcast's head had been a stone cast into a pool. People were staring, gaping—the surviving easterners as much as the women of the people.

"Enough," Penthesilea said. "It's over. My offer stands. Surrender and no penalty will attach to you. Refuse and die."

One by one they stopped fighting to stare at the dripping thing on the spear and at the woman who held it. To them it was no matter who had killed the false queen. It was a passage of power, as clear as any they knew, and more bloody than any of them would have chosen.

The men from the east were not constrained by the laws or customs of the people. They turned on the queen.

The people turned on them—gladly; they had won no love for themselves even while their false queen won power over them all. They were overwhelmed, cut down, trampled into the stones.

Penthesilea left them to it. She was deep into the army now; if they had not backed away from the thing she carried, any one of them could have destroyed her with a stroke.

That was the power in her. Even the dullest of them felt it. Selene, closest to it and attuned by her gift and her long familiarity, felt it like a blaze of fire.

When Penthesilea reached the center, a circle had formed itself around her. She grounded the spear. Selene braced it with stones, while the queen turned slowly, taking in as many faces as she could see. "It's over," Penthesilea said. "It's done. You can kill me now, or you can follow me. There's nothing in between."

She gave them time to ponder it. It seemed endless, but by the passage of the sun was remarkably brief. Dun Cow clan, mourning its chieftain, came forward first.

The people did not bow to queens. They offered respect with hands crossed on breast and head bent. For great favor, they would come together in an embrace.

Penthesilea could not embrace them all—there were too many. But as the people approached her, the warmth of her presence and the joy that she took in them left them dazzled. Some even bowed, or fell on their faces. Most offered deep respect.

They were falling in love as everyone did with that splendid spirit. The exile was gone, forgotten, even as her blind eyes and her stark dead face rose up above the surrender of the people.

Tanis and her troops opened the palisade and brought out what supplies they had left, which were barely enough to feed the army for that day. Laden with those, they all came up out of the valley that had become a trap, drawn on ropes to the freedom of the sea of grass. The few horses that had been in the valley had to stay behind, but there was pasture enough for them, and streams of water in the wood; they would survive until a way could be found to break them free.

The people buried the outcast in the valley, setting her body in earth where it had fallen. They heaped a cairn of stones above her and laid words of power on it, that her angry spirit might not rise and walk and trouble the people. Her easterners they left for the vultures.

None of the people would come back to this place. It was a place of shame, where kin had turned against kin, and a clan would have been slaughtered in the name of a lie.

THIRTY-SEVEN

By the time of the autumn gathering, the people had found their strength again. Bitterness lingered; memories would not pass quickly. But they had begun to heal.

The queen needed no crowning. She was what she was by the Goddess' gift and the free perception of the people. But Penthesilea had always loved ceremony: the more elaborate the better.

She had summoned the high priestesses from the nine temples. Unlike the seer, they could be commanded, although it was surpassingly rare for a queen to do such a thing.

The messengers that she sent rode with escort that was, very casually, armed. If any of the priestesses had resisted, they would have met with edged persuasion.

They were not fools, although they had resisted for so long and in such blindness to the Goddess' will. The exile's death had broken the spell. They had perforce to accept what they could no longer fail to see: that the Goddess had brought them a wonder and a marvel, a queen like no other.

They came, all of them, to the autumn festival. There in the midst of the games, the custom of which delighted Penthesilea to no end, they offered reverence to the queen whom the Goddess had made.

She received them at the center of the great circle, in front of the new shrine, where the Goddess' image had been restored to its place. She sat on the throne that had been in the queen's tent, a preposterous golden thing, far more apt for Persia than for the camps of the people; but it suited her admirably. She was dressed as queens had been from the dawn time, in the girdle of scarlet cords and no other garment or covering, with her bright hair flowing free and a crescent moon on her brow, a shimmer of silver amid the gold and red.

She did love a spectacle. The sight of nine priestesses in full procession with their servants and acolytes, coming one by one to offer her reverence, made her deeply happy. Whatever doubts they might still have had, the queen mare disposed of: she had come while they were still passing through the camp, and stood behind the queen. None of them could meet that fierce dark stare, or the queen's vivid blue one, either.

She gave them time to reflect thoroughly on the ways in which they had failed their calling. But she was not by nature cruel; she much preferred to be loved than feared. She came down from the throne and embraced them in order from eldest to youngest, and swept them with her to a banquet that waited in the field beyond the tents. Already as she went, she was inquiring after this one's children and that one's prized flocks and another's beautifully embroidered robe.

"She's happy," Nabu-rimanni observed.

He had not been forgiven for letting himself be captured and nearly killed, but in this time of mending and healing, Selene had chosen to forget that even he could be an idiot upon occasion. She slipped her arm about his waist and leaned lightly on him. "That was the great gamble," she said: "that that of all spirits could leave behind all that it had ever been."

"Not so much a gamble," he said. "Not for that one. She was always a seeker rather than a finder. How will she manage, do you think, now that she has to rule and not simply to win?"

"There's plenty of conquest left," said Selene, "with all the temples and the clans, and the villages that haven't seen her yet. Then I'm sure she'll find enough to occupy her. This time she is determined to leave a clear succession—and that means an heir."

His brows rose. "As in . . . ?"

"As in, she'll do it in the usual way."

"That's not as simple for a woman as a man."

"No," Selene said dryly, "it's not. But that's another world to conquer. Maybe when she's done that, she'll see the Ocean after all—or even find the half of her self again, when it's reborn."

"Or both," he said.

"Why not?" said Selene. "Anything is possible."

"So it is," he said, "and she is living proof."

He was smiling. Selene basked in that smile, and in the beauty of him that was so different from the beauty of the people.

She was happy, she realized—as happy as her queen. All that long journey: so much strangeness, so much sorrow, so much suffering, so many battles; and she had come to this place, this person, and this rather astonishing joy.

Still, she had to ask; to be sure.

"Regrets?" she asked.

"Never," he said without hesitation.

"Not one?"

"Not in this world," he said.